Alayziah:

When Loving Him is Complicated

B. Love

Soar young girl. Soar.

www.authorblove.com
www.blovesbooks.com

For information about bulk purchases, please contact B. Love via email – authorblove@gmail.com

To join my mailing list and be the first to know about my latest releases click this link right here -> http://eepurl.com/bYzdcr

Interested in having your book published under B. Love Publications? Send the first three chapters of your manuscript to blovepublications@gmail.com

Alayziah

Pronounced – Uh – lay – zhuh

Meaning – The product of undying love.

To say that I was pissed, embarrassed, surprised, and even more pissed would not begin to describe how I felt when I walked into Andrew's home last night and found him having sex on his couch – **with another man.** Andrew and I had been dating for about six months before he started talking about engagement and marriage.

Now I'm not going to lie, I would have married him. Not because I was madly in love with him; but because he was the type of man I always dreamed of marrying. There was just…something…that was off with him. With us. I thought that it was the fact that he wasn't the usual bad boy that I go for.

He was a musician. He spent more time getting ready than me. Hell, he knew more about fashion and trends than me. And he loved New Orleans. Now I have nothing against New Orleans. But the part that he went to was known for drag queens and prostitutes.

Even with all of that I continued to entertain the idea of me and him. So he had been talking about getting married a lot lately and that kind of scared me. It caused me to fall back with my feelings for him.

Eventually I started feeling bad about it, so I went to his place last night to make up for it and that's when I found him inside another man. Inside another man. Another man – a man! It wasn't the fact that he was gay that pissed me off because I slick felt like he was anyway. I just wasn't ready to face that truth about him. It was the conversation that we had after I found him that pissed me off.

They were getting it in on his couch. Guess they couldn't wait until they made it to his bedroom. When I walked in and shrieked he immediately removed himself from his boyfriend and pulled his pants up.

I tried to walk out but he grabbed my hand and almost dragged me into his bedroom. Leaning against his dresser I watched as he paced. He didn't owe me any lies or any explanations. I just wanted to leave and erase that sight from my brain. After what seemed like forever he stopped pacing and stared into my eyes.

He disgusted me so much I couldn't even face him. I hate liars and I hate half-truths. I hate frauds and people who live with facades, and he knew that.

But he played with me anyway.

"Alayziah," he mumbled my name like he would a child's name who'd just asked a question that you didn't want to try and explain. Like this was the most dreadful thing he'd ever had to do in his life. Like he was about to tell me my dog died or some shit.

"I'm sorry that you had to see that, but now that it's out in the open I'm glad that you did. Now that you know that I'm...into...men...I can be completely honest with you."

"What are you talking about Andrew?" I couldn't lie. He'd piqued my interest. *What else could there possibly be that he had to come clean about?*

"I chose you to be my wife because I thought that you would understand my situation. That you would be cool with me having my affairs. You help me keep up my façade and I can help you with school and your businesses. I know you want to open up a creative arts center, I can help bring in sponsors for you to do that. I think it would be a good exchange. You would never have to worry about your finances. Whatever you want I can give. But I wouldn't be able to have sex with you while I'm...you know...with...someone...else."

I shook my head and chuckled lightly as I crossed my left ankle over my right.

"So let me get this straight..." I started before crossing my arms across my chest. "You want to marry me...not because you love me and want to spend the rest of your life with me...but because you need a fake wife? Someone who won't tell the world about your secret? That's all I am to you Drew?"

"That's not what I mean at all Alayziah," he mumbled as he walked towards me and tried to take me into his arms but I pushed his cheating behind away. "I care about you deeply. More than I have ever cared about any other woman. You're a great woman and friend. That's why I chose you. I would love to spend the rest of my life with you."

"Do you hear yourself Andrew? Did you really think I would agree to this? Did you think that I would overlook the fact that you've been cheating on me? With a fucking man my nigga? A man!"

I was clapping my hands together and yelling louder than I wanted to before trying to open his door; but his hand around my forearm stopped me.

"Let me go Drew. I am not about to let you bring me out of myself. I'm trying to remain calm and respect you as a man. So let me go, now."

Reluctantly he let me go and dug his hands into his pockets. I refused to shed a tear over this trifling nigga. My ego was bruised. Here I was thinking a man saw my value, and wanted to commit to me because he knew that I would be his good thing, but all he wanted was a trophy.

"Don't worry Drew. Your secret is safe with me," I continued in a softer tone opening the door.

"Alayziah please, forgive me."

As much as I wanted to be bitter and resentful it wasn't even worth it, he wasn't worth it. The combination of us wasn't worth it. I didn't love him. I didn't really even want him. I just loved the idea of him and me. I loved the idea of us together. I wasn't hurt. I wasn't sad. I was, however, terribly, terribly disappointed.

Alexander

When I walked into the writing center inside my fiancée's church and I saw this peanut buttered complexion beauty sitting at the piano I couldn't help but stare. She was beautiful. I've never believed in love at first sight. *Until now.*

Now I love my fiancée Carmen, and I love her three children. I would never do anything to jeopardize my relationship with her, or the relationship I have with her children as their father, but when I saw this woman sitting at the piano...she awakened something inside me that I didn't even know was sleeping.

I watched as she tried to compose a piece on the piano. I could tell that she was a beginner and that she was struggling. I was going to let her get it on her own until she sighed and grabbed her papers and stuffed them in her purse as she tried to walk away.

I felt myself walking over to her and I couldn't stop staring at her. Her jet black hair flowed in a bob that brushed her shoulders. I'd never seen her smile before in the church. Honestly she was kind of intimidating.

She was about 5'1 and couldn't have been more than one hundred and five pounds but she never smiled. Much smaller than Carmen, this beauty was the perfect size for me. She had the type of body that made me want to lift her up and just have my way with her. Shaking the thoughts of lust from my head I grabbed her hand lightly and turned her back to the piano. She looked at me skeptically at first but her face softened when she realized who I was.

We'd never spoken to each other before, but I played the piano at her church every once in a while. I'm a full time musician and I am engaged to her Pastor's daughter. I stopped by the church to pick my girl up after choir rehearsal. When I heard someone playing the piano, well attempting to play the piano, I couldn't help but look in and see who it was. And I'm so glad I did.

After I sat her down on the bench I sat down as well. Taking her hands into mine I played what I thought she was attempting to play. I must have been right because she smiled. And it pissed me off.

How could she rob the world of such a beautiful smile?

Her high cheek bones lifted even higher and I noticed the dimple in her chin. She looked at me briefly. Allowing me the opportunity to look into her deep brown eyes. Her eyes were so beautiful. They were so bright it's like they shined. Literally.

"I suck," she said in a low voice with a smile. Her voice was so light and hypnotic. I couldn't help but wonder how she would sound moaning in my ear. And that smile, God I was falling for that smile, maybe that's why she didn't do it often.

"How long have you been playing?" I asked tearing my eyes away from her.

"Ummmm I've only taken a few lessons. I don't really *want* to play. I just…want to have guitar and piano to go with my poetry CD and I can't seem to find anyone who can understand my concept and how I want it to sound. So I figured I'd learn and play it myself."

I nodded my understanding before glancing over at the paper that was sticking out of her purse. "Is that the poetry you're working on now?"

She nodded as she pulled it out of her purse and smoothened it out.

"Yea. It's kind of hard for me to focus on my message and my delivery and learn the piano at the same time."

There was that smile again. That smile was going to get my ass in trouble. Deep trouble.

"Why don't you do your poem and let me see if I can vibe with you," I offered. She looked at me with a frown on her face that caused me to chuckle.

"What?" She asked, like she ain't even realize what she was doing. "What?"

"Your face…" I replied staring into her eyes.

"I'm sorry. I suck at hiding my facial expressions. That's why I walk around stone faced."

"Oh, so that's why I never see you smile?"

"Yes. I don't want to hurt anyone's feelings. I show all of my emotion on my face. Good and bad."

"I got ya. That makes sense. I thought you were going to be mean because I have never seen you smile before."

"You've been watching me?"

Fuck. I was slipping.

"I mean…yea…you're beautiful. It's hard not to. I can't help myself when I see you. Even when I'm sitting next to Carmen I can't help but stare at you. You're beautiful."

She blushed before looking away. "That's right. You're Carmen's fiancé. I'm not mean at all. I'm probably the goofiest soft hearted emotional person you'll ever meet. It's just I give it all or nothing. In my face, my life, my relationships. That's just how I am."

"Right. Right. I feel you. So…let me hear what you got…"

After she inhaled deeply she picked up the paper and began to recite her poem. It took me a while to even begin to play because she'd captivated me. Her voice. Her face. Her delivery. Her passion. Had a nigga craving her in the worst way.

Eventually I gathered myself and began to play along with her. When she saw that I knew what I was doing it's like she let herself go. She put the paper down and started going off the dome. Closing her eyes as tears fell. Took all my strength not to stop playing and kiss her tears away.

I couldn't help but feel connected to her; like her pain was my pain, my pain was hers, and she was telling my story. I started to adlib and sing some runs as her background. I must have caught her off guard because she opened her eyes and smiled.

"You can sing," she said wiping her face. "You can really sing."

I smiled lightly. I'd been playing the piano since I was six, now twenty three I'd say I was pretty good. Been singing for just as long. I was blessed to be able to say I was able to do what I loved professionally.

"Thanks…" I didn't even know her name.

"Alayziah."

"Thanks Alayziah. You're quite talented yourself. I love your poem. I could feel your passion and emotion. Your voice is amazing as well. Just with you speaking. You don't sing?"

I watched her as she rubbed her hands against her leggings. I guess I'd made her nervous. That was cool. For the way she had me feeling in this church she could stand to feel some type of way too.

"Thanks um…"

"Alex."

"Alex." She blushed before stuffing her poem into her purse. "You got me. You got my vision. You played just what I needed."

"Yea I vibed with you. That's what it's all about. Energy vibing. Feeding off of each other."

I ain't mean to look her up and down but I couldn't help myself. She blushed again before pulling a piece of her hair behind her ear. Giving me an even better view of that pretty face.

"I've been looking all over for you. You're supposed to be picking me up and you all in here giving piano lessons," Carmen's voice was surprisingly annoying to me at this moment. And her kids running and yelling really didn't make the situation any better. I went from this peaceful exchange with this beautiful soul to nagging. Sighing heavily, I looked at Carmen before returning my attention to Alayziah.

"Well it was nice to finally meet you Alayziah. Good luck with putting your CD together." I said as I stood. I wanted to offer my services to her but I figured that wasn't the best idea. If I was lusting after her in a church where I knew my fiancée was I can't imagine how I'd feel inside a studio with her alone. Especially while she poured out her heart and soul.

"Thanks Alex. I really appreciate your support," she replied without looking at me or Carmen. Instead she stood and walked out of the room. Ignoring Carmen's stare. I could tell that she was back to her stone faced self. I felt bad. I wanted to be the one she could be her true self with, but that was over now, and as much as I love Carmen and knew how I was feeling was wrong, I was kind of pissed that she ruined it.

Alayziah

When Alex sent me a message on Facebook after I posted a status about my performance tonight I was stoked. He offered to play the piano for me at my poetry set. I was a little in my feelings when I left the church a few days ago because of my exchange with him.

He was a very good looking man, he seemed to be a genuinely nice guy, and he had to be patient and loving to accept a woman with three kids and three different baby daddies – none of which belong to him. Now that is love. I want that... not with him of course, but with someone who is for me.

Here I was all in my feelings just a few minutes before I had to go on stage and perform. I was tired of performing about heartache. I wanted to write love poetry for a change. When I heard the door slowly creak open I looked at Alex and smiled. He looked good without even trying.

No I don't want to date him, I know he is in a committed relationship and that isn't how I get down, but I can't lie, the nigga looks good. Without even trying. He had on a Kendrick Lamar snapback with the lowercase *i*. A tight fitting white tee. A pair of black sweats. And some white and black Nikes.

Oh my God, he smiled at me, genuinely, and as much as I didn't want to smile back I did. Widely. Sometimes I was insecure about my size but the way he stared at me let me know that I didn't have anything to worry about. I chose to wear a royal blue custom made jumpsuit. I love getting my dresses and jumpsuits custom made because they accentuate the curves I have. The suit was so tight it looked as if it was painted on, but because of the material it was extremely comfortable.

I finished my look off with a pair of red pumps and red lip stain. I wasn't big on makeup. Occasionally I'd do a gold or brown eyeshadow to complement my skin with some mascara but that was about it. He was staring at me so hard I was starting to get uncomfortable so I spoke hoping his eyes would center on mine.

"Thanks for coming Alex. I know this is really last minute."

"No problem. Glad I could help," he looked me in my eyes and I was starting to wish I let him continue to look at the rest of me.

"So how much do I owe you?" I asked grabbing my purse off the counter and walking towards him. His face shriveled up like I offended him.

"Nothing Alayziah I offered to help, remember?"

"Yea but this is what you do for a living right?"

"Right, but I'm not charging you. If you want to repay me why don't you write me a piece I can perform at my reception to my wife?"

"Okay cool. Sounds like a good exchange."

The knocking on the door cut off his reply. It was my best friend Marcel letting me know that they were about to introduce me.

"Thanks again Alex. I guess it's time," I tried to walk to the door but he wrapped his arm around my stomach and stopped me. Confused I looked into his eyes and asked, "What's up?" hoping he hadn't remembered he was supposed to be somewhere else.

"Let me get your number. I'd like to stay in touch with you after this. I don't have many friends and my schedule is pretty free because I'm a musician."

I guess my face was saying what I was thinking because he took a step back.

"I would never do anything to jeopardize what I have with Carmen. I just want to be your friend, honestly. You seem like a really sweet and cool person and you're incredibly beautiful and talented."

Against my better judgement I took his phone from his hand and entered my number. I mean…what would he want with me when he was engaged to her? This time when I tried to walk away, he let me.

Alexander

I found myself sitting outside the precinct again. I already had felonies and was on probation. The last thing I needed was for my probation officer to know that I'd been arrested for driving with a suspended license. I wasn't trying to go to jail for three to twelve. As usual Carmen's dad was giving me a hard time. When the nigga found out about my past he started tripping.

Yea I was trying to live right and my parents were Preachers but that didn't mean I had it all together. Back in my younger days I was a gang banger high up in rank. I fought, I robbed, I sold drugs, never killed, but I helped dispose of plenty bodies. Now that I was trying to leave the game alone I only sold drugs when I absolutely had to. I was done with all of the rest of that shit.

I didn't even know my license was suspended. Now I had to figure out what the hell to do to get that shit taken care of before my court date. After all I'd gotten away with I wasn't about to have my freedom taken away for some bogus ass charge like driving with a suspended license. Especially since I wasn't even driving when the cops checked me.

I'd just pulled up at Carmen's house and they were already there waiting for me. Her pops and I had gotten into it the night before. I guess when he found out who I was in the streets he feared for his life. So he had them there just in case I clowned. I wasn't finna do no shit like that though.

Her kids were there and like I said, I was already on probation. So when they came at me sideways I talked crazy to them and they looked my shit up. Now here I was sitting outside the precinct waiting for my brother to get off so he could come and pick me up.

I loved Carmen. She started out as my best friend and things just grew from there. But she was such a liar, and I was too. I didn't know how I thought that shit was gone work. And on top of having to deal with her crazy daddy and her baby daddies it was times like this that I wished I'd never proposed to her ass.

Everybody thought we were this perfect couple, but we were having our fair share of issues, and on top of that she was still married to her last baby daddy. A marriage that most of her family didn't even know about. I'd been with her for ten months. With two divorces of my own under my belt a nigga really wasn't trying to end this and start over. I just wanted to get it over with and be in it for the long haul, but the more I talked to Alayziah the less I wanted Carmen.

Alayziah was mad cool. Her energy was laid back and nonchalant, but at the same time she was so corny and goofy. We'd talk about anything under the sun. We had so much in common. She genuinely cared for a nigga. We prayed for each other. She prayed for my union with Carmen.

I ain't wanna let her know that her prayers weren't working, and I didn't want to burden her with my troubles, especially since I knew she was at work, but I pulled my phone out and texted her and asked her to let me know when I could call her because I was going through. I didn't even have to because shortly after she called me. I tried to hide my smile so she wouldn't hear it when I spoke.

"Hey..." I managed to get out.

"What's wrong Alex?" She asked immediately and as mad as I was at Carmen and her pops when I heard her voice all of that began to fade away.

"You got a minute?"

"I called didn't I?"

I smiled harder. She had a smart ass mouth, I loved it though.

"Mane, I'm so mad right now I don't know what to do. I didn't know who else to call..."

"Talk to me. Let me ease your mind."

"Okay...I feel like I can be honest with you and you won't judge me, am I right?"

"Right."

"Well...I never told you this but I used to be a street nigga, chief of my set too, getting into all kinds of trouble. Carmen's dad was cool with me until he found out about my past. Then he started tripping. We've been having some issues, too much to even get into. She's still married and for a good little minute she lied to me about it. I guess she was trying to please me and her father. It's just a lot of shit going on. Excuse my language."

"It's cool. Continue."

"I went to pick her and her kids up this morning and her pops had the cops there. We'd gotten into a lil' argument last night and let him tell it he feared for his life. So they ran my license through the system. Turns out it's suspended. I was arrested. I bailed myself out. Now I'm sitting outside waiting for my brother to come get me. It wouldn't bother me as much, but I'm already on probation. If she finds out about this, I'm getting locked up again. I can't believe Carmen would let him call the police knowing I'm on probation."

She was quiet for a minute but then she said, "Text me the address to where you are. I'm coming to get you."

"Alayziah, you don't have to do that. I didn't call you for that. I just called you to vent."

"You can vent when I get there."

Before I could protest she hung up. I wanted to be mad at her little feisty ass but I found myself smiling twice as hard as I texted her the address.

Alayziah

I brought Alex back to the restaurant I worked at. I was working double shifts today so I welcomed the opportunity to leave and get some fresh air. I hated the idea of a 9 to 5. That just wasn't me. I wanted to live out my dreams as a writer and a poet. I wasn't the college type.

So here I was, a college dropout, working as a waitress to pay my bills until my gift was recognized and made money for me. I promised my grandmother that if that didn't happen by the time I turned twenty five I'd either get a real job or go back to school. Since I'd just turned twenty four I had a year to pull this shit off.

When we made it to the restaurant I fixed Alex a plate and sat in front of him. At first he didn't want to eat but when he couldn't take the scent of the Asian wings in front of him he dug in. I smiled. We both loved hot wings and catfish. I watched him eat and wondered what made people lie so much. I never would have guessed that he and Carmen were having issues because according to their social media pages they were happy and in love.

But the more we talked, the more he opened up to me, and the more I realized that was untrue. I truly cared for him and wanted what was best for him, even if it wasn't her. So that's what I prayed for. I didn't want to take her place. I'd never even considered being with him. I just wanted him to be at peace. And if I could bring him that peace…so be it.

After eating a couple wings he leaned back in the chair and stared at me.

"I appreciate you," he mumbled before sliding the plate to the side and resting his elbows and forearms on the table. Crossed in front of him. I leaned in closer as well out of habit.

"It's nothing."

"You're a true friend. You really mean me well hunh?"

I nodded lightly as he sat back in his chair and stared at me.

"What Alex?"

He shook his head nothing before starting to eat again. I saw my coworker Pam coming to the table out of the corner of my eye and I sighed. Ever since I told her about Drew she'd been trying to hook me up.

"Well hello Al. Who is this nice looking young man you have here?"

I shook my head as Alex blushed.

"This is my friend Alex. Alex this is Pam. She's taken it upon herself to marry me off. So before you waste your time he's engaged," I spit out before she had a chance to say anything else.

"Fine. Fine. I'm just looking out for you boo. You're a good girl. You're like a daughter to me," she said before massaging my shoulders and kissing my cheek and walking away.

I hated when she did shit like that and got me in my feelings. Pam was a well off retiree. She only worked here because she was bored at home. I on the other hand needed this job and any other I could get.

My mom died when I was fifteen and my dad struggled to keep a job and provide for us. By sixteen I was working at McDonald's to help pay the bills but we still ended up losing the house. I guess that was too much for his pride to handle because he left town and shipped me to my grandmother's house.

Since then he's returned to Memphis to visit on a regular basis and we've strengthened our relationship, but it was rough there for a minute.

"She seems cool," Alex said breaking me out of my thoughts. I smiled lightly.

"Yea. She means well."

"So why are you single?"

I shrugged. "Just haven't found the right one. I keep giving myself to the wrong one and it just ends horribly."

"That's messed up baby. I'd love to have you. I honestly believe if I'd met you a year ago we'd be together. You're so loving and supportive. Who wouldn't want to do right by you?" I couldn't help but blush as his phone rang. "Yea what's up? Oh, you outside? Here I come." He stood and I pouted. I was disappointed. He walked over to me and lifted me up by placing his hand under my chin.

"Walk me out. I texted my brother and told him to pick me up from here." I walked behind him slowly and unwillingly. He looked back at me and smiled.

"You know I'm gone text you the whole time you're at work Alayziah. So stop pouting."

Scrunching my face up I mugged him before smiling.

"Fine."

When we made it to his brother's car he introduced us to each other before closing the passenger door and leaning against it, looking down at me.

"Thanks again baby – for everything."

"You don't have to thank me for that. What are friends for?"

His hands found their way to my waist and he pulled me into him. I wrapped my arms around his waist as he kissed me on my forehead.

Damn my panties got wet.

"Call me on your break," he instructed still holding on to me. A second passed and I looked into his eyes. His pants growing under me. I guess he was turned on too. He smiled, I smiled, and removed myself from his arms.

"I'll call you when I get off," I said over my shoulder.

"That's fine, but still, call me on your break."

I shook my head and chuckled as I made my way back into the restaurant. After I closed the door behind me he opened his and got inside the car.

Alexander

I kind of felt bad. I'd been texting Alayziah all day every day for the past few weeks. Hell I was talking to her more than I was talking to Carmen. We just had so much shit going on that I welcomed the distraction that was Alayziah. She was so loving and sweet and good to look at.

A nigga didn't mind just sitting in silence staring at her or just sitting next to her and just being. No conversation, no sex, no kids running around... just being. I hadn't spent any time alone with her though. After I gave her a kiss on the forehead and hugged her and my dick got hard I knew that probably wasn't the best thing to do.

I kind of felt like I was using her. I'd dump all my problems on her and she'd just take it in. Let me vent and say nothing, or she would pray, or offer me some advice. She knew just what to do when I needed her to. I told her that I was seriously considering ending things with Carmen and she wasn't even on no shady shit.

She told me that I needed to do what was best for me, what would give me peace and what would help me to become a better man. I was constantly arguing with Carmen and her father. Felt like she wasn't respecting me. Submitting to me. Felt like she was putting her pops above me. Like she was more concerned with pleasing him than me. And I wasn't about to have that in my marriage.

It was making me question whether or not she was the one for me, especially after talking with Alayziah.

She never talked against my marriage or Carmen for that matter. She just always was concerned with what was best for me, and I'd never had a woman do that before. She had a nigga wide open, so much so that I was at Carmen's youngest baby's birthday party texting Alayziah. I wanted to see her again but I knew that wasn't a good idea.

Even though I didn't really want to be around Carmen right now I adored her children like they were mine so I was happy to be there for them. I paid for them to go to school. I'm at every event and every game. I pay for whatever they need. I'm the one that paid for this party for baby girl. I just spent the money I had saved up putting a new transmission in Carmen's car.

I was struggling financially because I was providing for her, her kids, and my parent's. I was helping my mother pay the bills because my father had just had heart surgery so he wasn't working.

I had to move back in with them. I lost my car. I was basically starting over and now looking at expenses to take care of my license and hire a lawyer to get me some more time, I felt like the world was caving in on me.

I had a daughter of my own that I had to pay child support for. Plus, probation fees and a balance for stealing out of a jewelry store that was three hundred a month.

A nigga was struggling and Alayziah was definitely my peace. So when I saw one of Carmen's baby's daddy's walk in I was pissed. The nigga was abusive and did nothing for his kid but she had the nerve to invite the nigga to the party I paid for.

Now I knew for a fact that she had been lying to me because she told me that she wasn't talking to any of them anymore. So if she wasn't...how this nigga find out about the party? Her ass was about to get it and if he came at me wrong he was about to too.

Alayziah

Even though me and Alex texted all day we didn't actually talk unless something was wrong and he needed to vent. What they had going on was so toxic. I didn't want to seem jealous and tell him that I felt like they needed to slow down, but I just didn't believe in starting a marriage with so many issues. So much fighting. That just seemed like setting yourself up for failure.

Like, how can you expect a solid marriage with a rocky foundation?

I tried to be there for him as much as I could, but it was starting to get to me. I was tired of being the friend. Tired of being the one they went to when they needed to talk. While the woman they had wasn't taking care of business.

And I was home, alone and lonely.

He called and I didn't even want to answer. I wanted to dead the friendship completely. It was getting closer to their wedding day and I knew I was going to have to get used to not talking to him as much. I figured we might as well start now, but I couldn't even ignore him no matter how much I wanted to.

"Hello?"

"Why you sound so dry?" He asked and I shrugged like he could see me.

"No reason. What's up?"

"I had to go ahead on and break things off with Carmen."

My heart dropped immediately. I'd been telling him lately that I felt bad about talking to him so much. He'd been making comments about how he wished he was the man to marry me and calling me baby, telling me that he loves and appreciates me and I just felt so bad. I felt like I was distracting him, but every time I told him that we needed to talk less he talked me out of it. So how was I supposed to feel now?

"Why? What happened?"

As he told me about the fight that he had with her and one of her baby daddy's I sighed. They had way too much drama going on, and she had just uploaded a picture of him and her daughter to Facebook talking about how in love they are. How lucky she is. How he's a great father to her children. How they call him daddy. And here he is telling me that they're over.

"Well Alex. You gotta do what you gotta do. You gotta do what's best for you. I'm behind you no matter what."

"I know you are. That's why I want to do something for you to show you how much I love you and appreciate you. I know we've only been talking for a month but I love you baby. You're the best woman I've ever known. You show me what a real woman is. I want to do something special for you. I want to plan a special evening for us. Can I do that?"

I was skeptical. I didn't want to be his rebound. But at the same time, I'm a damn good woman and he's been honest with me so far, so why would he stop now?

"You sure it's over between you and her?"

"Positive. I'm done with her. I'm going to still be around for the kids because they had nothing to do with this. But I'm done with her. I want you."

I couldn't help but blush. I guess there was no point in hiding my feelings now. Alex had everything I thought I wanted and needed, and now that I had the opportunity to be with him I was going to take full advantage of that.

"Okay. I would love that Alex."

Alexander

Alayziah had just texted me and asked me for the room number. I looked out the window and saw her grabbing her bag and a white box. I rented us a hotel room for the night. I ain't gone lie, I wanted to get inside her; but that wasn't the only thing on my mind.

Really I just wanted to hold her and be in her presence. She filled me with such peace. I had so much going on and I needed that peace. I pulled my eyes away from the window and lit the candles I brought.

After cutting the volume on the TV down I cut some music on and dimmed the lights. I had a tray of fruit and a bottle of wine waiting for her as well. It wasn't much, but I knew she was going to love it because she liked simple shit like this.

I paced around the room waiting for her to make her way to me. I have never been so nervous and excited in my life. Lightly she pecked against the door and it sounded just like the beating of my heart. As bad as I wanted her up here I found myself slowly walking to the door to let her in.

When I did she scrunched her face up immediately and I realized I didn't have on anything but some boxers and basketball shorts. I'd just gotten out the shower and hadn't had time to dress. She always told me that she didn't want to see my body because of my color and my tattoos. Said that shit turned her on. So I know she was going crazy at the sight of me.

"I'm sorry baby…" I said opening the door laughing at her silly ass.

"Why don't you have on any clothes?" She handed me the white box.

"I just got out the shower baby."

"Umhm," she mumbled putting her bag in the chair by the window.

"What's this?" I asked as she sat on the bed.

"Just open it."

I did as I was told and my heart melted. Strawberry cupcakes. I told her that I loved strawberry cake. Really strawberry anything. Here I was trying to do something special for her and she surprised me. I looked at her through the mirror and she blushed.

"You do listen to me hunh?" She nodded. "You gone make me buy you a house one day girl."

I was serious too. The way I was feeling for her she was going to be wife number three. And you know they say the third time is the charm. I sat the box of cupcakes down and walked over to her as she took off her jean jacket.

She had on a pink romper with blue and black flowers. The sides were cut out so I could see her sides and the sides of her breasts.

The fuck was she thinking teasing a nigga like this?

I already told her that I wanted to make love to her. How she expect a nigga to keep my composure under these circumstances?

"I can't get a hug?" I asked with a smile as I looked down on her.

She got up reluctantly. I guess she was thinking about what happened the first and last time we hugged. I grabbed her and pulled her into me and she rubbed my back up and down.

"Why you rubbing on me like that?" Shit was getting my dick hard.

"I missed you," she practically moaned.

"I missed you too," I said before cupping her face between my hands and placing my lips on hers.

I'd wanted to kiss her since I first saw her. She had some sweet plump lips. And they felt so good I moaned. Must've turned her on because she pulled me closer to her. I couldn't help myself. I was tired of pecking at her lips.

Slowly I eased my tongue into her mouth to see if she would allow me entrance, she did. Our tongues danced against each other like they'd done it before. This time she was the one who moaned. I started massaging her scalp. She started sucking my lips. I lifted her up and wrapped her legs around my waist and tossed her on the bed.

Looking up at me she smiled. Her eyes had lowered like she was high. She looked so fucking good. I knew we were rushing, I knew we were moving fast, I knew she wanted to go slow and not be so reckless, but none of that mattered. I had to get inside of her. As I crawled between her legs she pushed me away gently.

"What's wrong?"

Running her fingers through her hair she sat up in the middle of the bed.

"You promise that it's over with her?"

I could see the fear in her eyes. I wanted to reassure her. Not because I wanted to have sex, but because I wanted her to know that I wanted her and her alone. Yes, I loved Carmen, yes I was still spending time with Carmen, and yes people still thought we were together, but I wanted Alayziah No matter the cost.

I had to have her.

"I promise baby. It's over. I want you. We don't have to have sex. I know you think we're moving too fast with our feelings. But I can't help that I fell for you. I'm just trying to get our bodies to catch up with my heart I guess. You can't help who your heart wants and my heart wants you. Only you." She smiled lightly before running her hand down my face. "I love you Alayziah."

"I love you too."

After getting out of the bed I grabbed one of my t-shirts and handed it to her for her to put on. She went into the bathroom to change. While she was in there I heard my phone vibrating. I looked at it and it was Carmen asking me where I was. I shot her a lie back quickly before Alayziah came out.

"You don't want to wrap your hair up?" I asked her.

We were going to end up falling asleep in each other's arms. She smiled as she crawled over to me. Kissing my lips lightly she shook her head no. As we both laid on our sides, chest to chest, I wrapped my arm around her, and she wrapped her arm around me, stroking my spine lightly with her fingertips.

I shivered under her touch.

"Stop," I warned.

"Why?"

"That's turning me on."

"So?"

"Kiss me."

Lifting her head slightly she did as she was told. My lips found their way to her neck as I flipped her onto her back. She spread her legs and allowed me to lean against her as I nibbled on her neck.

"Ummm..." she moaned taking my face into her hands and kissing me. I couldn't help myself. My hands went from her stomach to her thighs to her pussy. I stopped kissing her abruptly and stared down at her. "What?"

"You don't have any panties on. You giving you to me hunh?" I twirled my middle and ring finger against her clit.

"Mmmm..." Alayziah moaned again.

I knew her moans would be like music to my ears. I had to hear it some more. Pushing my shirt up and over her head my mouth began to lick and suck on each of her nipples while my fingers still worked their magic on her clit. She grinded against me. Getting wetter and wetter. Her breathing was short and choppy as her mouth opened slightly.

I looked up at her as I kissed down her stomach, stopping at her clit. Sliding one finger inside her and covering her clit with my mouth at the same time I flattened her stomach as she arched her back. I needed that ass flat so I could find and tease her spot. Her legs wrapped around my shoulders and I smiled as I pushed and pulled my finger inside of her. Licking. Sucking. Biting. Blowing on her clit. Her moans were sending me over the edge. I was about to nut and I wasn't even inside of her.

Taking my free hand, I pulled my shorts down and ate her until my dick was free. When it was I positioned myself on top of her so I could enter her. Taking the lips on her face into mine I slowly eased myself inside of her. She moaned and bit down on my lip as I put all of me inside of her. She was so tight. So wet. So hot. I couldn't even move. I just laid there. Inside of her for a few seconds. And stared at her. I truly was in love.

Alayziah

The past two months of my life have been awesome. For the first time in years I was happy and in love. Alex wasn't perfect, but he was perfect for me. He made me feel so special. It's like, he valued me and appreciated me and I loved him for that.

We weren't in a committed relationship yet but I didn't even care about titles. We had a connection, or at least that's what I thought – until I walked into my church for the first time in months and saw him with Carmen. I didn't want to let it faze me. I didn't want to act a fool in the church. I didn't want to get all in my feelings, but I couldn't understand for the life of me why he was there with her.

After he had been in me a few times out of the week every week. After he'd constantly came inside of me trying to get me pregnant. I was on birth control though. I was struggling to provide for myself. I couldn't take care of a baby too. He had been telling me on a daily basis that he loved me and wanted to marry me. Wanted to have a family with me.

We'd even started looking at apartments to rent. I was even considering getting off my birth control after he proposed. Which he said was coming soon. But here he was, in church, sitting next to her. And they were all hugged up. Smiling. Like they didn't have a care in the world. I can't lie, I'd been feeling bad about what I was doing with him.

I never meant to be the reason he left her and he swore that I wasn't. That I had no reason to feel bad, but I did. So much so that I stopped going to the church. Couldn't face her or her father, but something inside of me was telling me to come to church today and I see why.

I sat on the back pew and logged into my Facebook account only to find more disturbing statuses and pictures of them together. One was taken just a couple of days ago. A day that he told me that he couldn't see me because he was sick from food poisoning. But here he was, having lunch with her. Served his ass right if he did get sick. I was so pissed looking at that shit.

I stood, about to leave the church and my eyes connected with his and his expression immediately changed. Deep down I was hoping that he would get up and run after me. Tell me that it wasn't what it looked like. Give me some excuse as to why he was all hugged up with her; but I realized he wasn't going to when she wrapped her arm tighter around him. I couldn't even make it out of the sanctuary before tears were flooding my eyes. I can't believe it.

That nigga played me.

Alexander

It broke my heart to see Alayziah upset, and at that moment I felt like shit because there was nothing I could do. I couldn't run after another woman with my fiancée sitting right next to me. Yea I lied to Alayziah about my situation with Carmen, but it was complicated. I didn't plan on falling for her, and I didn't plan on her giving me a chance but when she did, I took it.

Carmen and I were still letting people think we were engaged. We were still kicking it tough. I was still having sex with her, but I made love to Alayziah. I was with Carmen, but I wanted Alayziah. I was just in a tight place.

Carmen and I had history, but Alayziah and I had chemistry.

I love Carmen's kids, I couldn't just dip on them, and it was hard spending time with them and not laughing and tripping with Carmen and remembering why I fell for her in the first place. I fucked up. I know I did. I never wanted Alayziah to find out. I planned on ending it with Carmen completely when I got my court stuff taken care of and got on my feet financially; I just needed Alayziah to ride it out with me for a little while longer.

After three long church services and dropping Carmen and the kids off I made my way to Alayziah's place. I was surprised she answered the door. When she did she didn't even look at me. She looked so good. Her hair was wrapped with a scarf around it. No makeup. Just puffy eyes and red lips from crying over me.

That shit hurt.

She was wearing my shirt.

That shit hurt worse.

She turned slightly to the side and opened the door wider so I could walk in. I had this whole speech planned full of lies that I thought would pacify her so she would keep satisfying me. But when I saw the pain in her face, all of that went out the window. I just wanted to make her feel good. Feel loved. I grabbed her hand and led her to her couch.

"Let me have it. Get it off your chest," I spoke preparing for the worst.

At first, she remained silent as a single tear slid down her face.

"Why did you lie Alex?"

"*It's complicated.* I didn't really lie. I just didn't tell you everything."

"Whatever Alex. You're still with her. After I asked you constantly what was up with y'all. We still could've done our thing if you were with her. I just wouldn't have given my heart and body to you. Why did you lie?" More tears fell from her eyes.

"I'm sorry Alayziah. I never meant to hurt you. I just didn't want to tell you the truth because I didn't want to change the way you look at me. Yea I'm still messing with Carmen but I'm single. She knows that I don't want to be with her anymore. She's just helping me financially because she feels bad about her pops calling the police on me and I agreed to act like we are still together because she's been in so many failed relationships and she didn't want to hear her parent's mouth about being right about me," I grabbed her face and turned her towards me. "I'm just using her. I love you and I want you Alayziah. Do you believe me?"

She removed my hand from her face and stood. "You got me out here looking like a fool Alex."

"You not looking like a fool. Is this where you want to be? Or not?"

"That doesn't matter."

"Yes it does. Is this where you want to be or not?"

"You know it is."

"Then that's all that matters. I'm yours. You just have to trust me. When I get my court stuff taken care of I promise I'm going to commit to you. You just have to trust me Alayziah."

She didn't trust me right now and at this point I didn't blame her, but I couldn't lose her. I had to make this up to her.

"How did you even get here?"

"My mom's truck."

That was a lie too. I was in Carmen's truck. I don't know why I lied to her so much. I guess because I thought she couldn't handle the truth.

"When do you have to take it back? Let me follow you home so you can drop it off. I want to spend the night with you."

"You don't have to do all that baby. I'll just go home and get my brother to drop me off on his way home."

She looked at me skeptically before shaking her head and walking into her room.

31

Alayziah

When I found out that Alex was still messing off with Carmen things got really awkward between us. I was so paranoid. I wanted to trust him, and wait for him, but I'd been hurt and played so many times that it was hard. I found myself checking their Facebook pages every day and almost every day they'd be posting a status or picture talking about how in love and happy they were.

Then, I'd call or text him and flip out, and then he'd ignore me for a few days, and then he'd get horny and show up at my house, and then we'd have sex and everything would be good for a few days. Until he stopped calling and texting as much.

Until he stopped coming around as much. Then, I got paranoid again, and I'd go on Facebook again, and I'd see them together again, and I'd act crazy again, and he'd ignore me again, and we'd fuck again. Ugh. It was a cycle that needed to end.

I didn't want to let him go. Now they were saying they were married, and he swore it wasn't true. Who fucking lies about being married? Their bitch asses. I knew it wasn't true because I was checking for their marriage record every day, but the shit was pissing me off. It was like I was his dirty little secret. His mistress. His side chick.

And I couldn't understand that.

I begged him to be honest with me. He could've came to me and said, 'Alayziah, I like you and I love her, but I want to see what's up with you while I take a break from her.' I would have been cool with that, but all these lies and secrets is bullshit. We'd been fighting more than anything lately. I wasn't his peace anymore. I was a source of pain, and I felt like that was pushing him right back into her arms. I knew he was going to leave me. I just didn't know when.

I'd been blowing his phone up and of course he was ignoring me. Finally, he decided to show his face and I was pissed. As soon as he walked in the door I started going in on his ass.

"Alex why do you insist on lying to me? If you with her say you with her. If y'all married say you married. If it's just about the sex say that. Just be honest for once so I can let you go."

"Mane I'm so tired of having this conversation. I'm single. I don't belong to nobody. I can do whatever the fuck I want to do with whoever the fuck I want to do it with. I got too much shit going on to be fighting with your ass. I can be with her for that. I gotta cut grass and shit just to make some extra money. I'm trying not to start back to selling weed but the harder I try to do right the harder it is to survive.

I gotta come up with five hundred dollars by Friday to pay my lawyer. Then I need another sixteen hundred if they agree to give me the continuance. I got a home visit with my probation officer Friday. And I gotta pray that she don't know about my court date otherwise she gone be shipping my ass back to jail. My daughter's birthday is Sunday and I don't have any money to buy her anything.

And on top of all of that I gotta come over here to hear this bullshit from you? Yea I'm still fucking with Carmen. Yea I love her. I was with her ass for ten months. And I love her kids. I love the little family we got going on. I love spending time with them. But I also like what I have going on with you. I'm sorry. I didn't plan on falling for you. I'm sorry for putting you through this. But she's helping me with my money. And I ain't trying go to jail just to prove to you that I love you.

You and my daughter are my every day reason to smile. I'm willing to do whatever it takes to be able to come home to the two of you every day. Even if that means I gotta fuck around with her for a little while."

My emotions were all over the place right now. I wanted to be his peace and give him what he needed but how was I supposed to ignore the fact that she gave him what I couldn't? *A family.* He loved those kids. He loved her. I fucked around and started to love him. I didn't say anything. I just went into my kitchen, opened my cookie jar, and pulled out half of the money I had saved. I walked back into my living room with tears in my eyes and handed him the five hundred dollars.

"What is this?" Alex's eyes and voice softened.

"You said you needed it."

"I could never ask you for anything. Do you know how bad I feel for you to even have to know I'm struggling like this Alayziah? I don't even feel like a man right now. I feel like I don't have anything to offer you. Maybe that's why I'm still messing with her too. I don't deserve you."

I walked over to him and put the money into his pocket before kissing him deeply.

"I love you Alex."

"But why. Why do you love me? Why me?"

I smiled lightly and shrugged. "You just make me want to love you. I feel like you need it. And I thought you would appreciate it."

"I do baby. I do need it. And I really do appreciate you. I promise I do. I'm so sorry," he took me into his arms and started covering my face with kisses.

"I'm so sorry Al. I love you. Please don't leave me."

Before I knew it his hands were under my shirt and my mind was gone.

Alexander

After I finished sexing Carmen up I thought she'd be satisfied for the week. I took her son to the zoo the day before and had already planned on going to her middle child's graduation in a couple of days. I'd done my job as far as she was concerned.

Now I needed to go check on Alayziah. She was going to be pissed. I blocked her number so all her calls went straight to voicemail and I didn't know she texted me until I scrolled through my log. I told her that my phone was broken. That I didn't have her number blocked.

She actually believed the shit. Carmen was getting suspicious so she deleted Alayziah from both our Facebook pages and I knew that's what Alayziah was calling me to trip about.

I watched as Carmen laid across our bed and rolled my eyes. Some days I couldn't stand her. Some days I couldn't stand to be away from her. It was like, the worse things were between Carmen and I the better things were between Alayziah and I; but the better things got between Carmen and I the worse things got between Alayziah and I.

Carmen was going hard for a nigga ever since I broke it off with her. She stopped going to her dad's church. Stopped being around them as much. Started spending all of her time with me and her kids. I couldn't deny her of me when she was genuinely trying to change and do right, but Alayziah had been down for me at my worst time.

Now that I had moved in with Carmen she was really pushing a nigga to get married. I didn't want to because I knew once I made that commitment to Carmen that things were going to be over with me and Alayziah. Call me selfish, but I wanted them both. And I didn't plan on letting Alayziah go no time soon.

Carmen sat up in the bed and smiled at me.

"What's got you all happy?" I asked her. I knew the dick was good but that wasn't nothing new.

"Well...I'm just glad that you finally decided to move in and we can be a real family now. Now that your court stuff is over and you've gotten us both new cars...I just feel like we're moving in the right direction."

I nodded in agreement.

"I've done all that you've asked me to Alex. You need to choose. If you want me then you need to commit to me. We need to get married. Today. And you need to end whatever it is you have going on with Alayziah."

"We're just friends."

"Whatever. You need to choose."

"I don't appreciate you giving me no ultimatum."

"What do you expect Alex? We've been telling people that we were married a month ago. We don't have anything to show for it. My daddy is getting suspicious. It took you forever to move in. And now that you're here he's really pushing for us to get married."

I sighed heavily. Here we go with this shit.

"Look… just… wait until my birthday, okay? Give me a couple of weeks to take care of some stuff and then we can get married."

"You promise?" She asked standing and walking towards me.

"I promise."

She fell to her knees and sucked any thoughts of Alayziah clear out of my head.

Alayziah

Alex and I were talking less and less but despite that today was his birthday and I wanted to do something special for him. He had a fascination with Jacuzzi tubs so I rented us a honeymoon suite at a hotel downtown.

I had candles lit with rose petals all over the floor and bed. Soft music playing in the background. Chocolate covered fruit and wine chilling in the refrigerator. Lavender scented massage oil for the full body massage I was going to give him after his soak in the Jacuzzi tub and shower and his favorite strawberry cake with candles.

I told him to be here at seven. Now at eight I was starting to get frustrated. Not with him, but with myself because I should have known he wasn't going to do right. Adele's *One and Only* was playing in the background as I did something that I knew I shouldn't have done – checked their Facebook pages.

He posted two hours ago about how special his wife was making him feel on his birthday. She posted a picture of him with her kids an hour ago. I was tired of getting played. Tired of being hurt. Tired of being pissed. So I stood, took pictures of everything in the room, and sent them to him via text.

Me: *You know what nigga? I'm so done with your lying ass. I spent all this money and time trying to do something for you on your birthday and you couldn't even respect and appreciate me enough to say you couldn't make it. All you had to do was say you had plans and I would have canceled the shit or rescheduled instead. Now I'm here. Alone. But that's alright. I'll call my ex and have him to enjoy this with me.*

Ex-Factor: *I didn't know she was doing this shit Al. It was a surprise. What was I supposed to do? Tell her I had to leave because you had something planned for me?*

Me: *Fuck you nigga. Delete my number. Oh yea...happy birthday.*

Ex-Factor: *That's what this is about? You mad at me because you want some dick? I'll be there in a few. Text me the room information.*

Me: *No. Stop texting me.*

Ex-Factor: *Stop texting you? First you was mad because you wasn't hearing from me. Now I'm texting you and telling you I'm on my way and you got an attitude? You crazy mane.*

Me: *I'm crazy? Why am I always crazy Alex? Because you don't know how to communicate? You always lying to me and leading me on. You always hurting my heart and you don't even care. You put me in these crazy situations and then you get mad when I react crazy. Just leave me the hell alone. I deserve better than this. I deserve better than you.*

Ex-Factor: *SO YOU WANT TO BE WITH SOMEBODY ELSE? YOU MY WOMAN. SEND ME THE ROOM INFORMATION ALAYZIAH.*

Throwing my phone on the bed I went into the bathroom and sat on the toilet. His ass was so full of shit and I was a fool to love him and want him, but what can I say? I love that nigga and love will have you doing some crazy things. Even though I told him I was going to have another nigga to come by I wasn't. I was too loyal for that. I wanted no one but him and he knew that.

He didn't even take my threats seriously anymore. He knew I wasn't going anywhere, and I hated that he knew the power he had over me. My phone started to ring and it was him. I wanted to ignore him but I couldn't be a hypocrite because I hated when he did that to me so I went back into the room and answered.

"Hello?"

"So you not gone give me the room information?"

"Why should I? You haven't cared up until this point. Why start now?"

"Alayziah you knew my situation when you started messing with me. What did you expect? I can't just drop everything for you sometimes like you want me to, but I'm doing the best that I can. Her kids are like my kids. This is my family. I can't just drop them and lay up with you. I wish I could but I can't."

"That's bullshit Alex. I didn't know your situation when I started messing with you because you lied! You told me that you were done with her! So if y'all aren't in a relationship why the fuck are you with her now?!"

"Ima need you to lower your voice and stop yelling at me. What hotel are you at Alayziah?"

"I don't want you here Alexander," I said softly with tears filling my eyes. I was so weak for him, and because of that I felt so stupid and insecure.

"Why not baby?"

For a moment he almost sounded like the sweet man I'd fallen in love with. Sitting on the bed I sighed into the phone as I wiped tears from my eyes.

"Are you crying Al? Baby…"

"I'm fine," I lied. "Just…enjoy your birthday Alex. I'm sorry to have interrupted your family time. I love you, bye," I hung up as he called my name.

Standing I went to the closet and grabbed my bags as my phone sounded off again. Shaking my head, I put him on speakerphone as I packed my clothes up.

"Yea?"

"Will you just tell me where you are so I can make you feel better?"

"I don't need you to make me feel better Alex. I need you to do better. Can you do that?"

I stopped packing and looked at the phone as if I could see him. He was quiet for a second before breathing deeply.

"You've been on my mind. I grow fonder every day lose myself in time. Just thinking of your face. God only knows why it's taken me so long to let my doubts go. You're the only one that I want."

He sang *One and only* into my ear and I tried not to slide down the wall.

"Is that how you still feel about me baby?" he asked before singing more.

"Promise I'm worthy to hold in your arms so come on and give me a chance to prove I am the one who can walk that mile until the end starts. If I've been on your mind you hang on every word I say. Lose yourself in time. At the mention of my name."

By now I'd slid down the wall, my face saturated with tears. His voice was like cream in my ears. It always did something to me. He sung to me on my voicemail for my birthday and I'd saved it and I play it at least once a week. He always got the best of me when he sang. There was a power in his voice that…captivated you. Drew you in and made you believe in whatever he was singing about.

"Is that still how you feel about me baby?"

"Yes Alex."

"Then. Tell. Me. Where. You. Are."

"Peabody Hotel."

"Damn. You really went all out for your boy hunh?"

"Yeeees Alex," I whined.

My heart was hurting terribly.

"I'm sorry Noelle. I love you."

I hated when he called me by my middle name. No one else called me that and he knew it. Every time he called me that I got weaker for him. Like I was his and his alone. The way he said it made me question if anyone had ever said my name before. He looked at me in a way that made me question if I'd ever been seen before. Made love to me in a way that made me feel like I'd never been loved before.

Damn.

I'd fallen in love with another woman's man.

And I had no intentions of letting him go.

"I love you too Alex."

"Text me the room number, or is a key waiting for me at the front desk?"

"It is."

"I'm in the car. Be there in about twenty minutes."

"Okay Alex."

"Noelle…"

"Yes?"

"I love you."

Alexander

I fucked up again. Alayziah had been telling me that she had something special planned for me for my birthday for weeks and I was genuinely looked forward to it.

She was so excited because I'd gone all out for her birthday a couple of months earlier and her competitive ass wanted to one up me, but when I woke up this morning Carmen had the kids to bring me breakfast in bed and I'd been enjoying my day with them ever since. I was making my situation even harder to get out of by continuing to spend time with Carmen and her kids but I'd gotten used to us being a family.

Alayziah tripped all the time about not being able to compete with what I had with Carmen because she knows how much I want kids and a family and she can't give me that. I try to convince her that she doesn't have to compete. That she gives me things that Carmen can't, but she don't be trying to hear that shit, and I guess I can understand that because I spend all of my time with them.

To be honest I'm getting sick of having this same conversation over and over again. I'd been ignoring Alayziah's phone calls and text messages a lot lately simply because I didn't like to fight with her.

The reason I fell for her so hard in the beginning was because she was my place of peace, but if I'm gone be arguing with a woman I might as well stay with Carmen. Yea I know she hates to be ignored and I shouldn't do the shit but she just irritates the fuck out of me with her feelings and shit. She always wants me to reassure her that Carmen and I are over. That we're not having sex. That I don't want to be with her anymore. That we're not really married. I hate lying to her but I don't want to lose her, especially when she does shit like this.

I walked in the room a couple of hours later than I told Alayziah I was. Carmen gave me the hardest time when I tried to leave. I think she knew I was coming to see Al that's why her ass put up such a fight when I tried to leave.

Alayziah had consumed the entire bottle of wine that I'm sure was for the both of us. The candles she'd lit were burned out by now and she was knocked out in the middle of the bed. I felt like shit. I didn't mean to keep hurting her, but I just couldn't seem to get it right. Not wanting to argue with her I just stripped, got in the bed, took her into my arms, and held her until I fell asleep.

Alayziah

"He did what?" My best friend Marcel yelled.

We were sitting across from each other at The Republic Coffee House and I should have known not to tell him about Alex while we were in public. In the beginning he loved Alex because he thought Alex loved me; but the more I let him in on what was going on with us the more he started to hate him.

"See that's why there are so many fucked up women in the head now. Because niggas like him do shit like this. Mane I wish a woman would do some sweet shit like that for me. I'd wife her ass immediately, but nah niggas like him get that kind of treatment and fuck it up for the next nigga when they don't appreciate it. Mane show me where this nigga live. I'll beat some sense into his stupid ass."

I shook my head and laughed at my crazy best friend. Really he was the only friend I had. People thought we were more than that but we'd never cross that line because I dated his cousin a while back. That's how we met.

"Marcel…"

"Nah Love I'm for real. You don't deserve to be treated like this. You are too good of a woman. You deserve better baby."

Wiping the tears from my eyes I sighed heavily. I knew in my mind that he was right but my heart wasn't trying to hear that.

"I know Marcel. I'm just trying to wait it out. He told me that in a month once he went to court for the last time he was going to end things with her and get serious about us. If things don't change by then I'm going to end it."

"You promise?"

"I promise."

"Cool. Now…let me tell you this hoe ex of mine did. Would you believe she came to the church telling folks I gave her an STD?"

Alexander

When Alayziah and I first started talking I had the craziest dream. I dreamed that I was bungee jumping and something went wrong. I was in a coma. She was the only person there with me. Carmen wasn't there. My parents weren't there. Her parents weren't there. The only person that was there for me was Alayziah. When I woke up from my coma I looked at her and she grabbed my hand. I was so surprised to see her there and she said to me, "I'll always be here for you."

I believed her. Maybe that's why I started to feel so comfortable around her after I had that dream.

Now I'm sitting in the hospital alone and I want her here with me but I know that's not possible. I'd been having some health issues lately. I've been tired a lot and I've been having some crazy migraines. I haven't been able to eat or sleep and the shit has really been fucking with me. It's been killing me on Sunday's with all of the music surrounding me. The only person I told about it was Alayziah and she told me to see about myself but of course I didn't listen until it was too late.

I couldn't take the pain anymore so I decided to make myself an appointment. I know I shouldn't have called her because she wouldn't be able to come up here and I knew she'd worry but I just had to hear her voice. I pulled out my phone and called and hoped she didn't answer. I'd settle for listening to her voicemail.

"Hello?"

"Hey."

"…Hey."

"How are you?"

"I'm good, how are you?"

"Listen…I know I haven't been talking to you much lately…"

"It's cool Alex. What's up?"

"I'm in the hospital."

"What? For what? Are you okay? What hospital? Who's there with you? Is Carmen there? Do you need me to come up there with you?"

I smiled lightly.

"The migraines. I'm sure I'll be okay. I just…wanted to hear your voice. You know you bring me peace. I called Carmen. She's on her way up here." She remained silent. "Al?"

"Call me when you leave and let me know what they say."

"Okay."

She hung up. It was selfish to put that weight on her but it eased my mind.

"I don't even know why he called me knowing I wasn't going to be able to be with him. Now I'm going to drive myself crazy worrying about him. Especially since I know about the dream he had. What if it's something serious? What if something happens to him and I'm not there for him?"

I was standing outside of my job pacing back and forth yapping Marcel's ear off. He always seemed to have a way to ease my mind.

"Relax Love. I'm sure he's going to be okay. He probably just needed to hear your voice and for you to tell him that everything was going to be okay. You know that's what you are to him. Someone he vents to when he's going through shit. Someone that encourages him and lifts him up. He knew what his ass was doing."

"I couldn't even do that this time. I just told him to call me and tell me what happened after he left. I'm just so drained emotionally. I want nothing more than to be there with him. Holding his hand. Supporting him. And to know that at a time when he needs me most I can't be there for him..."

"So what you want to do? Go up there? I'll go with you. You know I'll knock him and his bitch out for you if need be."

I smiled.

"No crazy. I'm just going to go home for the rest of the day. I won't be able to function right until I hear from him and know that he's okay."

"Well alright. Call me if you need me. I love you."

"I love you too."

When I ended the call I noticed I had a text from Alex. I smiled at his name in my phone. Swear I changed it every day depending on how he had me feeling.

Honey: *Why am I at the hospital horny thinking about you?*

Me: *Well it's good to see you're okay physically hehe.*

Honey: *Lol yea I'm straight baby. They're giving me a prescription and hoping these migraines don't affect my vision.*

Me: *Good! I was worried sick about you. I was about to leave work.*

Honey: *Whatever. You didn't care about me. You just wanted to use me as an excuse to leave work early lol.*

Me: *-_- Whatever nigga. I was worried about you. You know I care about you. But I'm about to go back in so I'll talk to you later.*

Honey: *Or you can stop by the house and give me some pussy.*

Me: *Where is Carmen? Why don't you get some from her?*

Honey: *Alayziah I want your pussy. My pussy. You're the best I ever had. I don't want nobody else's but yours.*

Me: *You sure you up for that?*

Honey: *HELL YEA*

Alexander

When I walked down those stairs and saw Alayziah walk through the door my eyes lit up. Literally. I missed her so much. I was so happy to see her. I immediately took her into my arms and couldn't help but laugh as she looked at me skeptically.

"I missed you," I spoke almost dragging her up the stairs. She didn't answer me back. She was getting tired of my shit but I didn't care. I love her and she ain't going anywhere and I was about to get her pregnant to make sure of that.

"Aye why the hell you got this little ass dress on?" I asked her. She started working at this office and she was always wearing some tight dresses or leggings showing off all of my assets.

"Why? I'm single I can wear what I want."

"That's what you think," I said pulling her onto my lap and kissing on her neck. "You mine Alayziah. I don't want no other niggas looking at you."

She looked at me like I was crazy and laughed. "You are something else."

"Whatever. Don't wear this shit to work anymore," I leaned back and took her with me. I kissed her and caressed her for a few seconds before she leaned up and grazed my nipples making my dick jump involuntarily. "I missed you Alayziah. I want you so bad," I leaned back up and kissed her again but she pushed me away and sat on the bed.

"I want you to wear a condom this time."

I looked at her ass like she was crazy. I'd been going in raw since the first time. No way in hell I was about to start wearing a condom now.

"Why Alayziah?"

"Because I was taking some antibiotics to keep my allergies from flaring up and I don't want them to cancel my birth control out. My doctor said that if I was on birth control it would be best to use a second form of protection until the antibiotics were out of my system."

"I don't want to babe. I want to feel you."

"You can feel me with a condom on. I don't trust you. And I'm not buying anymore plan B pills."

"I'll pull out," I lied.

"Fine."

I knew she was getting tired of buying them and she was tired of taking them. Think it ate at her emotionally. When we first started messing off we both wanted to have a baby together but when she found out about Carmen she started getting them along with the birth control she was already on. Her ass was avoiding my seeds at all costs.

I positioned her in the middle of the bed and kissed her deeply while I allowed my hands to roam her body. I removed her panties and went down on her and started pleasing her with my tongue like I knew she liked. She never could take that shit. She always put up a fight. Like she hadn't realized that the harder she fought the more determined I was to make her come.

"Okay stoooppp…" she moaned as I felt her legs begin to shake. As she came I pulled my dick from my boxers and entered her before she could recover.

"I love you Alayziah. I missed you. Did you miss me?" Finally, she shook her head yes. "Say it," I commanded pulling most of my dick out. Leaving just the head in.

"I missed you Alex."

"You love me?" I plunged deep inside of her. She tried to keep from moaning but there was no fighting it now.

"Yes Alex. I love you."

Hearing all I needed to hear I focused on making sure she felt my love for her.

Alayziah

He had been sending me flowers all week. I don't even know how he found out that I started working a new job to even send me flowers here. Knowing Andrew, he probably knew someone in my office and found out that I was here. I removed him from all of my social media sites after I walked in on him and his...boyfriend. And I hadn't talked to him since.

I can't lie there were times when I missed him. I missed things about him I guess I should say. I missed how he used to provide for me. Give me security. I missed how he used to cater to me. Take me out and show me off like I was his most prized possession.

I miss the way he used to just...stare my body up and down. We never had sex. I thought it was because he was a gentleman with self-control. It was probably because the thought of being with a woman repulsed him as much as the thought of being with a woman repulsed me.

Whatever the case we never took it there and I was glad we didn't. I didn't want to waste a number on my body count on him. Since I was bored at work I decided to call him and see what was up.

"Hey Alayziah. What's up?"

"You tell me Drew. What's up with all the flowers?"

He chuckled into the phone and I smiled. I really did miss him.

"I've been thinking about you since that day Alayziah. I really do love you. As much as I can you know? I just...I'm messed up. But I do love you. And I miss you."

"So how did you find out where I worked?" I asked ignoring his confession.

"Your boss is one of my old college buddies. He was telling me about the baddie he'd just hired and I asked him to show me a picture."

I blushed. "Oh."

"So what's new? You seeing anyone?"

"Umm..." Seeing as Alex and I had no titles I really didn't know how to answer him.

"Umm what Alayziah? It's a simple question."

"Yea."

"Yea you're seeing someone? Or yea it's a simple question."

I smiled again. "Both."

"Oh. Is he taking care of you Alayziah?"

I shrugged as if he could see me. No matter what I could say negatively about Andrew one thing I could say about him was that he took his role as a man seriously when it came down to providing for his woman and his family.

He's four years older than me with a daughter. He's the boss at this pharmaceutical company and he makes a pretty good salary. The entire time we were together he paid all of his bills and mine. Never once did I ever have to buy anything while I was with him. Whatever I wanted or needed he took care of it, and I'd always appreciated him for that.

"I mean…not like you Drew. Everybody ain't able," I joked trying to lighten the mood. If anything I was taking care of Alex but I wouldn't dare tell Drew that.

"If he can't take care of you he doesn't deserve you Alayziah."

"Drew…what do you want exactly?"

"I want you Alayziah. I miss you. I didn't realize how much you meant to me until I lost you. I know you might not want to be with me and I honestly couldn't take you rejecting me so you don't even have to answer. I just…want to be a part of your life. Can I be a part of your life Alayziah?"

Tapping my pen on my desk lightly I thought about it. I didn't see anything wrong with us being friends. The feelings that I'd had for him had withered away. I just didn't need him trying to move in on me.

"If you promise to only keep it on a friendship level that's cool."

"Really? Great. Okay. Cool. Are you going to church this Sunday?"

"Nah," I hadn't been to church since I saw Alex and Carmen there together a while ago.

"Well…would you like to come to church with me? You know I won't be able to sit with you the whole service because I'll be playing but I'd love to have you there."

"Yes. I'd like that. I need to go to church. It has definitely been a while."

"Cool. Can I pick you up around nine? Let's have breakfast before service. I don't need you bitching after service because you're hungry."

"Whatever. I am not that bad."

"Girl whatever. You are straight up evil when you're hungry."

I shook my head and laughed lightly as I sat back in my chair and continued our conversation.

∞

When I walked into the church with Drew and saw Alex sitting in the choir stand my feet just…stopped moving. Drew realized I was no longer by his side and he turned around to face me.

"What's wrong?" He asked as Alex stood. He hadn't began to make his way to me yet and I wasn't sure if I wanted him to.

"Nothing," I lied. I hadn't talked to Alex all week and I wasn't expecting to see him. Not today. Not here. This wasn't even the church that he normally played at.

"What is he doing here?" I asked as Alex finally started to walk towards us.

"Who Alex? He's playing second piano under me this morning. How do you know him?"

"I…we talk."

"Y'all talk? Alayziah, that nigga is married."

"No he's not. That's a lie."

"You believe that?"

Before I could answer Alex was standing in front of us.

"Where do I need to sit?" I asked Drew ignoring Alex's presence.

"Anywhere. I'd prefer it if you sat up close so I could look at you."

"So you gone act like you don't see me standing here?" Alex asked.

"Yea. Pretty much." I tried to walk away but he grabbed my arm.

"Can I just talk to you for a minute?" I looked at Drew and when he got the hint that I wanted him to leave he walked away.

"What Alex?"

"I miss you."

"You don't have to miss me. What's stopping you from talking to me and seeing me Alex?"

He looked at me as he ran his hand over the waves in his head.

"I'm sorry Al."

"You're always sorry Alex. You don't care about me and my feelings."

"I do care."

"Yea you care. You just don't care like I care and that hurts. You care more about her than me, and that's cool. I've accepted that I'm not a priority in your life. I'm just the one you call when something is wrong or when you need some sex."

"Alayziah you know that's not true baby."

"Yes it is Alex and that's cool. Just let me go. Leave me alone."

Before he could reply I walked towards the front of the church and found a seat. As service progressed I actually started to relax and enjoy the atmosphere. When I saw a woman that resembled Carmen come and sit next to me with a baby bump the walls of the church seemed as if they were about to close in on me.

My ears started ringing. Chest tightened. Hands started sweating. I didn't even want to look at her and confirm that it was her, but the sadness in Andrew's eyes and the fear in Alex's eyes let me know that it was her.

"Bitch, I'm four months pregnant. Alex and I are married. Stay the hell away from my husband."

I chuckled lightly. "That's funny. I've been messing with Alex for eight months and the whole time he's been telling me that he was done with you. Obviously that was a lie. That's cool though. But I'm gone tell you straight up...I see that you're pregnant...but that baby ain't in your face. Disrespect me again and I'm gone beat the shit out of you."

I stood and tried to walk away but she put her foot out and tried to trip me. I lost it. This bitch was the reason I couldn't have the only man I ever really loved. She didn't respect and appreciate him and now that I was giving what she lacked she wanted to fuck around and get pregnant and trap him?

I fucking lost it.

In church and all.

I punched the shit out of her ass before a man who was sitting on the same pew picked me up and carried me out of the church. Another grabbed Carmen and took her in the opposite direction. Drew and Alex ran after me as I bawled my eyes out. I was pacing outside of the church by the time they both made it outside. Alex made it to me first and I punched his ass too.

"Why didn't you tell me she was pregnant? Why couldn't you be honest nigga all you had to do was tell the truth! Why would you take away my choice and force me to deal with this bullshit because I fell in love with you? Why did you lie Alex?" I yelled. He just stood there with his head hanging in shame.

"Answer me!" I yelled slapping his ass.

"Mane Al you just…started acting crazy. I didn't like that side of you. When we first started talking you were so nice and sweet and respectful but then you started tripping and acting crazy so I fell back. I wasn't sure if I really wanted to be with you anymore and she stepped up and confused me."

"Nigga I was acting crazy because you are a liar! And I love you! But you don't love me! You only love what I can do to and for you. How I make you feel. How I take your stress away. Nigga I gave you my all and this whole time you've lied to me while you were with another woman. You love her. And that had me jealous. And insecure. And that made me hate you. To know that you don't appreciate me but she don't appreciate you. You…you…"

"I'm sorry. I ain't shit. I know I ain't shit. I feel like shit. I didn't mean for you to find out like this. I…I just didn't know how to tell you. I didn't want to lose you."

"So you're really married to her…hunh?"

"I haven't been married to her the whole time. We got married a week ago. I wanted to tell you but I didn't know how. She came to me and gave me an ultimatum. Told me she was pregnant and that she'd been doing all that I asked her to. She stopped going to her pops church. She ain't been spending time with him or letting him disrespect me.

She's been keeping the kids' daddies away so that's less drama. And her divorce was finalized. She told me if I wanted to be with her we had to get married that day so I just…did it. But I haven't sent the signed license in yet. I don't know if I'm really married or not Al. I don't know if I really want to be with her because I love you. I didn't mean to fall for you but I fell for you. I'm just…in a fucked up spot right now."

I took a step back and sighed heavily. I was officially done. I guess it took him getting married for me to actually have the strength to let him go. Sitting here looking at him and listening to him made me realize just how much I loved him. I love him more than I love myself. What other reason would I allow him to disrespect me this way?

"You don't have to worry about me calling you and texting you anymore Alex. You don't have to worry about me acting crazy. I'm done."

"You done? What do you mean you done? You can't leave me."

"Nigga...you're married."

"So? I love you. I want you. I need you."

"No you don't need me. You don't need my love. You don't appreciate my love. If you did you wouldn't have married her."

"You still love me?"

"I will always love you."

"Then don't leave me."

"What the fuck Alex? You think I'm finna be your side chick while you out here fronting like you living the married good life? Nah. I'm not finna play with you. You've lost all access to me."

I tried to walk away but he grabbed me by my waist and pulled me into his chest. Tears had begun to fall again and I was getting weaker as he held me tighter.

"Please Noelle. Don't leave me baby. I need you. You bring me peace. I miss and love you so much baby. No other woman loves me the way you do."

"Yea but you don't love me the way you love her," I sobbed.

"Baby..."

"Let me go Alex please. If you love me or care about me at all...please...just let me go."

"Noelle..."

"No Alex. Let me go!"

Unwillingly he released me. Only to turn me towards him and pull me into him. His hands cupping my face. His nose and forehead on mine.

"I'm sorry Noelle. I. I never meant to hurt you. And I'm sorry you had to find out like this." I wrapped my hands around his waist as he kissed my lips lightly. "I love you baby," he whispered.

"Let's go Alayziah," Andrew interrupted.

"No. You stay. You have to play. I'll call Marcel and have him to pick me up," I said removing myself from Alex's grip. He just stared at me with the most pathetic begging eyes.

"I'm sorry Alayziah."

I couldn't face him anymore. It was hurting too much. I turned my back to them both and walked to the curve and sat down. After pulling out my phone I texted Marcel and asked him to come and pick me up. He asked me for the address and I shot it to him before placing my face in my hands and crying until he pulled up.

Alexander

After two weeks of not talking to Alayziah I couldn't take it anymore. I called her and apologized and she accepted. Told her I loved her and she told me she loved me too. Told her I needed her and she told me I was a fool. I agreed, but that didn't change anything.

She rushed me off the phone to get ready to go out. Said she had a performance tonight. So I figured I'd swing through and let her know in person just how much I missed her. When she walked on to that stage my dick stood and my heart fell. I don't know if it was even possible but she looked more beautiful than she did the last time I saw her.

But, as much as I wanted to, I couldn't ignore the sadness in her eyes.

She looked around the crowd and her eyes fell on mine. Her eyebrows wrinkled in anger and she closed her eyes. After inhaling and exhaling deeply she looked me dead in my eyes and started to recite her poem.

"Said you wanted me to write you a poem to recite to your wife at your reception.
Well here you go…
To the woman I've committed myself to for the rest of my life three days before I
made you my wife I was inside the poet who wrote this piece for you. She gave me
everything I needed while you were trying and failing to satisfy me and your father.
Told her I'd marry her so she agreed to take our friendship farther. Filled her head
with lies like I planned on leaving you. Lied to her for so long I almost believed it
was the truth. But then I got my court stuff together and I started making some
extra money; you and I started getting along better so I started acting funny.
Stopped calling her as often started texting back less. Told her I loved her still but it
was really just about the sex. She had no problem giving it up even though I was
driving her crazy. Told her I was coming in her and that she could be having my
baby.
But I never came inside her I just wanted to keep her close. She had to know I was
playing her. She had to know my feelings were a joke. But she loved me so much she
kept riding with me and giving me money until she was broke. Spread them legs and
blew my phone up until I couldn't take it anymore. Started going off on her like I
never had before.

Figured if I disrespected her that she would get a clue but she stuck around anyway because I told her she was going to replace you. Let days go by without giving her some attention. Until I got tired of screwing her and her feelings. Told her I loved her and missed her and sexed her one last time. Then I started ignoring her without taking into consideration the effect that would have on her mind.

Guess her woman's intuition was screaming too loud because she looked up our marriage record. Threatened to expose me on Facebook so I left her the most disrespectful voicemail yelling at her. But she so stupid she still wants me and cries over me every day. She even kept her word to write this poem for me to read to you on our wedding day. And what makes this even better is I don't even feel bad about being the worst man she ever had.

And even though I call and text her every week or two I'm all yours now and I vow to love and be with you forever. And I'll love you twice as good because I stole her heart placed it inside of mine and now it's like we loving you together.

And I know I left her heartless but that's none of our concern. She said she wanted to love me unconditionally so I was her mistake and lesson to learn."

By the time she finished she had tears rolling down her cheeks. And I can't lie, they were running down mine as well. I couldn't believe she felt like my love and feelings for her weren't real. Like I'd been lying to her, using her, and leading her on all this time. That was so far from the truth I felt insulted, but I couldn't blame her looking at how fucked up the situation looked.

She walked off the stage towards the back and I made my way to her. When I made it to the dressing room that had her name on it the door was locked. I rested my head against the door. She was crying and I caused her this pain.

"Noelle…open the door baby."

"No!" She yelled.

"Alayziah please. Open the door."

"No Alex. Leave me alone!"

"I can't do that baby. I'm not leaving until I see you. There's no other way for you to get out so you might as well open the door and get this over with. I'm not going anywhere."

After a few moments of silence and a lot of sniffles later she opened the door and stood behind it as she let me in. She closed the door and I got all in her personal space to reach behind her to lock it. Her hands pushed me in my stomach as she tried to create space between us but I stepped closer. Pressed her body into the door.

"Alex…stop…" she whined. I ignored her as I stared at her. "Alex…"

"I miss you."

"I don't care."

"I love you."

"No you don't."

"Yes I do baby. My love for you was never a lie."

"Just get away from me Alex. I hate your lying ass."

"That's how you feel Al?"

"Yes! I hate I ever met you! You ruined my life. I can't stand you!" She yelled before punching me dead in my jaw.

Out of reflex I hemmed her little ass up against the door.

"Alayziah I ain't gone take too much more of you putting your hands on me!"

"Then leave me the hell alone! You didn't want me remember? You got tired of me and my crazy attitude right? You wanted to ignore me and cut me off didn't you? So leave me the hell alone!"

She kneed me in my dick and I let her go but before she was able to turn around and get out of the door I grabbed her again and threw her against the wall.

"I love your crazy ass girl! I promise I do. I tried to let you go but baby I can't get enough of you."

I kissed her. She didn't resist. In fact, she pulled me deeper into her. I wrapped her legs around my waist as I kissed her as passionately as I could. As she unbuckled my pants I pushed her panties to the side.

I couldn't wait to get inside of her, and when I did she yelled out so loud I know anybody in the hallway heard her, but I swear I didn't care at all. I planted my hands on the wall, with the back of her knees positioned in the bend of my arms and I stroked her deeply.

"I miss you so much Noelle. I love you so much. I'm so sorry," I confessed as she wrapped her arms around my neck and pulled me deeper into her.

"Why did you do this Alex? Why?" She cried as I licked and sucked on her neck.

I didn't answer her. I couldn't answer her. I just focused on trying to show her how much I loved her in this moment. I felt her tighten her legs around me and I figured she was about to cum so I slowed my strokes down and she got even wetter. I didn't want to cum so fast but feeling her pussy throbbing against me made me cum right along with her.

I slid down the wall and tried to catch my breath. She stood and pulled her dress down. Rushing to get her purse she tried to hide the tears that were falling but I'd already seen them. As she walked sideways out of the room I stood.

"I love you. Call me," I said to her, but she didn't reply.

Jabari

When I saw her sitting at the table alone I immediately wanted to walk over to her and be her companion. She looked stressed as hell. Her leg was shaking quickly. Three shot glasses were sitting in front of her and she had three cigarette butts in her ash tray. I hated when women smoked cigarettes. The occasional blunt or cigar was cool but I couldn't do cigarettes. Especially when the woman was as beautiful as this one was.

Her skin was a little lighter than cinnamon. She had the prettiest set of beauty marks on both cheeks. Each cheek had five of them sitting perfectly on her face. Her cheek bones were high and well defined and she had the most captivating brown eyes I'd ever seen. It was like…they glowed. Her black hair was a little past her shoulders in this feathered layered cut. Every time she rocked to the side it flowed effortlessly. Full of body.

Speaking of body, she was short and slim. Her body was like that of Jhene Aiko. She was small but toned and sexy. I definitely was feeling her. But I couldn't understand why she was sitting here in the middle of the day smoking and drinking, and alone for that matter.

As crazy as it sounds I felt the need to see about her. Protect her, but I didn't want her taking her frustrations out on me so I decided against it. Now if she wanted to take her frustrations out on this dick we could talk. She looked like she wasn't the type to give it up that easily so I admired her from a distance. I know I probably looked crazy standing here staring at a woman I didn't even know but I didn't care.

Ever since she came in and placed her order and made her way out to the patio I couldn't help but want to be close to her.

It started out with me coming out of the kitchen and going behind the bar. Then I sat at a table near the window. Now I was standing outside leaning against the wall. When I heard the door open and close and the scent of Japanese Cherry Blossom filled my nostrils I sighed. My little sister was about to come out here and start some shit.

"Will you just talk to her already so you can go back in the kitchen? I'm tired of cooking. I want to go back to serving and making my tips."

"Talk to who?" I asked her playing dumb.

"Nigga don't play with me. The girl that's got you acting all stalkerish. You want me to go talk to her for you?"

Before I could answer her Jessica was making her way to the cutie's table. I hemmed her nosey ass up real quick. Bumping into a table in the process. She looked at us for a moment but returned her attention to her phone.

"Girl are you out of your mind?" I loudly whispered.

"What is wrong with you RiRi? You've never been scared to talk to a girl before."

"I ain't scared now. I don't want to talk to her. I just…I was just admiring her."

"Well can you stop admiring her and get back in the kitchen and do your job?"

"Somebody sent their food back on your ass hunh?"

That was the only time Jessica tripped about covering for me in the kitchen. She couldn't get down like I could. Nobody that I knew could frankly. That's why I was the head chef here.

"Yea. Talking about the middle of his chicken was cold. I'm like…nigga…it ain't my fault you let it sit there and get cold. The shit ain't have no blood in it so I know it wasn't raw."

"Watch your mouth lil girl. I'll be in there in a minute."

"So you gone talk to her? She *is* pretty."

I looked over at her again before shrugging. "I guess. I don't know man. Nah. I'm not."

"What? RiRi…why not?"

I ignored my sister as I returned to the kitchen. There was something about this chick that I loved…and feared at the same damn time.

Alayziah

It had been three months since I found out that Alex and Carmen were married. I slipped up and had sex with him a few times before I changed my number, deactivated my social media accounts, switched jobs, and moved to a new apartment complex.

Yes, it was that serious.

I couldn't shake him. It was like…he was my weakness. Like I was addicted to him. I just couldn't turn him down, and he knew that, that's why he kept coming back; but I felt so bad so I was committed to doing whatever it took to get over him. My cousin hooked me up and I've gotten a job as a copywriter and with my salary I was able to rent this banging studio apartment downtown by the river.

With me feeling all that I was feeling I wrote a poetry collection and I was spending my weekends traveling and doing open mic nights and slam poetry contests to promote it. That was definitely my release and way to get over Alex. Along with smoking cigarettes. People were always talking about how they calmed them down when they were stressed so I tried them one day and now I was hooked.

It was a stinky and expensive habit to pick up but for now it was getting the job done. There's this cool restaurant down the street from my apartment that I stumbled across that I frequent a lot. I hate being in the house alone. Gives me too much time to think. About him. With her. So if I'm not at work or out of town that's where I spend my free time.

Andrew finally found a woman to marry him so I didn't have him to entertain me anymore, and with Marcel working and going to school I didn't want to always bother him with my issues. I'm lonely as fuck. But seeing as I don't have any girl friends and I refuse to meet any new guys all I have are my cigarettes and my poetry.

I don't usually do the lounge scene but my nigga Red had been telling me about some chick that performs at the poetry night that he goes to on Monday's. He swears he's in love with her even though he's never spoken to her before.

Seeing as I have the same situation going on with the chick at the restaurant I decided to go and give him some moral support if he decided to make his move. We'd been there for an hour or so when he almost pushed me out of my chair nudging me.

"There she is nigga that's her." He said all hype.

I laughed at his ass before following his hand to the stage and laying eyes on *my* woman. My smile immediately faded. She was standing on the stage with her hands wrapped around the microphone. After inhaling deeply, she looked out into the crowd and locked eyes with me.

"I…I think she looking at me," Red whispered.

"No my nigga. She's looking at me. That's the chick from the restaurant I was telling you about."

"Oh shit. I won't stand a chance against your ass."

I chuckled as I sat deeper into my seat. She opened her mouth to speak but closed it before walking off the stage and out of the side exit. I wanted to run after her; but something was just keeping me away from her.

"Has she ever done that before?"

"Nah. Never. She always does her poetry with no problem. Guess I'll have to read her collection and imagine her reciting something to me."

"She has a poetry collection?"

"Yea. They sell them here. Go get you a copy from Fred."

Nodding I stood and made my way over to the owner of the longue. Maybe I could figure a little bit out about this mystery woman by reading her poetry.

Alayziah

I don't know what came over me. When I saw him my mind went blank. He literally took my words out of my mouth and left me speechless. Though his face was a little familiar I don't think I know him, and I don't think I've ever seen him that close up before. He was sitting down but I could tell by the way he was seated and his legs were positioned under the table that he was tall.

His skin was the same color as mine. He was slim built with hooded eyes and the fullest eye lashes I'd seen on a man. His lips were thick and blunt brown and his teeth, oh my God his teeth, he had some pretty white teeth but what made me pine over him was the fact that he had two pointy vampire like teeth that showed when he smiled. I couldn't help but want to see how they'd feel as he licked, sucked, and bit my skin.

I had to get out of there. I didn't want to like. I didn't want to lust. I didn't want to love. I didn't want to feel. I'd numbed myself to that and he was waking up things that I'd put to sleep. Even though I was hoping I'd never see him again it probably wouldn't have mattered if I did. After my mini meltdown he probably thought I was crazy.

Jabari

Weeks had passed since she came back to the restaurant. I'd been reading her poetry collection so much that I was pretty sure I had every poem memorized. She walked into the restaurant and for the first time since she'd started coming in she didn't order any alcohol. Nor did she sit on the balcony to smoke.

She sat in the back of the restaurant with a legal pad in front of her. Her hair was pulled into a bun on the top of her head. She had on some glasses so I couldn't look at those beauty marks that I'd grown to love but I could tell that she was more rested and at peace and I was curious to know why.

After she ordered her usual fettucine Alfredo and chicken Caesar salad I decided to take it to her.

I don't know why the fuck I was so nervous.

I could have any woman I wanted and here I was nervous to talk to this one. Her running out that night didn't make this shit any easier.

As I walked towards her table I tried not to drop her food and pull her move of running out. I was going to figure out what it was about her that was messing with me. Today. I sat her food on the table and she thanked me without looking up.

"You're welcome," I replied causing her to look up. Her mouth opened slightly at the sight of me. I blushed. She took her glasses off and smiled. I don't know what came over me but I couldn't speak. As she looked at me, all I could do was stare back at her.

I know I probably looked crazy and awkward as fuck but I couldn't help it. The only thing that came to my mind was her poetry collection. So I took it out of my pocket and asked her if she'd sign it.

After staring at me skeptically for a few seconds she took the book from my hands, signed it, stood abruptly, and rushed out.

I tried to chase after her but she was too fast and to be honest the shit caught me off guard. When I looked back at the table I saw that she'd left her pad, phone, and purse. Sighing I went to the back to get two boxes for her food before going through her wallet to get her address off of her ID.

Alayziah

"Ugh shit!" I yelled.

I couldn't believe I left my purse and phone at the restaurant. When that fine nigga asked me to sign my poetry collection for him my bottom set of lips started crying. Leaking. Throbbing. Aching. I had to get the fuck up out of there. Now I'm going to look even more stupid when I walk back down there to get my purse with my keys in it.

"Forget something?"

It was him.

I couldn't turn around. I was so embarrassed. With my head down I held my hand behind me. He placed my keys in my hand and laughed lightly. *God could this get any worse?* Once the door was open I held my hand behind me again. This time he handed me the legal pad I was writing my poetry in. I threw it inside my apartment and held my hand out again.

When he placed my phone in my hand he asked, "Why can't you look at me?"

I shrugged as I slid my phone in the pocket of the sweats I was wearing. I wasn't planning on being seen by him or any other good looking man today. My hair was a mess on the top of my head. I had on my red and white Tupac and Janet Jackson Poetic Justice shirt with some black sweats and a pair of white socks and Nike sandals. I even had on my glasses instead of my contacts. Today was not the day.

"Am I ugly to you or something?"

I shook my head no as I held my hand out for my purse. Instead he gave me containers of food.

"Shit I didn't pay for my food. I'm sorry. Give me my purse so I can pay you."

"You curse a lot. That's not ladylike. Neither is smoking cigarettes."

"What are you? My daddy?" I asked with my back still to him.

"No Sweetheart. Just a man."

"Well...I haven't smoked all week." *Why was I explaining myself to him?*

"That's good. That's great. That's really great. Why were you anyway?"

I shrugged again. "Just...had a lot on my mind at one point. It...relaxed me."

He grew silent but recovered by saying, "I can relax you if you let me."

Scratching my head, I slowly turned to face him.

Damn.

He was even more handsome up close.

Jabari

Damn.

She was even more beautiful up close.

I couldn't imagine how crazy I looked holding her purse so I handed it to her.

"Everything is in there. Just looked at your ID for your address."

She nodded as she looked away. Wrapping her arms around her stomach she bit the inside of her jaw. I took a step closer. She took a step back.

"What is it Sweetheart?" I asked. My heart was breaking for her and I needed to know why. Why did she have this effect on me? She shook her head no as if she had a choice on telling me or not. I grabbed her by the front of her shirt and pulled her closer to me.

"Talk to me…" I pried.

I wasn't the most emotional nigga, but I had no problem being honest and expressing myself. Being that I was close to my mother and younger sister I understood that women were emotional creatures. I took pride in my ability to empathize with them. Shit I had to learn, otherwise they would've drove me crazy in my younger days.

She opened her mouth like she wanted to tell me but closed it instead. I cupped her face so that her chin was resting in the gap between my thumb and pointing finger and she looked at me.

"Thanks for bringing me my stuff," she said finally.

I nodded and stepped back. She wasn't ready to talk now. That was cool. I knew where she lived now. If she did another disappearing act, I'd be at her front door again.

"Wait…" she called out stopping me surprisingly after I turned to walk away. "Do you…have to leave…right now?"

I smiled lightly. "I think it would be best if I did. Don't you?"

She shrugged again. "I don't want to be alone," she whispered. This time I grew silent. I walked towards her and gently grabbed her by her hand. Led her into her apartment. Closed and locked the door behind us. Texted my junior chef to let him know I was going to be gone longer than I expected.

"Make yourself comfortable," she said walking towards her kitchen with her food. She had a cute little studio apartment. All across the walls were quotes, bible scriptures, and pictures of Musicians. In one corner she had a desk and book shelf. In the opposite corner she had her bed and a lamp. Towards the center she had her couch and beanie bags. On all of her tables and even on the floor she had candles and incense.

"Are you hungry?"

"Nah," I replied lighting a few of her candles.

"Thirsty?"

"What you got?"

"What you want?"

"Red Kool aid."

She smiled genuinely for the first time and I melted. Her smile was so beautiful. So beautiful it made me mad that I had to wait this long to see it.

"Got you."

She pulled a jug of Kool aid out and I laughed. I wasn't expecting her to actually have it but she did. I wanted to know more about her but I didn't want her to lock up on me again so I decided to just vibe and feel her out.

After she poured my glass of Kool aid she walked towards me and sat next to me on the couch. I took a swig and nodded my approval. I looked at her and she blushed as she looked away. I gripped her chin and forced her to look at me. Her hand covered mine as she closed her eyes.

"Look at me," I commanded. Pouting she unwillingly opened her eyes and looked at me. "What do you need from me? Just to sit here and be a body so you won't feel alone? Random conversation? You need to get something off your chest without being judged? You need me to hold you? What? What do you need from me?"

She scratched the side of her face and avoided my eyes again. "Can you just hold me?"

Nodding I stood and held my hand out for her. She obliged. As I led her to her bed I cut the lights off. When we made it to her bed I undressed her. Leaving her in her bra and panties. I took off my clothes as well. Once I was down to my boxers I gave her one of my t-shirts.

Let her be somewhat inside of me because I desperately wanted to be inside of her.

She put it on and slid into her bed. I was about to get in with her but when she took her panties off I stopped. After she threw her bra on the floor she looked up at me briefly before turning her back to me and getting under her covers.

I got in the bed behind her and pulled her close. Her arm wrapped around mine and she exhaled a deep breath that I didn't even realize she'd taken.

"Would you ever lie to me?" She asked.

"Never."

"How do I know you're not lying now?"

"What reason would I have to lie Sweetheart?"

She grew silent before speaking again. "Would you think I was a hoe if I asked you to make love to me?"

My dick swelled immediately. "No. I'd think you were a broken woman that needed love and affection. Intimacy. Is that what you want me to do?"

"When was the last time you were tested?"

"I get checked every three months when I go in for my physical. So...two months ago."

"Do you have a girlfriend?"

"Wouldn't be here if I did."

"Do you have a wife?"

"Not unless that's your way of proposing."

"Do you have a boyfriend?"

"Hell nah."

She sighed heavily before turning to face me. "I don't know what it is about you but it scares me and makes me feel peaceful and content at the same time."

"I understand. I feel the same way about you. That's why I want to do whatever it takes to make you feel better."

A tear fell from her eye. I wiped it away with my thumb before resting my hand on her face. She covered my hand with hers and closed her eyes. Breathing peacefully. And within a few minutes she was snoring lightly.

Alayziah

I can't lie…the shit with Alex got to me. It changed me. It broke something inside of me that I didn't know was so fragile that it was even capable of breaking. Since him I've been drifting through life meaninglessly. Nothing that I've been doing has had substance besides my poetry.

Yesterday when…I don't even know his name. I don't even know his name. I'll just call him *he*. Yesterday when he was here with me I felt like the pieces of me that Alex took had been returned.

As crazy as it sounds he made me feel normal. When he held me his energy consumed me and it literally put me to sleep. It was so loving and peaceful. I didn't know anything about this man besides he worked at a restaurant near my house. And he'd read my poetry book enough times for it to be raggedy along the sides.

Other than that I knew nothing about him yet I had him in my bed and I felt at peace. When I woke up this morning he was in the shower and I just laid there. Not wanting to say goodbye I pretended to be sleep when he made his way to my side of the bed. He kissed my forehead, pulled my covers up slightly, and rubbed my back a few times before walking out.

I couldn't help but shed a few tears. He was so patient and gentle with me. Like he knew that that was what I needed. But I didn't even know. I wasn't sure what the future held for us. I didn't even know if I believed in happily ever after anymore.

What I did know was that I wanted him to be my happily right now. And as soon as I got off of work I was going back to that restaurant to find out what his name is.

Jabari

"Well what's got you all happy today RiRi? And where were you yesterday? I stopped by your house and you weren't there," Jessica asked. I didn't even realize I was smiling until she spoke to me.

"Nothing that concerns you little girl. Stay out of grown folks business," I replied mushing her face.

"Ugh stop you know I hate when you do that!" Jess yelled grabbing her entrees off the counter.

"Why do you think I do it?" I asked walking over to the sink to wash my hands before I started preparing for my dinner shift.

"Well before you get ready to start dinner I thought you'd like to know ole girl is out there asking for the chef with the pretty eyelashes and vampire teeth."

Jessica was cheesing with her hands folded under her chin. She had put her plates down and was searching my face for a response. And that's when I remembered, we'd never exchanged names or phone numbers.

After snatching my chef coat off I rushed out of the kitchen and made my way to her. When I reached the dining room she was standing with her back to the kitchen. The red pencil skirt she had on accentuated her curves and I couldn't help but wonder what those pumps would look like wrapped around my shoulders.

Shaking the thoughts from my head I walked over to her. I wrapped my hand around her forearm and gently turned her to face me. She smiled. I smiled. As good as she looked in her glasses I was glad she didn't have them on today. I got to look at those beauty marks.

"Hey Sweetheart. Everything good?" I asked.

"What is your name?"

I chuckled. "Jabari. Jabari Henderson. And you?"

"Alayziah. Alayziah Oliver."

"Alayziah can I take you out on a date tonight?"

"A date?"

The confused look on her face confused me. "Yea. A date. What? You've never been on a date before?"

"I mean…I kick it with guys but…" She shrugged and pulled a piece of her hair behind her ear.

"Well I would love to take you out on a date tonight if you would allow me to Alayziah."

Blushing she nodded her head slightly. "I'd like that."

"Cool. You hungry? We're about to start the dinner rush but I could whip you up something really quick."

"No, no. It's cool. I don't want to hold you. I just…wanted to know your name. I can't believe I had you all in my bed and I didn't even know your name."

Her cheeks turned red and that was the first time I'd ever seen that happen on a brown girl before, and the fact that it happened because of me turned me on.

"Damn baby, you're beautiful."

She bit her lip and scratched the middle of her scalp as she looked me up and down. "Jabari I'm going to be honest with you…I'm not easy. I've only had sex with three guys in my life. But I do fall in love fast. And hard. And passionately. And I like to make love. A lot. My sex drive is high. And I want you to respect me. So I need you to not say things like that and look at me like that."

I took a step closer to her and for the first time she didn't move back.

"I'm a grown ass man. And you're a grown ass woman. If I was to take you into that restroom and fuck you right now that ain't nobody's business but ours. I wouldn't judge you nor would I respect you any less. If you want to fall in love with me fall. I promise you I'm going to catch you. So don't fight how you feel. And don't hold back. I can assure you I won't. I'll pick you up at eight."

Nodding okay she took a step back and left without saying another word.

Alayziah

I'd been sitting on my bed for the past hour. Jabari was going to be pulling up any second but...I was stuck. I'd taken my shower and lotioned down. I had a few outfit choices laid out on my bed. I had my hair wrapped and ready to go. All I'd have to do was comb it down and fluff it up, but I just couldn't force myself to get ready to go out.

Yes, I know all men aren't the same. Yes, I know that Alex was...a fucking fool, but I love that nigga – and the thought of being with someone else... I just can't. I don't want to waste my time getting to know someone only to be hurt again. I'd rather just find someone to sex every once in a while and do my own thing.

No strings. No commitment. No expectation. No disappointment. But this nigga Jabari, I don't see myself being able to do just that with him, and that scares me.

Deciding not to completely give up all hope I called Marcel but he didn't answer. After I leaned back on my bed he called back.

"Hey Love. What's up?"

I smiled instantly. "How are you Boo?"

"I'm cool. How are you? What's wrong? I hear it in your voice."

"You know I'm supposed to go out with Jabari tonight right?"

"Right."

"I can't."

"What you mean you can't? You on your period or some?"

"Marcel!"

"What? You saying you can't like you bleeding or some shit. That's the only excuse I'll take at this point."

"Marcel..."

"No Love. You need to go. I don't even want to hear it. You've been cooped up in that house for too long. And there's only so much I can do for you. You not the type to move on by being single. You need somebody to love on you. Let Jabari take care of that. From what you've told me he seems genuine. Give him a chance and see what's up."

I couldn't even respond. He wasn't going to take no for an answer anyway.

"Now get ya lil skinny ass up. I know you sitting there naked and ain't did shit to get ready and the nigga bout on his way."

"Aye! I took a shower and lotioned down!"

"Well look at you! I'm surprised you did that much!"

"Fuck you Marcel!"

"Nah save that for Jabari! Call me in the morning and let me know what happens. I love you my Love."

"I love you too Boo."

Jabari

Alayziah is probably the cutest thing I have ever seen in my life. Period. I knocked on her door and her silly ass opened the door wide enough to poke her head out. She smiled at me as I tilted my head to try and see the rest of her body. Her hair was wrapped around her head so I figured she was nowhere near ready. I chuckled as I took a step back.

"Hey beautiful."

"…Hey handsome. I'm not ready."

"Yea I figured. No rush. I can wait for you in the car."

"No. Just. Close your eyes and give me your hand and I'll lead you to the couch. I don't have on any clothes."

Why did she have to say that?

Nodding I bit my lip and closed my eyes. She placed her hand inside mine and mine enveloped hers. She was so little. So petite. So fragile. Made a nigga wanna cuddle and shit. Wrap her inside me and then dig inside her. Shit. I don't know how long I'm gone be able to keep my hands off of her. As much as I wanted to look at her body I kept my eyes closed as she led me to her couch.

When we made it to the couch she sat me down and I pulled her onto my lap. I couldn't help but wrap my arms around her waist. Keeping my eyes on hers briefly I closed them as she caressed my shoulder lightly.

"Sorry I'm not ready," she mumbled regaining my attention.

"You planned on backing out didn't you?"

She nodded. I inhaled deeply. Taking in more of her scent. I'd never smelled the perfume she was wearing; but it was intoxicating. It was a mix of two things that seemed like they didn't belong together, but in their complexity they blended well. Kind of like how I figured she would be.

"Why Alayziah? What is it that's keeping you from letting me in?"

"It's a long story and I'm sure you don't want to hear about the men in my past."

"No I do. I need to know what I'm dealing with."

She smiled lightly. "Let me at least go and get dressed."

"Do I need to close my eyes again?"

"Yes Jabari."

Damn. That was the first time she'd said my name and I must say...I love the way it sounds rolling off of her tongue. I closed my eyes and she removed herself from me. Since she had a studio apartment her bed was behind the couch where I was sitting.

She had a covering that she could have used but she didn't so I saw her silhouette as she maneuvered around her bed piecing her outfit together. When she was done she walked past me and went into the bathroom to do her hair I assume.

And when she came out all I could do was stand up and hug her. Hold her. She looked so fucking good. She was wearing a pair of high waist slacks that were loose fitting and a red crop top. Her hair was flowing against her shoulders and the only thing she had on her face was red lipstick. I don't know what the last nigga did to fuck up but there was no way in the world I was going to do anything to ruin her or what I could have with her.

"You are so beautiful. Do you know how beautiful you are?" I asked taking another whiff of her scent as my lips grazed her neck.

"Jabari..."

"What perfume are you wearing?"

She chuckled. I let her go so I could look in her eyes.

"It's a mix of this apple body spray and With Love by Hillary Duff."

"Yea I figured that was some mixed shit. It didn't smell like something you could buy. It smells really good on you."

"Thanks Jabari," she blushed.

"So you ready to talk now? We might as well get it over with now before we leave for our date. I want and deserve your undivided attention. I play second to no man. Not even in your mind and heart. If you're with me physically I need you with me mentally and emotionally as well. So what's up?"

I could tell I'd taken her by surprise because she just stood there for a second staring at me. When she did move finally she went into her kitchen. Grabbed a bottle of wine and went out to her patio. She looked back at me and nodded for me to join her. After standing there and praying for enough self-control to not bend her over the railing on her patio I walked towards her.

Alayziah

This nigga. First he comes in here looking all kinds of enticing in his pale blue tailored slacks and a red button down with navy blue flowers on it and a pair of navy blue loafers. I could tell his hair was freshly cut and he had his goatee trimmed slightly. He was wearing one of my favorite colognes for men. Blue de Chanel.

Then he talks to me like he cares.

About me.

Like he wants me.

Me.

Like he's just as possessive as me. Like he wants to be a priority in my life. As I would be in his. I wanted to trust him and his sincerity but I couldn't risk being lied to and played again. My nerves were too bad for this shit. I grabbed the pack of cigarettes I had on the table on my patio and tried to take one out but he took the pack from me and put it in his pocket.

"The hell?"

"Watch your mouth. Why you stressing?" I sighed and leaned forward putting my forearms on my thighs. "What is it Sweetheart? Is it me? Am I making you nervous?"

I shook my head no and tried to fight back my tears. "It's not you Bari. You're everything right now. I'm just scared."

"Talk to me about it. That's what I'm here for. If I can't make you feel better, I'll give you these cigarettes back but I promise you I can make you feel more at ease than these ever will."

I smiled lightly as I sat upright and turned to face him. His eyes were the same color as Bow Wow's and every time I looked into them I wanted to melt.

"Okay...well...The first guy that..."

"Ruined you."

"Yea. Ruined me…we were in high school. He was more concerned with being cool and fitting in than being faithful and loving me back. He slept around yet pressured me to give him my virginity. Our senior year I did and I got pregnant. He told me that he wasn't ready to be a father. That we both had too much going on in our lives to be held back with a child. My father was willing to help me raise the baby on my own but he didn't want people to see him as a deadbeat. So he had his mother to invite me over for dinner one night."

I tried to shake the tears from my eyes but they began to fall. I'm glad I didn't put on any makeup. Before I could wipe them away he grabbed my hands with one of his and used the other to wipe my tears and encouraged me to continue.

"He put Mifepristone in my food. Here I am thinking he's coming to his senses but he was feeding me abortion pills. I was so fucking scared Jabari. Out of nowhere cramps. Contractions. I started bleeding. Throwing up. When I got to the hospital they told me that it was side effects of the medicine I'd taken to abort my baby. And I was like, that can't be right. You know? But it was in my system. And by the time I got there, there wasn't anything they could do to save my baby."

"Damn. I'm so sorry Alayziah. No one should ever have to go through some shady shit like that."

I half smiled as he squeezed my hands tighter.

"I got over it eventually, but I waited a while before I dated anyone else. After him it was a guy that I loved way too hard who couldn't appreciate and return it. So then I took another break and when I did give another guy a chance it was a guy who was bisexual. He wanted me to marry him so he could keep up his façade and have his little boyfriend on the side," I laughed at the thought of Andrew.

"Damn. Where they do that at?"

I laughed again. Causing him to smile. God I loved his smile and his teeth.

"I guess he was scared because he's a musician. He's a few years older than me and his parents and church had been trying to marry him off for a while before me. I think they were starting to get suspicious. I walked in on him and the guy having sex and I flipped. But I wasn't in love with him so…I got over that too. But this last one."

Tears filled my eyes at the thought of Alex. I inhaled deeply as my leg began to shake. He released my hands and wrapped his hands around my thighs. They stopped shaking under his touch. Our eyes met and he smiled.

"Let it out."

Nodding I inhaled deeply before continuing. "I fell in love with him. Hard. But he didn't catch me. He…couldn't catch me. Because he was holding someone else. Long story short I fell in love with another woman's man. They married and for a while he wouldn't let me go. I had to move and change my number and block him on my social media just to get away from him. He swears he loves me."

I rolled my eyes and scoffed at my stupidity. "But if he loved me he wouldn't have married her. Without telling me. He wouldn't have been having sex with me and her and gotten her pregnant. He lied about so much and I felt so stupid. So foolish. I just…Jabari my heart can't take another break."

I was crying harder now. For a while he said nothing. He just…absorbed me and all I'd said. Then he kneeled before me. Ran his fingers through my hair before cupping my cheeks with his hands. I looked down at him as he wiped my tears away with his thumbs.

"Is that it?"

I nodded yes.

"Let me apologize to you for them. The way they treated you was foul. You didn't deserve that shit. No one deserves that shit. I can tell that you love hard. And easily. So I want us to take things slow. I want to give you time to see that you can trust me. That you can trust me with your love. Alayziah I will never lie to you. I will never keep anything from you. I will never disrespect you or cheat on you. I will leave you before I do that.

Now I'm not perfect. We will fight and I will hurt you, but you have to trust that I'd never do anything to intentionally hurt you. And no matter what happens between us bad it will never outweigh the good."

It all sounded good…but how could I trust him? Why would he want me? Why would he want to love me?

"Why me? Why do you want to love me?"

"Because you need me to. I need to love you. And I need to be loved by you."

"But how can I trust you? Trust this. How do I know that you won't change your mind?"

"You don't. You won't. You can't. You just have to be open. Be vulnerable. Be brave. And take a chance with me. But I will tell you this, I have a mother and I had two sisters that I adore. I know how to treat women because of them. My older sister ended up spiraling out of control and overdosing because the man she'd given her best to left. He left holes in my sister that she tried to fill with drugs. And instead of her waiting for a real man to love her she just…kept smoking. Kept drinking. Kept trying to fill that hole."

I saw the gloss cover his eyes. I knew he was getting choked up. But he looked away. Trying to keep me from seeing it. Naturally my hands covered his face and I forced him to lock eyes with me.

"Is that why you don't like for me to smoke?"

He nodded. "I just don't want you to think you need a substance to numb you. I don't want that to lead to something else. I know you might think I'm overreacting but…"

I couldn't even let him finish. I covered his lips with mine. But when I realized what I was doing I stopped and stood. Tilting my head back I exhaled deeply. I never initiated or made the first move.

He stood and walked over to me. Turned me to face him. Wrapped my arms around his waist. Placed his hands on my cheeks. Lifted my face so he could see me. Ran his thumb across my lips. Felt so good. So intimate I closed my eyes. Pulled me closer. Put his lips on mine. And pecked them until I smiled.

When I did he slid his tongue into my mouth and kissed away any doubtful words I had on my tongue. Once he released me he looked at me intently as I smiled.

"What?" I asked.

"I just don't understand why a man would want to do anything but love you."

"Jabari…what I tell you before about saying stuff like that?"

"And what did I tell you in response to that?"

Before I could answer him he was covering his dick with my hand. "Damn," I mumbled at the feel of him.

"I'm like this every time I'm around you. I doubt if that will ever change. I want you just as bad as you want me. So when you ready…just let me know."

Jabari

When I finally got her to open up to me things were smooth for the rest of the night. We ended up staying in. I cooked and we just vibed. We stayed up talking for a while and fell asleep on the couch. I'm used to waking up when the sun came up so when it did I went home and got ready for my shift at the restaurant. Hearing about all that she'd gone through in the past because of niggas made my blood boil.

I felt like it was my responsibility to protect her heart from this point forward. If she allowed me to. After watching my sister kill herself over a nigga who didn't care enough about her to even see about the child they had together there was no way in hell I could ever toy with a woman's heart and emotions.

I was supposed to be meeting her after my shift was over so we could go to the gun range. I figured if I introduced her to some other ways to relieve her stress she wouldn't depend on anyone else to do it for her.

I wanted her to know that she could always depend on me; but realistically, I wasn't gone always be able to get to her like we may have liked for me to. This way she'll always have an outlet besides smoking and drinking.

Alayziah

"Damn girl! You sure you ain't did this before?" Jabari yelled cheesing.

He brought me to a gun range and I must say I did pretty well. And letting off them bullets definitely gave me a rush that I can't explain. I just kept shooting. Even after I ran out of bullets. That shit was like one of the ultimate highs. He had to take the gun from me to regain my attention. But when he did, his sexy ass had it.

"Yes this is my first time. I love it here! I'm so glad you brought me. This definitely helped me."

I wrapped my arms around his waist and he did the same to me. Kissing me on my forehead.

"I thought that was your voice," I heard him before I saw him.

I buried my head into Jabari's chest and prayed I was hearing things. Jabari's grip around my waist weakened as he tried to turn around to see who was talking to us but I held him tighter. Not wanting to acknowledge him.

"Let me go babe," Jabari spoke softly trying to remove my arms from around his waist. Reluctantly I let him go and he turned around to face him.

"I'm sorry…can I help you?" Jabari asked Alex.

"Nah. I was actually talking to Noelle."

"To who?"

"Alayziah."

"Alayziah…" Jabari looked back at me as I held my head down. "You wanna talk to him?"

I shook my head no as tears fell from my eyes. Nodding Jabari grabbed my hand and pulled me away.

"It's like that Al? You not even gone acknowledge a nigga you claimed you was gone love forever?"

As much as I didn't want to I stopped. So did Jabari. I couldn't turn to face him. I wasn't ready to see him again.

"I just wanna talk to you for a minute baby. Please," he begged.

My heart ached. I looked at Jabari and saw the love in his eyes and continued to walk to his car in silence.

As we rode back to my apartment we still hadn't spoken any words to each other. He didn't ask me who the man was. He didn't even seem bothered by it. I on the other hand was a nervous wreck. I tried to hide it but the way he kept looking at me with sadness in his eyes let me know he could tell.

"I don't want to leave you by yourself like this Sweetheart. If you want to talk we can. If you don't want to we don't have to. Whatever you need...just tell me."

"I'll call Marcel," I mumbled. He nodded before opening his door and making his way to mine. After walking me to my door he walked back to his car without saying another word.

Jabari

A nigga ain't gone lie...the fact that she brushed me off after seeing one of her exes kind of pissed me off. I could understand if she wanted to be alone, but for her to call her best friend... As if I couldn't be there for her? I ain't gone force my love and companionship on no woman. If she can't see that shit then it's gone be her loss.

She called me this morning but I wasn't ready to talk to her ass so I shot her a text and told her I would get up with her later. I was going to have to find out who this nigga was and make sure that when he sees her...he doesn't see her. He doesn't deserve to have his eyes rest on her. To speak to her. And whether we got together or not I was going to make sure they never did again.

Alayziah

When I made it to work this morning I felt like shit. Jabari wanted to make me feel better but I just didn't want to be around him at that moment. I didn't want to confuse me feeling bad about Alex with me feeling good about Jabari. I'd probably made him mad brushing him off and I planned on making up for that but I just needed some time to get my mind right.

That didn't seem like it was going to be happening any time soon when I walked into my office and saw Alex sitting there. I stood at the door for a while. Staring at him. He just sat there and smiled. His hands crossed over his lap.

I looked behind me before closing the door and walking towards my desk. Once I sat down I opened my laptop and he was still staring at me. When I couldn't take it anymore I looked at him and asked, "Why are you staring at me Alexander?"

"Just...making up for lost time."

I didn't want to but I smiled. "Why are you here? Who told you where I work?"

"Pam."

I shook my head and made a mental note to go up to my old job and get on Pam's head in a respectful way.

"Okay...well what do you want?"

"You."

"Alex, get yo life."

"I miss you baby."

"Alex you're a liar. Get the hell out of my office," I whispered to keep from yelling. He didn't look fazed at all. He just stared at me for a few seconds and gave me time to cool off before he spoke.

"I love you Al. That hasn't changed."

"Why are you doing this to me?" I asked with tears filling my eyes.

"Because I love you. And I know you love me too. I know this whole thing is crazy but baby you have to understand none of this was my intention. I didn't plan on falling in love with you, but I am. I tried to let you go, but I can't. I don't want to be without you."

"You should've thought about that before you married her."

"I'm getting a divorce when the baby is born."

"I don't believe you. And even if I did that has nothing to do with me."

"So you don't want me anymore? You don't love me anymore Noelle?"

I didn't answer him, just returned my attention to my computer. He didn't deserve my love or my emotions, but I couldn't lie to his face and tell him that I no longer loved him. So I was just going to ignore him. He stood. Walked over to my desk and kneeled in front of me. I tried to ignore him but he started singing and my whole body began to shake.

"I need your forgiveness and your mercy too. I must be all kinds of crazy for what I've done to you. I hope you understand that my heart is true. Mistakes I've made them but I'm making change for you."

He hit a high note and my heart ached. Burned. Missed a couple beats.

"I'm ashamed of me. I wish I never did you wrong. Every night of us I dream that I wake up in your arms. I know why you left me but since you've been gone my understanding has more than grown I come to this conclusion over and over again. I don't want an enemy I just want back my friend. I'm ashamed of me. I wish I never did you wrong. Every night of us I dream that I wake up in your arms."

A tear slid down his cheek and I had to wrap my arms around my chest to keep from wiping it away.

"Baby I'm so sorry. Please tell me you forgive me."

"I forgive you."

"Do you still love me baby?"

"Do you?" We both looked up and saw Jabari standing at the door. "Do you still love him?" Jabari asked again.

"Yes but…"

"But nothing. Let me make it up to you." Alex interrupted.

"Is that what you want Sweetheart?" Jabari asked.

"No Jabari I don't want that."

"Tell him you don't want him." Jabari said.

I can't lie the way he was handling this situation and not even acknowledging Alex was turning me on. I looked at Alex and saw the hurt in his eyes before I closed mine.

"I don't want you anymore Alex."

"Look him in his eyes and tell him Alayziah."

I looked at Jabari with tears in my eyes but he seemed unfazed.

"I don't want you anymore," I couldn't even get it out before I was sobbing. Alex tried to console me but Jabari stopped him.

"My nigga you need to leave."

Alex looked at him like he was crazy but stood. "I'll leave only if you want me to. Is that how you really feel Alayziah?"

I nodded. Alex nodded. Then he walked out. Jabari walked over to me and stared down at me. When I looked up at him he spoke.

"I don't believe you. And I know he didn't either. Until you get him out of your system..." He didn't finish his sentence. He just turned to walk away.

"Jabari wait..." I called out to him but he didn't stop. "Bari!" Ignoring me he left my office. Leaving me to deal with my own self.

Jabari

"Why would you do that RiRi? You know she's struggling right now. She needs you."

I side eyed Jessica before taking another sip of my Hennessey. I don't know why she felt like she could give me love advice. Only reason I told her about what happened with Alayziah is because she kept harassing me wanting to know what had me in a fucked up mood.

Truth be told, I used to be a dog ass nigga. I was in the streets heavy. And because I'm a good looking nigga it was nothing for me to get a female to drop the panties, but after seeing what happened to my sister years ago I threw all that shit to the side.

I witnessed for myself how low a woman will drag her own self because a nigga ain't doing what she thinks he should. I refuse to watch another woman self-destruct. Not even Alayziah. So if she wanted that nigga, and it was obvious that she did, she could have him.

"RiRi!" Jess yelled trying to snatch the glass from my hand.

"What mane?"

"You hear me."

"Yea I hear you. I ain't trying to though."

"Stop being stubborn and go see about her."

"Why do you care so much? You don't even know her to care about her."

"I care about you. And I see that it's eating at you."

"I appreciate that lil sis…but I'm not going. I'm not calling. I'm not going to allow her to think that she can do to me what he did to her."

She sighed heavily and stood. Staring down at me with disappointed eyes. "Fine Jabari. But if she goes back and gets hurt it's on you."

"No it's not. She a grown woman. I put what I had on the table. If she don't want to accept it that's on her."

"God you're so stubborn," she mushed my head before running to the bedroom I had for her in my crib.

Alayziah

I could tell Jessica was surprised to see me at their restaurant. Her face immediately lit up. A week had gone by since the whole ordeal happened at my job. I hadn't heard from Jabari since. Alex however had been at my job every day.

He just couldn't get over the fact that I was trying to move on. Like...he expected me to wait for him to realize what he had in me. True I loved him, but if loving him caused this much hurt I no longer wanted it or him.

"Hey pretty girl." I spoke as she pulled me into her arms.

"Hey Allie cat. I'll go get RiRi's stubborn ass for you."

"No...actually...I came for you." She looked at me skeptically as I continued. "I need your help. I know I may have made him mad and I want to make it up to him. What can I do to show him that I'm serious about him? About us?"

"Well...there is one thing that I know that will make him absolutely crazy about you. Can you cook?"

Jabari

When I walked inside my home the lights were off, candles were lit, Sam Cooke was playing in the background and something was smelling good as hell in the kitchen. Since I was old enough to cook for myself I've never allowed a woman to cook for me. Not even my mother.

In fact, the only time she's cooked for me is when I've been sick. Or if I've gone to her home for dinner with the fam. But for a woman to just...cook for me.

Nah.

I wasn't having that. Food was too sacred of a thing for me for it to be tainted by someone who couldn't satisfy my appetite and taste preferences. I'd never put that weight on a woman so I've always done the cooking.

I knew it couldn't have been Jessica because she knows I don't play about people being in my kitchen so it had to be Alayziah. I smiled at the thought of her going through all of this trouble for me. I just stood there for a moment. Taking in what she'd done for me. When I couldn't take it anymore I walked into the kitchen and saw her in her sexiest form.

She was barefoot with a pair of boxers and a razorback sports bra on. She was too busy singing along with Sam and poking a fork in her candied yams to notice me so I leaned against the wall and watched her work.

As Sam sung about his woman bringing it on home to him I was glad that she decided to come home to me. After she tasted the yams she turned around to put the fork in the sink and jumped when she saw me standing there.

"Good grief! Are you trying to give me a heart attack?" Al yelled grabbing her chest.

I smiled lightly as I walked over to her. Stood so close she had to wrap her arms around me to keep from moving backwards. I caressed her face and stared into her eyes for a second before asking, "What are you doing here Alayziah?"

She bit her lip and looked down. After lifting her face I asked her again.

"I'm sorry," she mumbled.

"For what?"

"For whatever I did to make you pull away from me."

I sighed as I took a step back.

"You don't even know why you're apologizing. You're just doing it because you think that's what I want from you. But it's not."

"Then what do you want Jabari?"

"I want you to be happy and loved and at peace. If you don't want to get it from me Sweetheart that's fine; but I refuse to watch you backtrack with any of your exes. And it was evident that day in your office that you want him. Is that the one that is married?"

Nodding lightly Alayziah wrapped her fingers around my belt buckles.

"Yes. And yes I want him. Yes, I love him. I gave him me Bari. I can't deny that. I also can't deny the fact that I know that he isn't for me. Or that he lied to me. Betrayed my loyalty and trust. And caused me so much pain. So yes I want him but I give you my word...I'm never going back to him."

I placed my forearms on top of her shoulders and grabbed her hair gently from behind. Forcing her to look up at me.

"I want to love the pain out of you, woman...but I'm not going to let you hurt me."

She started biting the inside of her cheek, fighting back tears and her emotions.

"Bari when you say shit like that..."

"Stuff. Stop cursing so damn much."

She smiled as she hugged my waist.

"How you gone tell me not to curse and you curse in the same sentence?"

"I'm a nigga. I can curse."

"No you're a man. A real man. And I'm so glad you found me. I appreciate you so much Jabari."

This time it was I who fought back my feelings.

"Are you hungry?" She asked removing herself from me.

"Yea. What you make?" I went to my refrigerator and grabbed a bottle of water.

"Smothered pork chops, cabbage, yams, cornbread, and sweet potato pie."

"Jess told you that was my favorite meal hunh?" I smacked her on her ass before sitting on the counter next to the stove. She blushed as she cut the burners off on the stove.

"Yes. She told me that you'd never let a woman cook for you before. So I wanted to show you that I can handle you."

"Is that right?"

Nodding she grabbed a fork and put a bite of the yams to my mouth. I must admit, they smelled good, but I was scared to try them. If her ass couldn't cook it was going to be a wrap.

"Taste it Jabari," she commanded. I looked at her skeptically as I closed my eyes and opened my mouth. She fed me the potatoes and they melted in my mouth. I moaned and she squealed.

"I passed? You like them?"

"Yea they good. Real good. Almost as good as mine. Gone fix me a plate before I make you my dinner."

"Oh yea?" She asked grinning.

"Yea. And I ain't playing either."

"What if I wanna be?"

I jumped down off the counter and walked up on her. When she didn't back away I lifted her off the floor and carried her over to the table. She watched me pull her boxers down with the sexiest smile I'd ever seen on a woman. Once I got them off I wasted no time as I pushed her legs so far back her ass lifted off the table faintly. I twirled my tongue around her clit before sucking it gently.

"Got damn Jabari..." she moaned grabbing my head as I dipped my tongue in and out of her pussy. "Shit...right there Bari."

"What I tell you about that cursing?" I asked taking her ankles into one hand and using the other to finger her.

"Ummmm I'm so-sorry..." she moaned as she started to move her hips up and down. Fucking my finger. Wetting it all the more. I released her legs and lifted myself and stared down at her. I pissed her off by stopping but I didn't care. I was about to teach her hardheaded ass a lesson.

"You don't listen. I keep telling you about your mouth," I said as I walked away.

She must have thought that I wasn't coming back because she started going off and cursing under her breath. I cut Sam Cooke off and made my way back to her. As I did I took my shirt off and pulled a condom from my pants. Immediately shutting her smart ass mouth up.

She bit her lip and watched me drop my pants. I handed her the condom after I opened it and she slid it on me. I pulled her ass off the table and slid inside her slowly. Inch by inch until all of me had filled her. She flung her head back in ecstasy but I wanted to see every face she made.

"Look at me Sweetheart," I said as I started to move in and out of her.

"Mmmm...uhhhh..."

Every time I dug inside of her she was grunting. Slapping her juices on me. Biting her lip. Raking her fingers up and down my chest.

"Umhm. That's it baby. Squeeze my dick just like that. Just like that."

She was coming and squeezing the shit out of me. Or should I say squeezing the cum out of me. Once her orgasm subsided she wrapped her arms around my neck and I lifted her off the table. Standing straight up I pounded into her. Hitting her g spot and brushing against her clit each time.

"Baarrriiii!" She yelled coming again. Her legs stretched out. Back arched. Head hung back. I laughed at her ass.

"That's not funny," she whined bouncing up and down on my dick. I gripped her waist tighter and tried to control her movements but she wouldn't let me.

"Shit," I moaned feeling my cum rise up. "Slow down," I pleaded but she didn't listen. Seemed like that made her go faster. "Aahhh..." I groaned slamming her into the wall gently as I stroked her until I busted my nut.

After I did we stood there for a second. Still connected to one another.

"Jabari..." she whispered like we weren't the only two people in the kitchen.

"Yes Sweetheart?"

"Can I curse one last time?"

I looked at her crazy ass and shook my head yes before kissing her forehead.

"You just fucked the shit out of my ass. Damn, I needed that."

When I looked in her face and saw the seriousness in her eyes I burst into laughter.

"Girl you crazy as hell you know that right?" She shrugged as I removed myself from her. "Thank you though baby. That pussy is A1 too. I see why these niggas don't wanna let you go."

Smiling she went into the bathroom and got us some towels to wipe off with as I fixed our plates. A shower could wait. A nigga was hungry as hell after that.

Alayziah

"Just...move...on Alex!" I yelled through my front door.

He followed me home from work and found out where I lived. Now he was randomly popping up trying to talk to me. Like he wasn't married. Like he hadn't spent I don't know how long lying to me and leading me on. I don't know why he was trying so hard to get me back when it's his fault that he no longer had me.

"How can I move on Noelle? How can I move forward when my future is in my rearview? It's you baby. It was always you."

I slid down my door and grabbed two handfuls of my hair. Resting my elbows on my knees I tried my hardest not to yell out.

He was driving me crazy.

"You made your choice Alex. And it wasn't me. You no longer have access to me."

"I made a mistake baby. I need you."

"No you don't."

"I love you."

"No you don't. You love what I did for you. How I made you feel. But you don't love me. There's no way you could have loved me and did me the way you did."

"Baby..."

"Go Alex. Let me go."

"I can't. I wouldn't be here if I could. I need you Noelle."

"If you love me at all let me go Alex. Please...let me go," I begged. He was wearing me down and he knew it.

"Noelle. Open the door baby. Please. I need you."

There was such desperation in his voice. I sat there with my head on the door. Looking up. Praying for strength and self-control. I licked the side of my mouth and shook my head as if I could shake the tears out.

"Baby..."

I stood. Turned towards the door. Placed my hand on the nob. Tapped the door with my forehead lightly.

"You're never going to let me go. Are you?"

"I can't Noelle. I promise you I've tried."

I opened the door and felt my heart hit my stomach at the sight of him. Fuck that it went down into my vagina at the sight of him.

"I don't want to miss you. I don't want to love you. But I do. That hasn't changed," he continued placing his hand over my cheek and pulling me into his chest. I stopped breathing when he wrapped his arms around my waist. And as much as I didn't want to want to...I wanted him to never let me go.

"You miss me?" He asked as I hugged him back. I nodded my head yes. He moaned into my ear as he squeezed me tighter. "I'm sorry Noelle. I know I fucked this up. But if you just give me some time I'm going to fix this. Fix us."

I didn't want to believe him. I couldn't believe him. I was tired of wasting energy on him. I just nodded okay and held him tighter. I didn't want to hear him. His words meant nothing to me.

"Make me feel your love Alex," I pleaded softly.

His arms went from my waist to my face as he kissed me passionately. When he lifted me off the ground and wrapped my legs around him I came to myself and jumped down.

"No. You. You have to go Alex. I can't keep doing this with you."

"Please Noelle. Just one last time."

"No. Go Alex. Please."

"I'm not letting go."

"You let me go the day you signed that marriage license."

He looked at me as if he couldn't believe what I was saying. Then he just...left. And I was glad he did.

Jabari

When I saw that nigga leaving her house it took all the Jesus within me to not hop out and tag his ass. Really, the only thing that saved him was the pissed off look on his face. I figured things must not have ended the way he wanted them to if he was mad. And I was proud of Al for standing her ground. Had that nigga came out smiling I don't know how I would have reacted.

Once he made it to his car and drove off I took a few deep breaths before I exited mine and went up to Al's door. I didn't even have to knock because the door was cracked open. I heard her crying so I went in and found her in the middle of the floor, laying there, sobbing.

She was that weak over this nigga that she couldn't even close the door and at least sit down before she let it out.

I can't lie...seeing her so broken...scared me. I didn't know if I was capable of taking on the challenge of fixing what this nigga had broken. I walked over to her and lifted her up. She panicked until she realized it was me. Then she rested inside my arms.

I took her and laid her in her bed. Took her clothes off and tucked her in. I tried to leave but she grabbed me and pulled me into the bed with her. I held her until she went to sleep.

When she did, I left.

Alayziah

When I woke up alone I called Jabari. He didn't answer so I got up, showered, and threw on some clothes. I walked down to his family's restaurant and just the thought of all of the different foods being prepared by his hands made my stomach growl. I saw Jessica before I saw him and she looked spooked as she walked towards me.

"Hey pretty girl," I spoke as she hugged me.

"Hey Allie cat. Um...RiRi know you here?"

"No. I just wanted to stop by and see him. Is he busy?" I asked looking towards the kitchen. It was thirty minutes before their dinner rush so I figured he was probably doing some prepping.

"Um...uh..."

Hearing her struggle to answer caused me to look back at her. "What is it Jess?"

Ignoring my question, she looked to the left of me. I followed her eyes and saw Jabari cheesing in some chicks face. I chuckled and shook my head in disgust.

"Allie cat..."

"It's cool," I said walking towards him. Towards them. He saw me before she did and he immediately stood and walked towards me.

"Sweetheart..."

"What the fuck is up Jabari? You leave me so you can flirt with the next bitch?"

He grabbed me by my forearm and almost dragged me to the other side of the restaurant.

"I thought you were different. You just like the rest of these dog ass niggas," I continued.

"Alayziah shut the fuck up and listen damn."

"No! I'm tired of niggas lying to me and leading me on. If you didn't want to fuck with me anymore why didn't you just say that?"

"I don't want to fuck with you anymore."

Taken aback by his honesty it took it a second to register in my brain, but when it did I nodded okay before I took a step back and stuck my hand inside my purse. I pulled out the tickets I'd purchased for us to go the Grizzlies game tonight and handed them to him.

"Take your girl. Have fun Jabari."

His face softened and he ran his hands down his face as I walked away. Jessica was standing there watching me with the most pitiful look on her face. I smiled to assure her that I was okay when really, I was breaking even more on the inside. I walked over to her and kissed her forehead as she wrapped her arms around my hips.

"He's just scared of you Allie cat. Please don't let him go."

I caressed her cheek lightly as she brushed a tear away from my eye.

"Call me if you need me Pretty Girl. I'm here for you for whatever, okay?"

"Al…hold up before you leave…" Jabari said.

I removed Jessica's hands from my face and sped my way out of there before he made it to me. As far as I was concerned there was nothing else for us to say to each other. I respected and appreciated his honesty, and the fact that he'd spared me from any more heartache. Now, I was done.

"Al...baby wait..." I yelled out to her.

Her ass was speed walking down the street. I could have easily caught up with her but I wanted to give her time to cool off a bit before I made it to her. I knew I'd messed up when I told her I didn't want to fuck with her anymore. It was true when I said it; but once I said it...I knew I didn't really mean it. I wanted her. *I guess I just wanted the healed and normal her.*

Not the one that's in love with a married man. Not the one with trust issues and paranoia issues. Not the one that's been so fucked up by men that she can't see a good one standing in front of her.

I'm scared of her.

Scared that I'm going to fall in love with her and she's going to do me the way he did her. I don't want to be her. I can't be her. I refuse to be her.

"Alayziah," the bass in my voice made her stop dead in her tracks. I made my way to her and wrapped my arms around her waist. She wrapped her arms around mine and leaned back into my chest.

"I'm sorry," she turned towards me, but she didn't look at me. "Let me explain."

"You don't have to explain. I appreciate your honesty."

"Look at me Sweetheart."

"I can't."

"Why not?"

"I'm tired of crying."

Hearing her say that literally made my heart burn.

"Lay..."

"It's cool Bari. You don't have to explain. It's cool."

"And you mean that don't you? You're seriously giving up on me already?"

She scrunched her face up as she looked at me.

"You just said you didn't want to fuck with me anymore. What you want me to do? Beg you to stay?"

"I don't know what I want you to do to be honest. I saw you in that floor earlier and that shit fucked with me Al. I can't even lie. Made me feel like what I've been trying to give you will never be enough. Made me feel like you was going to leave me for him like he left you for her."

"Bari…" Her hands cupped my face as she stared at me. Like she was trying to find the perfect words to say. "I would never inflict that pain on you or anyone else. I'm sorry that you even feel that way; but I can't lie…I'm struggling. But that doesn't have anything to do with you. It's…this…hold he has on me. He won't let me go."

"Do you want him to?"

"I need him to."

"But do you want him to?"

"…Yes. He doesn't deserve me. I know that in my mind. It's my heart that doesn't want to cooperate."

I sighed heavily before pushing her back slightly. "What do you want from me Sweetheart?"

"I just want you to love me Bari."

"I want to love you, but I'm not going to let you play me. If you want to continue to go back and forth with him you can't have me."

"I understand. You don't have to worry about that. I'm done with him."

I nodded. "Okay. I guess we'll see."

"Can you fix me some pasta? I'm hungry."

Time passed and Jabari and I are doing very well. Alex just randomly stopped reaching out to me and I must admit, that is kind of bittersweet. I love that man and I miss him so much, but I know that he isn't for me. Sometimes I find myself crying myself to sleep. In his t-shirt. Wishing it was him that was holding me.

I always said I'd never be a side chick. I'd never mess with a man who had a girlfriend let alone a married man, but I've learned my lesson.

Never say what you won't do because you never really know until you find yourself in that situation.

The love that I have for Alex had me doing things I never thought I would, and as much as I didn't want to love him, want him, miss him…I do. As much as I wish I was over him I'm not. To be completely honest, if he came to me with divorce papers I'd give his ass another chance. Not because of his love for me, but because of my love for him. That's how much I love him, and what fucks with me the most…is that I love him so much and he loved and cared for me so fucking little.

Yea he says he made a mistake and I was the one he should have chosen, but my God, did I not do enough for you to see what you had in me? Yea I had my crazy moments but there was nothing that I wouldn't do for that man.

I literally gave him the best of me and he took it and made a mess of me. Left the rest of me. Swore I wasn't enough. Maybe that's why I stayed, because I couldn't understand why he wouldn't want me. If I'm this great woman…this great catch…why would he need someone else?

Now I'm sitting here with this man that wants to love me deeply, and **I can't really give him all of my heart because I'm reserving pieces for a nigga who ain't even mine**. I'd invited Jabari, Jessica, Marcel, his new boo thang Whitney, and my cousin Erica over for a little set and in the midst of being surrounded by all of this love my mind just kept going back to Alex. I promised that I'd never call him or text him again so I called over to Marcel and told him to meet me on my patio.

"What's up Love?" He asked when he finally pulled himself out of Whitney's arms and met me on the patio.

"I got a funny feeling. Some ain't right."

"With?"

"Alex. He's been on my mind heavy these past few days."

He sighed and sat down. "Love…"

"I'm not saying I'm going to call him or anything. I just can't shake this feeling. I just feel like he needs me Marcel. I can't explain it. I know him. And I know when things aren't right with him. I feel it in my soul. Something is wrong."

"Okay. So how do you want to handle this? Do you want to call him? Check out his social media?"

"He's not gone say anything about it on there, but I don't want to call him."

"Then how are you going to find out if something is wrong?"

I sat next to him and inhaled deeply. "I don't know. I don't know."

"Just call him. Get it out your system."

I shook my head no. When I opened my mouth to reply my phone started to vibrate in my pocket. I pulled it out and Alex's number was flashing across my scream.

"Oh my God. It's him."

"Answer it."

With shaking fingers and a racing heart I answered his call. "Hey."

"Is this Alayziah?"

I pulled the phone from my ear and looked at it. There was a woman on the other line.

"Yea. Who is this?" I asked standing.

"This is Amy. I'm a nurse here at Methodist East. Alexander White is here. He's been in an accident. We had to put him in a medically induced coma because of the amount of pain he was in but before we did…he asked for you."

Dropping the phone, I fell to my knees. Marcel rushed towards me. I looked at him. Saw his lips moving. But I couldn't hear anything that was coming out.

I had to get to my baby.

Jabari

I saw Alayziah fall to her knees outside and my first instinct was to go and see about her. Before I could Marcel was lifting her up and she was rushing into her apartment. Tears were staining her face and she was shaking like crazy.

She ran past everyone in the living room section of her studio apartment, including me, and went over to her bed. After throwing her phone and keys into her purse she tried to run out of her front door but I stopped her.

"What the hell is going on? Where you going?" I asked her.

"He. I. I have to go!" She yelled crying harder.

"Love you can't drive like this. You need to sit down and get yourself together before you go anywhere," Marcel said walking towards us.

"No. I need to get to him. He needs me. I need to get to him. He's all alone. I gotta go," she sobbed. Her cries were getting louder. I pulled her into me and surprisingly she didn't pull away. She just cried into my chest as I looked at Marcel for an explanation.

"It's Alex. He's been in some type of accident. He's in a coma, but before they put him to sleep he asked for her."

I chuckled in slight frustration. Here I am comforting her while she's crying over the next nigga. I let her go and called for Jessica. When she made it to my side she asked what was going on.

"We heading out. I'm done with this shit."

"What? What's wrong?" She asked as Alayziah opened her door and walked out with Marcel on her heels.

"I'm tired of playing second to her ex. The nigga ain't even her ex. I'm done with this shit. If she loves him that much I'm just gone step back and leave her be."

"What happened RiRi?"

"The nigga was in some sort of accident."

"Okay...that doesn't mean she wants him. She obviously cares about him. She'd probably be acting the same way if it was you. You can't be mad at her for that. Don't be insensitive RiRi."

"Whatever mane. Like I said, I'm done. Get your shit. We out of here."

When we made it outside Marcel was still trying to convince Alayziah not to go to the hospital until she calmed down. She locked eyes with me as I walked to my car. After giving Marcel a hug she walked towards me. By the time she made it over I was in the car with the door closed. I rolled the window down and looked at her.

"I'm sorry," she mumbled. I nodded. "Can I call you when this is over?"

I shook my head no as I cut my car on.

"That probably wouldn't be for the best Alayziah. I'm not for this back and forth shit I told you that. Just…see about him. Do what you gotta do for him. And after some time has passed, once you're really free of him…you know where to find me."

"I don't want to lose you Bari."

"You never had me to lose me Sweetheart. Not because a nigga ain't fall for you; but because you didn't catch me. You was too busy holding him."

I used her words against her. She opened my door and sat on my lap. Took my face into her hands and stared into my eyes until I couldn't take it anymore.

"Gone Al."

"Thank you."

"For what?"

"Trying to love me. Showing me that there are some good men out there to love me."

"My love won't mean anything to you until you love you."

Her lips kissed mine sweetly. Then my cheek. Then my neck. Next she laid against my chest.

"Gone Al."

Biting her lip, she got out of the car. "I'm sorry Bari."

"Yea. Me too."

She stepped back and I closed the door. Drove off. And prayed I never looked back.

Marcel

I've never seen my best friend so distraught. I was there for the passing of her mother and she handled that better than she's handling this situation with Alex. I ended up driving her to the hospital because I didn't want to run the risk of anything happening to her.

When we arrived she ran up to the nurse's station and couldn't even speak. I went up there and told them who she was looking for. Alex's doctor came out and told her that until she calmed down he wasn't going to tell her anything about his condition or let her see him. So for an hour she stood outside.

Pacing, praying, and smoking cigarettes until I took her phone to find Jabari's number and called him. I tried to calm her down but she acted like the only thing that would soothe her was seeing Alex. I took her my phone and Jabari only talked to her for less than a minute, but whatever he said calmed her down immediately.

After listening to him she said okay, handed me the phone, put out her cigarette and went back inside.

A few minutes later his doctor appeared and took us into a private room. We sat down and he stared at Al for a moment before he started talking.

"Alayziah...Alex was in a car accident. He may have fallen asleep behind the wheel. Whatever happened he ran into an eighteen wheeler. Before he could make it out they both exploded. When the truck driver and the people in the gas station heard the explosion they ran out...but the flames were too insurmountable. They had to wait for the firefighters to get there."

"So they just...just...watched him burn?" Alayziah asked. She began to shake.

"There was nothing they could do Alayziah."

"How bad is it?" She put her forearms on her thighs and leaned her head down so low it almost went between her legs.

"Well...ninety five percent of his body was severely burned."

"What?" Her tears began to fall again as she jumped up. I grabbed her and pulled her away from the doctor. Tried to get her to compose herself. "So what's the plan? Is he going to make it? What? What can I do?"

"Honestly Alayziah, this is the worst case of burns I have ever seen in my life. It doesn't look good at all. He has less than a one percent chance of survival."

I held her tighter as her knees almost gave out on her.

"We put him in a medically induced coma. The pain was unbearable. No one deserves to go through that. We're going to scrape his skin to prevent infection. But after that, all we can do is keep him comfortable. Until...his...his vital organs are going to shut down Alayziah. His body has swelled. Right now we just need to keep him comfortable."

"Have you called his parents? His wife?"

"You're not his wife? He said you were. You're the only person we've called."

"When can I see him?"

"You can see him now; but I must warn you, he will look nothing like himself."

Al patted my arm signaling for me to release her. After I did she turned to face the doctor.

"Take me to him."

Alayziah

I stood at Alex's door for what felt like forever before I walked in. When I did I immediately burst into tears. Even though the doctor warned me about his appearance I was not prepared for what was before me. He was unrecognizable. The sight of him literally made me sick to my stomach.

My mind immediately went back to the last conversation we had. How I put him out of my house. Pushed him away. And he still wanted me here. I walked over to his bed and sat next to him. Put my hand inside of his and sobbed until I became weak.

I needed to contact his parents but I just couldn't pull myself to do it. I didn't want to be the bearer of this bad news, but if I didn't they'd be hearing about it soon so I looked his father up and called them. He's a preacher so it was easy for me to find his contact information online.

"Hello?" He spoke.

"Pastor White?" I tried to choke back the tears. I had to be strong. I had to be strong for him. I had to be the peace he'd always needed me to be. That's why he wanted me here. Because I bring him peace.

"Yes?"

"This is um…Alayziah. I'm not sure if you know me…"

"Of course I know you. My son was crazy about you. I still have a strawberry cupcake in my freezer that he's saving. Said he never wanted to forget that day with you."

His father chuckled as I pulled my phone away from me. Looking at Alex as I composed myself.

"Pastor White…" I couldn't find the words. They wouldn't come out. He sensed my apprehension.

"What's wrong Alayziah? Is my son okay?"

"Can you and your wife get to Methodist East? We're here. Um, can you get in touch with Carmen as well?"

"For what? He divorced her. Said he wanted to work things out with you. Just tell me…is my son okay?"

"You'll see him when you get here Pastor White. Call me when you're outside and I'll come meet you."

"We're on our way," he disconnected the call and I stood and caressed Alex's burned, rubbery cheek.

"I love you Alex. I don't know if you can hear me…but…I love you. Fight this baby. I promise if you do I'll never leave your side. I'll be with you every step of the way Alex. Please…don't give up on me. On us. I will always be here for you."

No longer able to hold my tears in anymore I sat down and cried until his parents arrived. When Pastor White called I wiped my face and stood.

"You're here?" I asked walking towards the door.

"Yes. What room are you in?"

"Just…wait by the nurse's station. I'll get his doctor and have him come out and talk to you."

"It's…it's that bad? Oh my God."

I hung up the phone. His cracking voice was about to send me over the edge. I walked out of the room and slowly made my way back to the waiting room.

When I saw an older man who looked just like Alex and who I assumed to be his wife standing next to him I finally let my body go. That's when it really hit me. I wouldn't be able to grow old with him. Not even marriage was able to separate me from him; but death…death was trying to. I called out to them and when I did, I blacked out.

Marcel

When Al passed out I thought all hell was about to break loose in this hospital. I called Jabari and him and Jessica came up here. I knew that she was trying to be Alex's strength but she needed someone to be hers. I was trying to, but there was only so much that I could do. When her body hit the ground Jabari, Jessica and I all jumped up and ran to her along with Alex's parents.

Jabari lifted her up and yelled for help. A couple of nurses came and led us to a nearby vacant room as they tried to wake her up.

When she finally did wake up she looked around at all of us as if she didn't know where she was. I guess she may have thought it was a dream but when she saw Alex's father she started crying again.

"Please. Go on and talk to his doctor and see about him I'll be fine," she instructed.

"Are you sure?" His father asked.

"I'm fine. I'm going to let you two have some alone time with him then I'll be back in."

His father nodded as his mother leaned down and kissed Alayziah's forehead.

"We're going to have to talk soon," his mother said.

"Yes maim."

When they left Alayziah sighed as if a weight had been lifted from her shoulders.

"What are they saying Alayziah?" Jabari asked as he stared down at her. Jessica was in the corner looking like a scared cat while all I could do was sit there and hold her hand.

"He was in a car accident. His car and the truck he ran into caught on fire. His...his body...he...doesn't even look like a human being. They've given him less than a one percent chance to live."

"Damn," I whispered and squeezed her hand tighter.

"Well...I know you're going to be here for him and his family, but I want you to know Jess and I are here for you," Jabari said kissing her forehead.

"That's right Allie cat," Jessica said.

"And you know I got you," I added.

She smiled lightly and looked at each of us.

"I appreciate y'all. I need to get back to him."

As she sat up in her bed we heard the loudest, most painful yell coming from the depths of a woman's soul, and then we heard a man sobbing, yelling over and over again, "My son. My God. My Son."

Alayziah inhaled deeply and got off of the bed.

"You sure you can handle this right now?" I asked her.

Nodding yes she gave me a weak smile. "That's why I'm here Boo. I gotta get myself together so I can be here for him and his family. I'm gone be okay. Y'all go ahead and head on out. I'll be fine."

"I'm not leaving you Love."

"I'm fine Marcel. Promise. If I need you I'll call you."

"I'll take you home," Jabari offered. I'd forgotten that I drove her here in her car.

"Aight cool," I said as I hugged Al tight. "Call me best friend."

"I will."

"I love you my Love."

"I love you too."

Alayziah

After his parents had calmed down and called some of his family and other Pastor's his mother tugged at my arm lightly and pulled me outside.

"Would you like a cup of coffee?" She asked. I shook my head no.

"But I'll go with you."

We walked to the cafeteria in silence. I decided to get a cup of coffee anyway. Once I filled half of my cup with sugar and cream we sat down. Face to face. I hated that the first time I met his mother was under this condition. After she took a sip of coffee and made the usual aahhh sound she looked at me and smiled. Which caused me to smile.

"It's good to finally meet you," she said.

"You as well. I didn't even know you guys knew about me."

She laughed lightly and shook her head.

"Girl my son talked about you on a daily basis when he was staying with us. We couldn't help but notice the change in him. Carmen and her parents had him so stressed out, unhappy, and angry. Then...all of a sudden, he just started walking around the house smiling. In his phone all day. Laughing and just...being at peace.

His father and I teased him until he finally told us that you were the reason behind his smile. You and his daughter. I thought you were going to be what pulled him away from Carmen but, he just, wouldn't let her go completely. I know it was those kids. That's why he stuck around. Had it been just her I feel like he could have moved on.

But he didn't want to hurt those kids. Their fathers left them all and he stepped up. She preyed on his desire for a family. Used that as a way to keep him around," she sighed and took another sip of her coffee.

"You know that baby wasn't even his?" She laughed lightly. Shaking in disgust.

"She was just trying to use that to keep him tied down. He'd already told her that he was leaving her when the baby was born for you. When she realized he was telling the truth she went ahead on and told him that there was a chance that the baby wasn't his. And sure enough she wasn't."

"Wow," I whispered more to myself than her.

"I know the way my son handled things with you wasn't the best way. He was...struggling Alayziah. Trying to be the man he thought he had to be for us and the church, the man he needed to be for his daughter and her kids, and the man he wanted to be with and for you. He needed you baby. And even though I know you two may have ended on bad terms I'm glad he had you for as long as he did. You loved on him and allowed him to be himself. When he felt like he couldn't be him with anyone else."

"First Lady..." I was trying not to cry and be all in my feelings but she was about to make me lose it.

"I'm sorry. But you need this. You need to hear this. My son loved you. Loved you as much as he could. And I'm appreciative of you loving him. He's been married before to women who didn't really love and appreciate him. He wants love and his own family so much that he settled for the first woman to come along and offer him that. But when he found you, you showed him what true love and support and friendship was.

He said that. He said you showed him what true love and support and friendship was about. He was just...dealing with the consequences of the choices he'd made and he couldn't get out. But he was trying. My God was my baby trying. He was coming home from playing in St. Louis. He's been playing more and more. He's never home. I told him he was doing too much. That he needed to rest. Said he'd rest when he died." I watched as tears began to roll down her cheeks. "They said he asked for you," I nodded. "They said, his chances of survival..."

"It's not about what they say. It's about what God says and what Alex does."

"All the same, you need to know that my son had a will. You know he was in a gang in his younger years so his father and I have an insurance policy for him. After his divorce he redid his will and left all that he has to you and his daughter."

"Ooww..." My heart literally ached as I grabbed my chest. "Why? Why did this happen to him? To us? Why couldn't he just let her go so we could be together?"

She stood and walked over to me. Pulled me into her stomach as I cried.

"I don't know baby. But everything happens for a reason. If God decides to show us the reason great, if not, good. All I know is my son needs you. So dry those tears and get back to his side."

I looked up at her and she smiled as she wiped away my tears. "Yes maim."

Jabari

He'd been in a coma for a week, and for a week straight Alayziah did not leave his side. His mother had to almost force her to go outside to get some fresh air. They were going to try and wake him up just to see if they could talk to him and see what he wanted to do.

We were all sitting around waiting for the coma to break. His doctor had warned us that depending on Alex's pain tolerance level he could wake up and just scream out from the pain. If so they were going to have to sedate him again. If he woke up and was calm initially so that they could talk to him and let him know what was going on they would allow him to stay awake for about two minutes before they put him to sleep again.

"I will always be here for you." I heard Alayziah say.

I looked up and her hand was on his chest as she stared at him. Broke my heart to see her this way, but it was beyond my control. I was just glad that she agreed to go home for a night or two once he woke up. They promised to call her if there was any change in his condition so she agreed to take some time to see about herself.

"Please Alex. Wake up. If you can hear me baby…wake up. I'm right here. I'm right here."

"Umm…" he moaned.

"Yes. That's it baby. Just…be still. And relax."

"Aahhh…" he moaned louder.

"Baby. Please. Try and relax."

"Noelle!" He yelled out in pain. Everyone jumped up as his doctors rushed in. His blood pressure was raising and so was his heartbeat.

"We have to sedate him or he's going to have a stroke. The pain is too much," his doctor yelled pushing his parents away. But Alayziah still stood by his side.

"I'm here baby. It's almost over. I love you so much Alex. I love you baby. I love you so much. I promise I do."

"I love you too Noelle," he opened his eyes finally and they were bloodshot red. "I'm sorry," he moaned as his doctor injected a clear liquid into his I.V.

"Don't apologize anymore. It's okay. I forgive you. I love you. And I'm going to be right here when you wake up again okay? I will always be here for you Alex. I promise."

"I love you Noe-" he drifted back to sleep.

His heartbeat and blood pressure lowered simultaneously. Alayziah wiped her face and rushed out of the room. Anger sketched across her face.

Alayziah

I was not angry, I was anger. I was not dangerous, I was danger. And I wanted to kill Carmen. I literally wanted to find her, wrap my hands around her neck, and choke the life out of her. Not because Alex chose her over me, but because she got to spend time with him that I couldn't. He couldn't be with me because he was with her. That shit was fucking with me.

Yes, I know it wasn't really her fault. I know that he made his choice. I know that he could've left her to be with me if he wanted to; but none of that mattered to me at the sight of him. I ran outside because I felt like I couldn't breathe in that room.

My head was spinning and all I could think about was the first night we spent together. How he held me all night, and every time I tried to get out of his grip he pulled me in deeper.

I got on Facebook and went to her page. Of course she's playing the concerned and heartbroken spouse when she hasn't stepped foot inside this hospital once. I messaged her ass and told her to call me. I was surprised when she did.

"Hello?"

"What?" She asked. I inhaled deeply to keep from spazzing on her ass.

"Where you at Carmen?"

"Why?"

"I wanna beat your ass."

Wasn't no point in lying or sugar coating it. I had so much pent up aggression and I needed to get it out. I was mad at her. Mad at him. Mad at myself. Mad at God for giving me a taste of the man and the love I'd always wanted and forcing me to watch him love and marry someone else. Now I had to watch him fight for his life. I knew it wasn't God's fault.

But, this pain, didn't care who it blamed.

"Girl if you don't get your crazy ass off my phone."

"Carmen I'm dead fucking serious. I'm gone be on your ass next time I see you. I don't care where it is. I don't care who you with. I don't care if you with your kids. When I see you...I'm on you." I hung up the phone and groaned.

"Now what do you think that's going to solve?"

I turned around and saw Jabari standing before me. I couldn't help but smile. Just the sight of him calmed me down instantly.

"I need to get this frustration out of me Bari," I said as he walked towards me.

"And you think fighting her is going to do that?"

"Damn right."

"What I tell you about your mouth and all that cursing?"

I blushed.

"Want me to take you to the gun range?" He asked. I nodded but I didn't think that was going to be enough to take this away. At this point though, I was willing to try anything.

Jabari

Alayziah with a fully automatic lusa was the sexiest sight I'd ever seen. She was letting it rip and even after she was out of ammo her finger was still on the trigger squeezing. I walked towards her and lowered the gun before taking it out of her hand completely. She stood there. No movement. No expression. She just stood there. I didn't know what to do so I just stood there as well. Waiting for her to make a move.

"Bari..." she mumbled.

"Yea?"

"Take me home."

Alayziah

Jabari took me back to his place. We sat in his car in silence for like an hour before I was ready to get out. He fixed me something to eat even though I told him I didn't have an appetite, but he insisted on cooking so I ate. When I was done I took a long hot shower and found him stretched across the couch. His hands folded behind his head.

I didn't know what we had between us; but I swear I'm glad to have him. I leaned against the edge of his couch for a while before I straddled him. His hands immediately wrapped around my waist. Looking down on him I traced his nipples with my fingers and my mind was filled with thoughts of Alex. He loved when I did that.

I didn't mean to start crying, but I couldn't help myself.

His fingers brushed my tears away as he lifted himself to face me. Taking my face into his hands he showered my lips with kisses.

"You said you would love the pain out of me," I whispered.

"I meant that shit too Al."

"Then do it. Love the pain out of me. Make me feel good Bari. I need to get these thoughts, him, out of my head. Even if it's just for a little while."

"Are you sure?"

"I'm positive."

Jabari wrapped my legs around him and stood. As he carried me to his bedroom tears slid from my eyes. He sat me in the center of his bed. I looked at him and thought, 'What in the hell is wrong with you Alayziah? This man is fine. From his brown skin and pretty eyelashes to his full lips and vampire teeth. His body is racked. He has a heart of gold. Sweet and soft as cotton candy but he don't play around. The dick is good. And he wants your crazy, confused heartbroken ass.'

I watched him remove his clothes and my heart was beating slowly. So hard. I felt so bad. Like I was cheating on Alex. When we'd never even been in a relationship for me to be cheating on him. I watched him slide the condom on his dick and my mouth watered at the sight of him. He was the total package. But he wasn't the package for me.

It's like...*Jabari was my me as I was to Alex*. He was showing me how Alex felt about me. It doesn't matter how good of a man Jabari was...Alex still had me. And it didn't matter how good of a woman I was...Carmen still had Alex.

They say he'd finally let her go. I hate I never had the chance to experience the real him. But there was no point in driving myself crazy over it now. Not right now. Now that I had this man crawling towards me.

His mouth covered mine briefly before he stopped and stared at me.

"What?" I asked.

"Turn around," he instructed. I did as I was told skeptically. I was expecting Jabari to be on some making love all night shit but I wasn't so sure now. Once I was positioned he spread my ass cheeks and said, "Now I can make love to you and have you sprung and crying when this is over, or I can fuck you and make you forget about anybody else that's ever been inside of you. What you want Sweetheart? What you need?"

"I...need..." I paused and thought. "I need you to make this go away Jabari. Fuck me." With no warning he inserted himself inside of me and I cried out. "Shit!" I yelled.

He didn't move. Just...stayed there. Still. I tried to throw it back on him but he wouldn't let me. He licked his fingers and used them to massage my clit.

"Bari..." I whined.

But he still wouldn't move. Before I knew it, it felt as if my pussy was on fire. Laying deeper into the bed I relaxed my shoulders and enjoyed the feel of his fingers against my clit. Just as my walls started to pulse and vibrate against his dick he pulled out and went deep inside of me. Giving me the longest and hardest orgasm I'd ever experienced in my life. I couldn't even moan. All I could do was shudder and struggle to breathe.

When it subsided he started long stroking me and I was able to voice my appreciation for what he'd just done.

Jabari

After I'd put Alayziah to bed with the dick she didn't want to leave me so I took off from the restaurant so I could spend the night with her. We were supposed to go back to her crib so she could pack a bag but when we got there an older man called out, "Ziah!" and I swear I've never seen her move as fast as she did when she dropped her purse and ran into his arms.

"Daddy!" She yelled as she squeezed him tighter.

He laughed and tried to pull away from her so he could look at her but she wouldn't let him let her go.

"Baby girl let me look at you," her father said but she wasn't trying to hear that.

"What are you doing here?"

I picked up her purse and took out her keys to open the door.

"Your cousin called me and told me you hadn't been to work. Just wanted to come home and check on my baby," he said carrying her inside as I stood at the doorway.

"Call me if you need me Sweetheart," I said not wanting to interrupt them.

"No Bari. Don't leave me," she pleaded.

Stepping inside I closed the door behind me.

"I'd shake your hand but she won't let me go," her father said chuckling.

"It's nice to meet you sir. I'm Jabari."

"You as well. Call me Laymont. My daughter is a handful hunh?"

I ran my hand down my waves and smiled. Not sure if that was a trap or not. She finally let him go and we all sat on the couch.

"So what's wrong baby?"

She looked from me to him as she ran her hands down her thighs.

"How did you get over losing mama?"

He inhaled and let out a hard breath as he sat deeper into his seat.

"Honesty Ziah I never got over her. I just...accepted it. You know your mother was my everything. I...loved that woman more than life itself. You know I say all the time I'd die for you and her. And I meant that. So when I lost her it was literally like I lost myself. I didn't want to live. I didn't want to love. But I know that she loves me and she would want me to be happy.

There is nothing that she can do for me in the grave. Loyalty is for the living. Yes, I miss her and I want her and I think about her still; but I had to move on. For me. So, I went through my little grieving stage. I didn't want anyone else. And when I was ready, not when women thought I was or my family thought I was but when I was ready, I started dating again.

It was difficult at first because I found myself comparing them to her and they all failed miserably. No one will ever be able to replace your mother. I felt guilty about moving on, but I couldn't let that consume me. I stopped looking for someone to replace her and I just...lived baby. And in living I loved. And it just flowed naturally. Now, what's going on?"

"It's a long story daddy. I just, I think I'm about to lose a man that I really care about and I don't know if I'm going to be able to handle it."

"You can do all things through Christ who is your strength. If all else fails, you can come back to Chicago with me. You know I think you're too young to be dating anyway."

She smiled and kissed his cheek. "Thanks daddy."

"Anytime baby girl. I'll be back to check on you a little later. I need to stop by your auntie's house or I'll never hear the end of it. I love you."

"I love you too."

We all stood and he walked towards the door as he talked to me. "It was nice meeting you Jabari. Take care of my Ziah."

"Daddy!"

"Yes sir," after she locked the door behind him I made my way to her kitchen. "You hungry?" I asked.

"Bari..."

I know what she wanted to talk about, but I didn't want to talk about it. I was hoping she'd let the shit go, but obviously she wasn't going to.

"Bari..."

"Yea?" I asked looking inside of her refrigerator.

"Look at me. We need to talk."

"Ion want to," I replied opening her freezer.

"Jabari."

"No. There's no point in us talking about this Alayziah."

"Why not?"

"Because."

"Because what."

"Because I don't want to."

"But we need to."

"Why?"

She walked behind me and wrapped her arms around my waist. I stood there. Letting the chill from the freezer put out the fire she had building inside of me.

"Jabari please."

"Fine. Fine."

She released me and grabbed a bottle of wine and one glass before walking back over to her couch. She poured a glass and sat it on the dining room table in front of me before taking a sip from the bottle.

"Talk..." I whispered.

"Jabari I like you. I really do. You're such a good man. But you said it yourself that I'm not ready for you. At first I didn't agree but I do now. I don't want to taint you. I don't want to hurt you. I don't want to be the reason you stop being as loving and open as you are. So as much as I want to be in your life I'm not sure if that's a good idea. You're so good for me, but Bari I know I'd be bad for you."

I nodded. It was the truth. She couldn't appreciate my love right now. But that didn't stop me from wanting to love on her.

"I don't want to take away your choice like Alex did me. So I'm telling you up front what it is and I'm allowing you to choose whether or not you want to stick around. But I'm going to be honest with you, right now, my heart wouldn't be in it."

I took the wine to the head before I said anything.

"I appreciate your honesty Alayziah. And I'm glad that you care enough about me to put me first like this. I'm going to be here for you while you go through this with Alex. And after that we can go our separate ways."

"Jess is going to be so mad at me," she said lightly as she flicked a tear from her face.

"She'll be alright. Everybody ain't meant to be in your life forever. Sometimes it's just for a season. This is our season. It's cool."

Alayziah took my face into her hands and kissed me deeply. So deep my dick grew. I pushed her away and licked my lips.

"I can't handle that Al."

Nodding she drunk a little more of the wine before laying her head on my lap. I ran my fingers through her hair as she drifted off to sleep.

Carmen

Before Alex and I became friends I was married to a cheater. There was also the abuser. And then the one that just meant me no good at all. I had children with each of them. I didn't think any man would want me. I became known as the hoe of the church.

But then, I met Alex.

He was known as the joke of the church because he'd been married twice and each of his marriages failed. We became friends and he accepted me. He accepted my children. And we were inseparable. Ten months into our relationship he proposed and obviously I said yes. Because of his past and my pervious encounters with men my father didn't approve and he gave Alex the hardest time, but Alex didn't give up on me. On my children.

Until he saw Alayziah.

The day they met he changed. He said they were only friends but I knew it was more. He would talk to her all day every day. I removed her from our Facebook pages and he would add her again. We'd fight or he'd get into it with my father and he would stop talking to me and spending alone time with me.

It got to the point where he didn't want to talk to me unless it was about the kids. He didn't want to see me unless it was with the kids. And I knew it was because of whatever it was he had with her. I told him that I didn't want him to be friends with her anymore and he promised me that it was strictly friendship; but I knew it was more.

When he moved in with me I thought that would keep him from talking to her but it didn't. So I started talking to other people too. I ended up getting pregnant and honestly I knew it wasn't Alex's baby.

We started using condoms. He told me it was because he didn't want to conceive while we were beefing but I knew it was because he was having sex with her. But I didn't tell him that I was having sex with anyone else or that the baby might not be his because I didn't want to lose him. He was the best man I ever had. Call me selfish but I refused to let him go.

So he married me and things just got worse between him and my father. I ended up trying to kill myself because it was just too much. But he was home and rushed me to the hospital. I don't know where he went but he left me and when he came back he was shut down emotionally. He probably went to her for comfort and she turned him down because we were married.

I'm sure people would wonder why I'd want a man that wanted someone else, but I wanted him. I loved him. And I was going to have him. I refused to have another failed relationship. Nothing but death was going to separate us.

So, since Alex wanted to divorce me, I made it possible for death to separate us. He always drinks iced tea while he's on the road. I put a few Sonata sleeping pills in his last bottle of tea. So by the time he made it into Tennessee he'd fall asleep. Sonata stays in your system for the shortest amount of time so I figured by the time he made it to the hospital and tests were ran there would be no sign of it, but because of how bad his condition was they didn't even run any tests to see if he was under the influence of any drugs or alcohol.

I couldn't watch him love her. Be with her. I know she thought he left her for me; but from the minute he saw her he was no longer mine. I couldn't handle that. How could I explain that to the church? To my following? To my friends? What was I supposed to say? That he fell for someone else? That yet again I wasn't good enough.

No.

I couldn't do that again. Not for her or anyone else. I couldn't hear my father say, 'I told you so.' I couldn't hear my mother tell me that I just need to focus on myself and my kids. So I did what I had to do. Alex falls in love so fucking fast. And he falls out just the same. I was the third woman he'd done that too. But I was going to be the last.

Yes, I practically killed Alex. And I don't regret it at all.

It took six months for his kidneys and liver to fail. Next would be his lungs. So his parents decided to wake him up and have a dose of the highest morphine so we could say goodbye. They went first. When it was my turn they left the room and gave Alex and I some privacy. His swelling had gone down but he was still badly burned. I'd gotten used to it by now so I was happy to see him awake.

He lifted his hand out for mine and I placed it inside. Caressed his hand lightly with my thumb. Stared into his eyes. Trying to keep tears from falling from mine. Kissed his cheeks. His nose. His forehead. His lips. As tears fell from his eyes.

"I love you Noelle."

Biting my lip, I closed my eyes and let my own tears fall. "I love you too Alex."

"I'm sorry baby."

"It's okay."

"You were my best friend." I removed my hand from his and took a step back. Tried to compose myself. "Noelle…"

"I'm here. You are my best friend Alex. Don't talk in past tense."

He smiled. "I wish I could get you pregnant." We laughed but stopped immediately when he groaned in pain. "Come…lay next to me."

I shook my head no adamantly as I wrapped my arms around myself. "No, Alex. I don't want to hurt you."

"What more can happen to me, baby?"

Slowly I walked over to his bed and climbed in. I laid on my side and faced him.

"Every morning when I rise I can just see heaven in your eyes. Makes me know this is not an everyday love. We've got something I'm sure we can be proud of. We've got so much so much love. We've got so much so much trust. Can't you see a halo? A halo. I can see a halo hovering over us. God blessed our love. God blessed our love."

He stopped singing and coughed.

"Alex…"

"Sing it to me Noelle."

Tears were saturating my face as I sat up in the bed. That was the song we said I'd walk down the aisle to when we got married. *God Blessed our Love* by Al Green. Rubbing his heart lightly I began to sing to him as best as I could through my tears.

He smiled as he closed his eyes. "Noelle…"

"Yes baby?" I took his hand into mine.

"God blessed our love," he whispered.

"God blessed our love. God blessed our love. He's on our side," I sung as his heart began to slow its pace. "Alex?" I called out.

"I'm…here…" he said.

"You've been on my mind. I grow fonder every day lose myself in time. Just thinking of your face. God only knows why it's taken me so long to let my doubts go. You're the only one that I want. I don't know why I'm scared I've been here before every feeling every word I've imagined it all. You'll never know if you never try to forgive your past and simply be mine. I dare you to let me be your one and only."

I sung. He clutched his chest. His smile widening.

"Promise I'm worthy to hold in your arms so come on and give me a chance to prove I am the one who can walk that mile until the end starts."

He opened his mouth slightly but closed it again.

"Baby?" I asked. He said nothing as his grip on my hand loosened. "Baby? Alex? Talk to me," I sobbed shaking him lightly.

"It was always you Noelle. You *were* my one and only. I love you," he said as he let my hand go.

"Alex, wait. Please! I love you. Don't leave me!"

The sound of his heart monitor flat lining filled the room.

"Alex! Alex!"

Selah

Part two

Alayziah

To the left of me sat Marcel, Jabari, Jessica and my work mother Pam. To the right of me sat Alex's mother, his father, and his brother Terrance. My eyes were puffy and red from crying but my sight was good enough to see Carmen standing over Alex's casket crying and acting a plum fool.

As my legs shook I found myself counting to twenty. Three didn't work. Ten didn't either. I was praying by the time I made it ten my desire to kill her and dump her in the casket with him would have subsided. But the louder her cries got the angrier I became. She was so fucking fake. So was he. And as much as I hated that about him I loved him even more.

His mother's hand found mine and she looked at me with a smile. I turned my head slightly and smiled at her. Wondering how she could be sitting here so strong and at peace as she buried her youngest son. I guess the Lord was definitely her strength.

Carmen started to moan and groan and I laughed. Alex's brother, Terrance, leaned forward and stared at me. I looked at him. Begging him with my eyes to give me permission to beat this bitch's ass. He looked from his mother and father back to me and nodded his head slightly and I jumped up and ran towards her.

Before I could get to her I felt a pair of strong arms wrap around my waist and lift me up and I knew it was Jabari. "Let me go!" I yelled, but he didn't listen. I watched as Terrance grabbed Carmen by her hair and dragged her out of the church. As ewws and oh my God's filled the church I followed behind Terrance and Carmen. With Jabari, Jessica, Pam, and Marcel following behind me.

Carmen

"Let me go Terrance! I just brought this weave!" I yelled trying to free myself from Terrance's grip with no success.

He had a firm grip on my hair and was not letting me go. I couldn't believe this nigga was embarrassing me like this. I was pouring my heart out to my husband and Terrance and his puppet Alayziah just had to ruin our moment. I know it's because she's jealous. Mad because Alex didn't leave me for her.

Yes, he served me with divorce papers but he was always going to be mine. Wasn't nothing but death going to separate us and I made sure of that.

Terrance and I never really got along. He felt like I wasn't any good for Alex. But he was crazy about Alayziah. Just like his lying, unfaithful, and unappreciative brother Alex. I couldn't even sit with his mother because her ass was sitting next to her. And when I finally had the chance to say goodbye to Alex she had to go and ruin it trying to run up on me.

Now Terrance was almost ripping my scalp from my skull dragging me out of this church. I hated his ass.

"Stay your ass away from my family Carmen," Terrance said as he released me.

"Nigga you don't tell me what to do! Today isn't about you! It's about my husband! And I have just as much of a right to pay my respects as you do."

He chuckled and placed his hands in his pockets as he licked his lips at me. "Carmen get your crazy ass on before I let Al tag you."

"Fuck you and that bitch! I ain't scared of her!"

"Bitch you ain't gotta be scared of her, I'll beat your ass!"

The little chick that was with Alayziah yelled as a man who favored her held her back. Alayziah stood there smiling with her arms crossed over her chest. Just the sight of her repulsed me. All I could think about was my baby wanting her instead of me.

"Bitch what the fuck you looking at?" I asked grabbing my keys from out of my purse. I knew they weren't going to let me back in. I was just glad I decided against bringing my kids to the funeral.

"Shit," Alayziah replied handing the older woman that was with them her purse.

"Alayziah chill the hell out. You not gone be outside this church fighting." The guy that was holding the younger girl said. He had the prettiest eyelashes I'd ever seen.

"Then follow me across the street Carmen. I owe you an ass whooping. I told you next time I saw you I was gone be on you. Didn't I?"

Alayziah was so calm I couldn't help but laugh. I couldn't even take her little skinny self seriously. I would have had no problem fighting her but I wanted to uphold my image in the church so I let the disrespect slide.

"Alayziah I have no reason to fight you honey. Alex was my husband. I had him. You were just the side chick."

She laughed as she tried to take a step towards me but the other guy that was with her grabbed her arm.

"Not here best friend." He stared at me like he wanted to hit me himself.

"Listen to me good Carmen… Alex may have given you a ring but that ring was nothing but a chain on his finger. All you had was his last name and I know you didn't even have that when he died. I had his heart. Marrying you was a mistake. You can front and make it seem like he wanted you before he died if you want to but you know the truth and I know the truth. And that's all that matters to me."

"Fuck you!" I yelled walking towards her but when I saw Terrance and her best friend square up at me I stopped. I knew I'd never win this fight. So I let it go. *For now.*

Alayziah

"Allie cat I swear I'll get that bitch for you! All you gotta do is take me to her and I'm on her for you baby I swear!"

I smiled at Jessica. She was a little firecracker. We were leaving the church and I didn't want to be alone so I asked her to ride with me. I'd calmed down but she was still mad at the situation with Carmen. Jabari was following behind us and we were heading to the restaurant to eat. Honestly, all I wanted to do was go home, crawl in my bed, and sleep. I couldn't bear seeing them lower Alex in the ground. I just...wanted to sleep. See if I could see him in my dreams.

"Aight pretty girl. You better watch your mouth. You know Jabari don't play."

"Mane fu- forget Jabari. I ain't thinking about him right now. I'm worried about you."

I looked over at her and smiled again to reassure her. "I'm okay Jess. I know it's going to take some time to get him out of my system but I'll be fine."

"I can't imagine how you feel right now. I can tell you really loved him. And to lose him before you ever really even had a chance to be with him..."

Looking out of her window she shook her head at the thought, giving me the perfect opportunity to dab away the tears that were filling my eyes. God. I missed him so much already.

Carmen

She had the cutest little snore I can't even lie. I guess she was really tired because a few minutes after she laid down she was asleep. When her snores stopped and she was deep into her sleep I stepped out of her closet and walked over to her bed.

I'd been watching her sleep for hours before my feet got tired. I found myself caressing her skin. Her hair. Trying to figure out what it was about her that made Alex want to leave me.

She was attractive, but so was I.

I sat on the side of her bed and inhaled her scent. Her neck smelled fruity. And her hair did too. My hands found their way under her shirt but I quickly removed them and stood when she moaned. I bet she was dreaming about him.

Bitch.

Alayziah

I never would have imagined that it would have taken losing Alex for me to realize just how much I loved love. The idea of love. Relation. Companionship. Romance. I craved it. Because I was so hungry for love I let any nigga come into my life and feed me. But, just like you can't eat from everyone's kitchen you can't mess off with every man that crosses your path.

I'm here, with rain pounding my skin, laying on top of a man's grave. Because I'm an addict. I'm addicted to love. I crave that shit. Just as someone craves crack or vodka; I crave love. I need it. The way their skin itches, aches without it, so does mine. Just like they would give their body and soul for a hit, so would I.

I need.

I needed.

I needed love.

I needed love to feel.

I needed love to feel complete.

And since love is my drug, men are my suppliers. Anything they asked me to do I did. Anything they wanted from me I gave. Whatever they needed to hear I said. Because I knew if I satisfied them they would satisfy me. I thought they would fill me when they would feel me. *Satisfy the longings I had buried deep down inside but their deep strokes could never reach it no matter how hard they tried.*

Now six months after Alex's death I've given up on love. I've given up on relationships. I don't trust these niggas. I don't want these niggas. And I damn sure ain't trying to love these niggas. All I want from a man at this point in my life is that gift between their thighs that I lack.

Other than that, there is nothing that a man can offer me that I can't give or buy myself. I'm tired of taking losses. Tired of being lied to. Led on. Picked over. I guess I'm going through life in rehab. Avoiding my drug. Trying to get clean and free. Trying to find peace.

Keeping my word to my grandmother I reenrolled in college to finish out my last two years. When I get my degree in Creative Writing I plan on teaching. I'm still writing poetry and performing. In fact, I want to do a poetry CD and DVD. There's a chick here in Memphis that did something like what I'm trying to do a while ago. Her name is Kailani. I'm supposed to link up with her after I take Jessica shopping.

She's like a little sister to me. Even though things didn't work out between Jabari and I, I could never turn my back on her. With me losing my mother and her losing her sister it's like...that connects us to each other somehow.

She'd been filling me in about him and this lil chick he calls himself being in a relationship with. I wish him nothing but the best. Jabari is a great man. But I've learned...every good man or woman ain't the man or woman for you. I've learned, I ain't for everybody. And mine is not meant every man's body.

Rell

"Are y'all niggas crazy? Ain't no way in hell I'm letting you two out of all people play matchmaker for me. I'm good."

I looked from Bishop, who had a smug look on his face, like he knew I wasn't gone go for this shit to Kai, who looked like she couldn't believe I didn't want her help before I took another sip of my water. Ever since they came back to Memphis they have been trying to hook me up.

I guess since they were married and a couple of months away from welcoming their first son into the world they wanted me to experience that love and happiness too. But shit, I was good with my first love. My music. Any woman that I entertained would be playing mistress to that.

Originally they were supposed to get a few months of traveling in before the baby was born but when Kai started having those hormonal mood swings Bishop hurried up and brought her ass back home. Said he wasn't gone be spending all that money to be arguing with her ass almost every other day. He could do that at home for free. That nigga is a trip.

I can't front, it felt good to have them back home. And it felt even better to have my best friend back. Yea we almost put them paws up when he found out about me and Kai but like real niggas do once the fight was over we put that shit behind us and we're just as close now as we were before she even came in the picture. If not closer.

Which is why they were taking it upon themselves to try and play matchmaker. Shit was starting to make my nerves bad. Every time we got together they brought this shit up. And I couldn't smoke around Kai because she was pregnant. She knew what she was doing. I stood and she grabbed me by my forearm and sat me back down.

"Prince." She started talking and I quickly dismissed her.

"Don't call me that Kai. And don't start with this shit either. I'm good. Bishop get your woman man."

"I agree with her nigga. You need somebody on your side. We getting old nigga. The late nights and early mornings is cool when you got somebody waiting for you and supporting you. That shit is played out now."

I looked at his ass like he was crazy and chuckled. "Oh so since you married now it's played out?" I asked standing again. "Look, I appreciate y'all looking out for a nigga and caring about a nigga...but I'm good. I don't have time to be getting to know nobody. Shit is time consuming. I got too much going on with my label to be weeding out who I can and cannot trust."

"That's why we're going to find her for you. Just let us set you up on one date Rell. And if you don't like her I won't bring it up ever again." Kai said rubbing her stomach.

I sighed heavily. "I'm not gone say okay. I'll just say...I'll think about it."

Kai jumped up and into my arms. "Yay! That's good enough for me."

Alayziah

Watching Kailani wobble over to my table was the cutest thing I'd seen in a while. She was little like me so to see her stomach sticking out as much as it was had me cracking up. I stood and we embraced before I helped her sit down.

"How you feeling mama?" I asked her. We'd talked and Facetimed a few times but this was the first time we saw each other face to face.

"Girl...I'm so ready to get this little boy out of me I don't know what to do."

"How much longer do you have?"

"Two months." She said with a pout.

"That's beautiful Kai. You and Bishop are beautiful together."

Blushing she rubbed her stomach absently. "Yea but it ain't always been beautiful between us Al. I love that man though. Wouldn't change him for anything in the world. What about you? Anyone special in your life?"

I chuckled before taking a sip of the wine I'd ordered. "No. Not at all."

She looked at me skeptically. "Why not? You're beautiful. I know you have men falling all over you."

"I'm just not into that right now. I'm focused on school and my poetry, feel me?"

"I hear you. That's how I was. I didn't want to have anything to do with love. But love found me. In Bishop. When I least expected it. And I'm sure the same thing is going to happen to you."

Leaning back in my seat I smiled. She had no idea. I was avoiding love at all costs.

Rell

When Kai invited me to see this poet she'd met I was a little skeptical. I felt like she was on some slick shit knowing how I'm drawn to creative women. Hell, that's why we were crazy about each other. Because of that vibe. But she assured me that it was strictly about business. Said shawty wanted me to produce her poetry CD so I agreed.

I met her and Bishop at the young lady's set. It was at a banquet hall. When I first pulled up I was a little skeptical because the building was so plain looking outside; but when we walked in I was pleasantly surprised. The lights were dim, but she had candles lit all over the place. In select areas of the room blue lighting shined down.

She had a band playing softly in the background. And our table had three candles and some sweet smelling incense burning in the middle.

"You owe me for finding her for you my nigga. You think I'm cold with the pen. This chick is a beauty and a beast with her writing. That's what she should call her album, Beauty on the Beat."

I nodded as Kai boosted her girl up. As much talking as she was doing I just hoped she lived up to her potential.

"We'll see about all that." I replied as our server came and took our drink orders.

The band stopped playing. The silence caught everyone's attention. When we were looking at the stage the band began to play again. And that's when I saw her. The most beautiful woman I'd ever seen. Not just physically, but she had an aura about her that drew me into her. As she walked onto the stage I found myself leaning deeper into our table. Trying to inch closer to her.

Her brown skin was smooth, while her arms were covered in tattoos. I couldn't see all of her legs because she had on a long maxi dress but from the split on the side I could tell at least one of her legs were tatted too. She was slim with toned arms and a flat stomach. Her perky breasts were sitting up perfectly without a bra. Her hair flowed to her armpits in loose waves that were jet black, complementing her skin.

Taking the mic into her hands she closed her eyes and inhaled deeply as a smile slowly crept across her face. When she opened her eyes they immediately met mine, and at that moment, I was her prisoner. Her eyes shined like honey. I should have looked away, but she had me. Dammit she had me. She ran her hand through her hair before looking down to the ground.

"Masterpiece." I heard myself say.

I saw Kai looking at the side of my face cheesing but I didn't give her the satisfaction of acknowledging her. I felt like I was holding my breath. Waiting for her to speak. I needed to hear her speak. And she was taking her precious time. Torturing me. *Like she knew I needed her to make my heart beat.*

Just as I was about to get frustrated at this game she didn't even know we were playing, that she was winning, she opened her mouth. Her beautiful mouth, and spoke.

"This is called, As I Wait." Inhaling deeply, she tilted her head to the side and looked at me briefly before looking at Kai and smiling.

"As I wait. Wait while you sleep. Wait as God molds me into who He wants me to be. As I wait. Wait for Him to bring me to you as He did Eve. As I wait I can't wait. Until the first time I see your face And He says to me, 'That's him Beloved he's awake.'

A poem for my future husband…

I am your Eve. Adam. I am your rib. How have you been able to survive without me? Have you been lonely? I'm here to save you from that. Give you the companionship you lack. Commune with you. And display God's mysterious equation of how 1 + 1 will equal 1 flesh never 2. I am your Eve. Adam.

I am your rib. I was created to protect your heart. I was created to love you. To support you as you fulfill the purpose God created you to do. I was created to give you life like no other woman can. To respect you. To encourage you. And to lift you up as a man. As my man. I am your Eve. Adam.

I am your rib. And I will not cause you to sin. No I will not use my influence to hinder you. No baby. I'm going to be your help… Meet. Your salvation and relationship with God will be safe with me. If anything I'll help you grow in your walk with God. That's what a real woman does. He will fill me with Him and I will drench you with His love. I am your Eve. Adam.

I am your rib. I will bear you a son who will want to grow up and be just like you. I will bear you a daughter who will want a man to treat her just like you do... Me. Baby. We will live. And we will love And we will serve. And nothing will separate us until the grave. And even then our bones will be side by side as our flesh rests peacefully. And I believe your spirit will recognize me. And we'll meet in heaven and if our hearts are visible your name will be tattooed across mine. And like eternity our love. Will not be constrained by time. I am your Eve. Adam. I am your rib. So I wait... Wait while you sleep. Wait as God molds me into who He wants me to be. As I wait. Wait for Him to bring me to you as He did Eve. As I wait. I can't wait."

Alayziah

I had the hardest time concentrating during my set. Kai invited the sexiest man I'd ever seen in my life with her and he was distracting me. Yes, he was a beautiful man physically. But there was also something about the way he looked at me that made me see no other man but him. From his dreads, to his thick eyebrows and chocolate brown eyes, full brown lips, tattooed arms and chest to his skin that was the same color as mine he was finessing these niggas. His dreads were in a high bun and he was wearing a white v neck with a pair of dark jeans and royal blue hi top Adidas.

It seemed like no matter where I looked my eyes always found their way back to him. And every time I would look at him, he'd smile.

Once my set was over I walked my way over to their table. After hugging her and speaking to Bishop she grabbed my hand and squeezed tightly as she said, "This is Terrell. Everyone calls him Rell. He's the producer I was telling you about."

Trying not to stare I smiled and waved as I took a step back.

"The sun is shining in your eyes beautiful," he said grabbing me around my waist and pulling me into his chest.

"I'm sorry...when did I give you permission to touch me?" I tried to push myself away from him.

"I don't need your permission to touch what is mine." His grip around my waist tightened.

I felt my face twisting up as Kai and Bishop laughed. Rell's face was serious. Like he meant what he said. Quickly correcting him I placed my hand on top of his forearm and tried to push him away again with no success.

"Nigga I am not yours. I don't even know you."

"You are mine. You my girlfriend. My woman."

I laughed. I mean I really laughed. And the more I laughed the more serious his facial expression was. Which made me laugh even harder.

"Yo, you crazy yo. I am not your girlfriend." I said once I finally stopped laughing. I was still smiling though. And he was looking at my lips like he wanted to kiss it away. I grabbed his chin and forced him to look me in my eyes. "My eyes are up here. Don't be staring at my lips like that."

"Fine…I won't stare."

I opened my mouth to respond but when I did he stuck his bottom lip between mine. Sucked the shit out of my top lip as he squeezed me tightly. I didn't want to moan but I did. Pushing him off of me I slapped his ass before walking away. I don't know who this crazy nigga was that Kai tried to link me up with, but I was going to have to find another producer. Soon.

Rell

I don't know why she was acting like she didn't wanna get down with a nigga. To be honest, I don't know what even came over me. I'd never done any shit like that before. But I just couldn't help myself. Her lips were taunting me.

I had to taste them.

And even though she slapped me I'm glad I did. I could tell by her moan that she was feeling my kiss, but before I could even slip her some tongue she was pulling away. Then she had the nerve to haul off and slap a nigga and try to walk away. Like I was just gone let her get away from me that easily.

I walked up behind her and wrapped my arm around her waist. Pulled her into me. She rested her head against my chest briefly before she could catch herself and try to fight me away. Then she started pushing the back of her body into me as she tried to remove my arm.

"Stop fighting and putting that ass on my dick. That's only gone make it worse Alayziah," I whispered into her ear before brushing it with my nose and burying my head into her hair.

Taking in her scent.

"Rell…let me go," she moaned with a look of frustration. Lust and frustration.

"Why?" I turned her around to face me. Making sure to keep her inside of my arms.

For a moment, she just looked into my eyes. I don't know what she was looking for, but I prayed she found it. As I caressed her cheek with my thumb she covered my hand with hers. Pulled it to her lips. Kissed it. Her eyes never leaving mine.

"What do you want from me?" She asked finally.

Honestly, I didn't know. I was done with relationships for the time being. So why did I want to be with her? I didn't even know anything about this woman. All I know is that I want her, and whatever comes with her.

"Rell…"

"I just want you." Was my honest reply.

"You don't even know me." She tried to release herself from me.

"I want to know you. I want to know you on every level possible Alayziah."

"I'm not tryna be on that love shit right now Rell. I'm just…tryna focus on school. My poetry. All that other shit…" Her eyes filled with sadness as she tried to pull away from me again. This time I let her go.

I nodded in understanding as I took a step back from her. Stared at her so long and hard she looked away.

"I feel you Alayziah. But let me tell you this…I'm not gone chase you. And I'm not the type of nigga to constantly pursue a woman once she lets me know how she feels. I know you want me just as much as I want you. I'm not gone wait for you and play with you because of what the last nigga did. So if you want to focus on you that's cool. We can link up in the studio and leave it there."

I took one of my business cards out of my pocket and handed it to her before I walked away. I didn't plan on acknowledging Bishop and Kai but Bishop stepped up on me with the biggest smile on his face and stopped me.

"So what's up? What y'all gone do?" He asked as Kai took one last bite of her burger and stood by his side.

"We ain't gone do shit. She on some broken hearted girl *I just wanna focus on my school and poetry* shit," I replied nonchalantly. I could see the disappointment in Kai's eyes but, what could I do?

"So you just gone give up? You niggas don't give up on what y'all want. Rell you can have her head gone by the end of the night if you really wanted to." Kai looked behind me at Alayziah.

"I ain't finna chase that girl mane. You know how I do. If she wanna keep it on a professional level so be it." I smelled her before I saw her. Her scent was fruity. Swear the shit made me want to pick her up, throw her on one of these tables, and feast.

"Al what's up? Why you won't give my brother no play?" Kai asked. I looked behind me and Alayziah was making her way towards us. She gave Kai a half-smile before she looked me up and down and bit her lip.

"Kailani I've told you before that I just want to focus on school and work."

"Well…just tell me this."

I rolled my eyes and groaned as I tried to walk away but Kai grabbed me by my forearm.

"Wait Rell. Al are you hungry?"

I looked at Kai in confusion and so did Alayziah.

"I could eat," she mumbled.

"Well I know Rell could too because he couldn't eat for staring at you. So why don't you two go out and grab a bite to eat and talk about your CD. Since you both are *so* into y'all careers why not start tonight?"

Bishop burst into laughter but stopped when Kai side eyed him.

"You crazy mane. Leave these folks alone and let them do them," he ordered wrapping his arm around her neck. "Al it was good meeting you. Hit me up tomorrow nigga." Bishop turned Kai around as she said goodbye and then started yelling at her for being messy and in other people's business. Sighing heavily, I turned to face Alayziah as she looked everywhere but at me. Figuring she wasn't going to make this any easier I gave in and asked...

"So...what you want to eat?"

Alayziah

When we made it to IHOP I just knew I saw Carmen through the glass window. I went outside and looked around for her while Rell was in the bathroom, but I couldn't find her. Maybe I was seeing things. I shrugged it off and went back to the table.

Trying to mentally prepare myself to eat and talk to this nigga.

The entire ride here I kept telling myself that this was strictly business. That nothing personal would come between us. That what I felt for him at my set was strictly lust. Now, if he wanted to be on some fuck shit we could do that.

But there was just something about him that was telling me that I would be setting myself up for failure if I thought I could have sex with him and let that be the end of it. So seeing as I'd sworn off love for the time being I had to be careful. Being with him was like an alcoholic being inside a liquor store.

I watched as he walked back to our table and I couldn't help but blush. His spirit was so commanding. As he walked everyone in the restaurant watched him, but the entire time his eyes were on me. Instead of sitting in front of me he sat next to me. I scooted towards the window and he chuckled.

"Why would you sit next to me?"

"I figured it would be too intimate for me to be sitting across from you. Staring in your eyes. So I figured this would be better."

I licked my lips inadvertently. "That was very thoughtful of you Terrell but I think this is worse."

"How is this worse Ziah?"

My heart immediately dropped. No one called me that but my papa.

"Out of all the variations for my name why that?" I asked as the server made her way to our table. He shrugged.

"Who else call you that?"

"Just my dad."

He smiled.

"You guys ready to order?" She asked.

151

Rell looked at me as he ordered. "She'll have...an order of strawberries and cream crepes, a stack of pancakes and...do you eat pork?" He asked. I smiled and nodded. "And an order of bacon. I'll have the breakfast sampler."

"I'll have it right out. Anything else for you guys?"

I looked at him and he smiled. "Did I forget something?" He asked. "I know...give her a cup of hot apple cider as well."

When she walked away he took a sip of water and I chuckled.

"What makes you think you know me well enough to be ordering my food?"

"How did I do?"

As much as I didn't want to admit it, he did very well.

"You did good Terrell."

"So what's up with you ma? Tell me about this project you want to link up to do." I watched as he licked his lips and turned to the side slightly. Giving me his full attention.

"Well, I want to do a poetry CD and DVD. I want you to produce my CD. I need someone who can vibe with me and get a feel of my sound and vision for my project. I wanted guitars and piano originally for this project..."

Thoughts of Alex immediately filled my mind and I stopped talking as tears filled my eyes.

"What's wrong Ziah?" Concern dripped from his voice and I don't know why but it pissed me off.

"Don't call me that." I snapped palming my face and resting my elbow on my thigh. I'd turned to the side as well and had one of my legs folded Indian style on the seat.

"Yo, what the hell is your problem? Talk to me..." His hand covered my wrist and he pulled my hand down. Tears were staining my face and I was so embarrassed.

"I'm sorry. Let me out so I can go and wipe my face." I avoided eye contact. He didn't move. Or speak. He just sat there. And stared at me.

"Rell..." I whined trying to push him out of the booth but his strong ass wasn't going.

"Look at me Alayziah."

"Ion want to," I mumbled reaching for napkins before his hand stopped me. "Rell."

"Look. At. Me." His voice lowered and I couldn't help but oblige him. I looked into his eyes as he took the napkin from my hand and patted my face dry. Which only led to more tears. And he wiped those too.

"I can't fix the shit if you don't let me know what's going on Ziah. Let me in."

"You can't fix it."

"Try me." He pulled my hand into his as I exhaled deeply.

"It's nothing. I just...thought about this guy that I was messing off with. He was supposed to help me with this but...things got personal and complicated and he...got into a really bad car accident and died. Talking about it just made me think about him and that messed me up."

"I'm sorry for your loss." He said as he squeezed my hand tighter. "Loyalty is for the living though Ziah. Ain't shit that nigga can do for you from the grave. I'm here now and I can take care of whatever he left unfinished. Professionally and personally."

My nipples hardened and his eyes fell on them immediately. He blushed before pinching my left nipple lightly through my dress.

"Rell..." I moaned pulling myself away from him.

"I'm sorry. You bring out the man in me woman. All I want to do is bury myself deep inside you. I'm trying to behave."

His voice was so husky. My pussy was so wet it felt like it was going to leave a stain on my dress when I got up.

"You wanna fuck me?" I asked him boldly.

"No." Sincerely. Shock covered my face as I smirked. His hand gripped my jaw and he pulled my face close to his.

"I want to make love to you. And I'm going to. But not right now."

"Why not?" I surprised the hell out of myself.

"Because if I do you won't respect me or take me seriously and I'll never have a chance to make you mine. We're going to do this right. Until you want to commit we're going to focus on business. But trust me...when you're ready...this dick will be waiting for you."

I looked up at our waitress as she smiled at us.

"Sorry..." She said putting our plates down. Rell released me but he kept his eyes on me. I blushed and ran my fingers through my hair.

What have I gotten myself into?

Rell

Once she finally started to loosen up our late night breakfast went by smoothly. She told me about her plans for her CD and DVD. And she even told me about what she had going on personally as far as school and work was concerned. We talked about her desire to build a creative arts center. What she didn't know was I was already thinking of ways to help her make that dream a reality.

I too opened up to her. Told her about how my label was doing. How I eventually wanted to venture into opening a community center with different types of studios in the hoods of Memphis. I wanted to create a space for kids to come and record music. Draw. Write. Dance. Whatever they wanted to do they could to. Actually, we both held the same type of vision.

Only difference was she wanted to do one and she wanted it to be a nonprofit and I wanted to open multiple centers with my own money so I wouldn't have to worry about depending on anybody else. She also wanted her main area of interest to be poetry and writing. She wanted to have plays and shit there. Mine was strictly for the kids.

But for now my main focus was the music. The music was my passion and it was going to fund my centers so that came first.

I can't lie...Alayziah had me.

She might not have wanted me but she had me. And when she did that poem, it was like she made it for me. Like she was waiting for me. We'd finished eating and we were sitting there talking for I don't know how long. But it had to be hours because we ended up getting a new waitress and I saw the sun peeping up. When I did I pulled out my phone.

"Damn," I said more to myself than her.

"What?"

Her back had pretty much been to the window the whole time. I watched as the sun rose and shined down on her face and I swear I fell in love with her beautifully damaged and complicated ass. The sunlight finally caught her eye and she turned to look out the window.

"Oh my God. Have we been sitting here talking…all night?" She pulled her phone out of her purse. "I have to go. I have to be at work in two hours," she continued going into her purse and pulling out her wallet.

"Girl if you don't put that wallet back in your purse…" I slapped her hand and the wallet down.

"Terrell I can pay for my own food. This was not a date."

I shook my head and chuckled at her stubborn ass. "Whatever Ziah. You will never need money as long as you with me. Don't do that shit again. That's an insult."

"Fine."

Alayziah stood and waited for me to stand up and let her out. I couldn't help but let my eyes rest on her center and think about how good she was going to taste.

"Terrell…" She nudged my shoulder and brought me out of my trance.

"My bad Ziah."

I stood and stepped out of the booth. After dropping the money on the table I watched her walk out of the restaurant. She was mine. Whether she wanted to accept it or not.

Alayziah

"So when you coming to the studio baby?" Rell asked me as he unlocked my car door. I shrugged as I resisted the urge to wrap my arms around his waist.

"When can I?" I asked when he turned to face me.

"Whenever you want to. I'll clear my shit for you."

I blushed. "You don't have to go through all of that trouble. Just...let me know when you're free."

"Fuck all that. You my woman. You my priority. You come first. So when you wanna vibe?"

"Terrell you are not my man."

"Well you my woman. You my girlfriend Alayziah. You might not be in a relationship with me but I'm damn sho in a relationship with you."

I smiled as he pulled me into him. Resting my hands on his chest I looked into his eyes.

"You're a mess." My smile deepened as he ran his fingers through my hair.

"The sooner you let me in the sooner I can make you happy and keep you feeling loved and at peace."

"So can I come by tonight after work and school?"

"You don't even have to ask."

"Okay. I'll call you and see if you've eaten yet."

Rell stopped running his fingers through my hair and looked at me skeptically.

"What?" He removed his hands from my hair.

"Nothing. Just...I ain't used to a woman seeing about me."

After standing on my tip toes I kissed his forehead lightly. His hands wrapped around my hips as he steadied me.

"Well get used to it. You put me first I put you first. That's how it works, right?"

Smiling he placed his arms around my neck and kissed both of my temples then my forehead.

"Right Ziah. Right."

When he released me he opened my door and I got inside. Once I was well on my way home I called Kailani.

"Spill it," Kailani said as soon as she accepted the call.

I smiled hard as I gripped my steering wheel.

"Kailani I just wanna say I love you girl."

She laughed and I laughed too. But I was dead serious.

"So you guys had a good time?"

"Girl…yes. We talked all night Kai. All night."

"Word?"

"Word. We're just now leaving the restaurant."

"Are you serious?!" She screamed so loud I had to pull the phone from my ear.

"Yeap. We just…vibed. He's cool I can't lie."

"So when are you guys going out again?"

"Well…I'm going to the studio tonight. I don't know about us going out though."

"What you mean you don't know? I know you not still on that keep it business shit Al."

"Kailani…"

"Unh unh. Alayziah, Rell is a good ass nigga. Give him a chance."

"Why? Why should I? Yes, he might be a good nigga but y'all don't know me Kai. I…" I stopped talking when I felt the tears forming in my eyes.

"What is it babe? What's wrong?"

"I just don't want to fuck it up because of what has happened to me in the past. I don't want to take my issues out on him. And I don't want to be hurt again either."

I drove in silence as she took her time to respond.

"Al girl I'm gone tell you like this…I was single for years before I met Bishop. And I did not want to give him a chance. But look at us now. He wouldn't let me go. Rell on the other hand is not that type of nigga. I get that you've been hurt before and you've gone through some shit but don't let that be the reason you lose him before you even get him. Rell don't play that shit. I know we don't know you but I can tell you'd be a good match for him. Just give him a chance. Give yourself a chance."

I nodded but didn't say anything so she continued.

"Where you at?"

"On my way home. Guess I'm going to try and get a nap in before I have to get ready for work."

"Text me the address to where you work. I'm going to bring you some lunch later."

"Girl you don't have to do that. If anything I should be bringing your pregnant ass some lunch."

"I need an excuse to get out the house. Let me use you."

I chuckled as I gave in. "Fine Kai. I'll text you when I get to the house."

Rell

The whole time I was recording today I couldn't help but think about Alayziah. Between texting her and Facetiming her on her lunch break that shit wasn't doing nothing but playing with a nigga's emotions.

I needed to be near her.

So when she called me and told me she was on her way I was as happy as a stripper seeing a team of basketball players coming through. She knocked lightly and stuck her head inside. I couldn't help but smile at her pretty ass.

"Come in Ziah."

She walked inside holding two containers of food and a smile. As I watched her walk towards me I took all of her in. From the patch of beauty marks she had on her cheeks to the way she dragged her right leg when she walked. Everything about her was beautiful to me. I was taught to stand when a woman entered the room so by the time she made it to me I took the food from her hands and hugged her like it had been years since I last did so.

"How was work?" I asked as we sat down.

"It was cool. Nothing to brag about. How has your day been?"

"Good. Besides missing you," I replied honestly as I opened my container. I had her to stop and get me a plate from Southern Hands. Best soul food in Memphis. Hands down.

"You just saw me this morning Terrell." She blushed as she opened her container.

"So...that was hours ago. I missed your face and your soul."

"Don't say stuff like that to me."

I stopped what I was doing and stared at her. "Why not?"

"Gets me all in my feelings."

"So?"

Ignoring me she looked around my studio and checked my set up out for the first time.

"This is nice. I can't wait until I'm doing what I'm passionate about for my career."

"What's stopping you?"

"Money. I can't do poetry and write books for a living right now."

"Just go for it. Save enough money to pay your bills up for about six months and just quit. That'll motivate you to do what you have to do to create a buzz for yourself."

"Is that what you did?"

"Yeap. Haven't looked back since."

She nodded as she coated a piece of chicken with ranch. After eating the bite of candied yams I had in my hand I reached into my pocket and pulled out my everyday money. It was about two stacks give or take. I sat it on the mixing board in front of her. She stared at it for a while before looking at me.

"What's that?"

"Money."

"I know but why is it there smart ass."

"I'm giving it to you."

"Why?"

"Because I want to help you make your dreams a reality."

"Terrell..."

"I want you to go home and add up all of your bills. Then multiply that by twelve. Let me know the total and I'll give you the rest in the morning. And when you go to work...put in your two weeks' notice."

I'd rendered her speechless. She sat her to go container on the floor and stared at me.

"Alayziah get your food off the floor country ass."

"Rell I can't let you do this for me."

"Why not? You wanted my help, right?"

"Yes but not like this. Not this much. This is too much."

I stood and walked over to the coffee table I had in the corner of the studio. After picking up her poetry collection I walked over to her.

"Where'd you get that?"

"I did my research. I needed to know if you were going to be worth the investment. And after reading this and watching your performances online I wholeheartedly believe that you are. If you don't want to take the money from me as your boyfriend take it from me as your producer. I see greatness in you Alayziah.

Between work and school you won't have much time to perfect your craft. We need to fix that. If you quit your job that's an extra eight to ten hours a day you will have for writing. Recording. Shows. Networking. You can travel when you don't have class. Build a name and brand for yourself. Or just spend it vibing with me. So just...take the money and do as I say."

"You are not my boyfriend Terrell."

We shared a smile as I grabbed the money and put it in her purse.

"Thank you."

"If you want to thank me...chase your dreams. And don't stop until you've lived them out to the fullest."

Biting the inside of her cheek she nodded as my phone began to ring.

"Shit...forgot to put this on silent." I said pulling my phone from my pocket. I was about to immediately swipe ignore until I saw the name on my phone.

Layyah.

"Answer." Alayziah said sitting back down and crossing her legs. Completely ignoring her food that was still sitting on the floor. I looked at her so long the call went to voicemail, but Layyah called right back.

"Yea?" I spoke... my eyes never leaving Alayziah's.

"Hey Rell. You busy?"

"I'm at the studio so you know how that goes. What's up? You good?"

"Umm...not...not really. I...I didn't know who else to call."

"What's wrong Layyah?"

"You know Mike and I moved to Miami right?"

"Right."

"Well...I opened my beauty shop here and shit. One of my clients came in and you know how bitches be gossiping and shit."

"Right, right."

"Well one of them was talking about her nigga from Memphis and how good he was treating her and all this and that and you know me..."

I rolled my eyes and shook my head.

"What did you do Layyah?"

"I um...we got into a fight and I was arrested. Mike bailed me out but when I saw his no good ass I started spazzing on him too. He pressed charges. Changed the locks on the house. All I have is my phone. He has the rest of my shit."

"Okay. So what do you want me to do?"

"Make him give it back."

I looked at my phone like she could see me.

"Layyah..."

"Please Rell. I just need you and Bishop to come and scare him a little bit so I can get my shit and dip. I promise I'm gone do right. I'm not even gone look his way. I'm just gone pack my bags and leave."

"Then what you gone do Layyah? You can't leave Miami because your business is there. What you gone do when you run into that nigga on the streets?"

"I'm not gone have to worry about that because you and Bishop gone make sure he knows not to fuck with me anymore. If you don't handle this, I'm going to end up in jail or dead Rell. You know how I am. I'm gone try to kill that nigga when I see him."

I sighed heavily and ran my free hand across my face. Swear I thought I was done with this shit when I let her go. Now she still dragging me into this craziness and I ain't even her nigga no more.

"Fine. Where you at now Lay?"

"Still at the police station."

"Aight. We'll handle the shit."

"Thanks Rell."

I didn't even respond. I just hung up the phone in her face. I cared about her wellbeing yea, but she was no longer my responsibility. Especially with me trying to build an empire with Alayziah. She was sitting there looking unfazed. I didn't know how she was gone respond to me leaving her to go and see about my ex.

I stood and grabbed her hands. Lifted her from her seat. She didn't want to look at me and I could understand that.

"She must be pretty special," she mumbled looking at the wall to the right of me.

"I just don't want to see anything happen to her."

Alayziah pulled the money from her purse before tossing it into the chair she was sitting in and trying to walk away but I grabbed her by her arm.

"The hell is wrong with you Ziah?"

"I'm not doing this shit again. I'm not gone be your rebound. I'm not gone sit around while you play with me on your free time and wait for you to let me go for her. I'm not gone do it Rell. I can't."

"Mane ain't nobody on no rebound shit!" I yelled louder than I wanted to. I didn't raise my voice. I didn't go back and forth. Alayziah was bringing me out of myself. And I don't like that shit at all.

"Whatever Terrell. Just go see about whoever that was. I'll record somewhere else until you get back."

"Fuck that. Your poetry is like your pussy. I bet not ever catch you letting another nigga handle either one."

I watched as her jaw muscles clenched. I didn't care how mad she was we weren't leaving this studio until we were on the same page.

"You got some you wanna say?" I asked her. She crossed her hands over her chest and mumbled something inaudibly as she continued to look everywhere but at me.

"Alayziah..." She ignored my ass.

The shit was so cute it almost made me laugh. Almost. I stood directly in front of her and blocked her view. When I did she tried to look in the opposite direction but I covered her cheek with my hand and turned her to face me. With closed eyes and pouted lips Alayziah was breaking a nigga down and she wasn't even trying to.

"Why are you so fucking stubborn? I'm not them niggas. I'm not gone lie to you. I'm not gone play with you. I know you might not want to trust a nigga but I'm gone show you that you can. I don't expect you to just take my word on the strength of me saying the shit. I wish you would...but I can understand that you can't. Them niggas bullied your heart. I get it. But you will respect me Alayziah."

Her shoulders loosened a bit and she opened her eyes but instead of looking at me she looked down to the ground. "Besides...I'm not your boyfriend...remember?" That caused her to look at me with anger in her eyes.

"Ugh I can't stand you Terrell. I told Kailani this wasn't going to be a good idea but nooooo she didn't want to listen to me." She grabbed her purse and her food as she continued her rant. "Gone tell me he ain't my boyfriend. Ha."

Once she had all of her belongings she came and stood in front of me. This time I was smiling with my arms crossed over my chest as she started talking to me.

"You don't get to say you're not my boyfriend. I say that. I don't give a fuck if you my boyfriend or not. You mine. And I don't appreciate the fact that a bitch can just call you and you cut me off to go and see about her. But that's my own personal issue and it has nothing to do with you. You just make sure you hurry home and keep your hands to yourself."

I pulled her into me. "Are you done?" She nodded. "Watch your mouth. Don't be cursing at me. I'll be back in the morning. And when I come back I want that total and for you to tell me that you put in your notice. I'll walk you out. Call me and let me know you made it home safely Alayziah."

"Fine."

Carmen

I stood back and took in the work that my hands had put in. I spray painted all of Alayziah's walls. Ripped up her couches and mattresses. Shattered her plates and cups all over her kitchen floor. Took a hammer to her TV's. Put all of her underwear in a bag that I was taking with me. And poured bleach on the rest of her clothes. She was going to learn the hard way. *Never fuck with a nigga that ain't yours!*

"Just slow down...I can't understand a word you're saying Al. Where are you?"

Jabari yelled through the phone. He couldn't understand me because I talked really fast when I was upset and crying. But these weren't sad tears. These were angry tears. My apartment had been destroyed. I took great pride in my apartment. It was my escape. My place of peace. And to know that someone came inside and violated my place of peace had me boiling mad on the inside.

"My...my apartment Jabari. Somebody has been in my apartment. They fucked my shit up! All of my shit is ruined! I can't even go in the kitchen because there is glass all on the ground!"

I yelled stomping my foot. Trying not to have a spazz attack. Wouldn't do me any good to right now because I didn't know who was in my shit.

"What the hell? Have you called the police? I'm on my way to you."

"No. No you don't have to come. I can't stay here. I'm going to go to Marcel's for the night and try to get my mind right."

"Fuck that Alayziah. Go sit in your car. Call the police. I'll probably get to you before they do. You need to file a report just in case some shit pops off. They will have this attack documented."

"That makes sense."

"Gone to the car. I'm on my way."

"Jaba..."

He hung up in my face. Sighing heavily, I grabbed my purse and the contents that fell out when I dropped it and walked back to my car. By the time I made it Rell was calling me. I wasn't really in the mood to talk to him but I didn't want to hear his mouth about me not answering so I did.

"Rell..."

"Didn't I tell you to call me and let me know you made it home safely?"

"Something came up. When I made it home and walked in...all my shit is fucking ruined."

"What you mean?"

"Somebody came into my apartment and trashed the place. Spray painted my walls. Broke glass and my TV's. Ripped up my furniture. And I know they had to be in there for a while because they even took the time to crumble my candles up."

"Why didn't you call me Alayziah?"

"Call you for what? You already on your way to play hero for somebody else. I'm good."

"No you're not. If nothing was stolen somebody clearly has it out for you and as your man it's my job to protect you. What's your address?"

"All that ain't necessary Terrell. I'll be fine. Take care of what you have to take care of. I'll be good."

"Alayziah..."

"Seriously Rell. I'm good. I'm going to my best friend's house tonight. I'll be safe with him. Don't worry about me. If they wanted me they would've came at me and not where I sleep. Coward."

"Him? Your best friend is a he? And you think you finna spend the night over this nigga house?"

"Terrell, Marcel does not want me like that. Besides, he has a girlfriend."

"I'm just gone let Bishop take care of Layyah. What's your address?"

"I'll be fine. I promise. You said you'll be back in the morning anyway right? I'll get up with you then."

"Fine. Call me when you get there. And before you go to sleep. And as soon as you wake up in the morning."

"Okay. Okay. Be safe."

"You too baby."

After I'd calmed him down enough to get off the phone and out my hair I tried to think of who knew where I lived and would want to bring me and my apartment some harm.

Rell

"You wanna turn around hunh?" Bishop asked me.

I did.

I knew Layyah was waiting for a nigga but Alayziah was my main priority right now. I was tired of constantly having to get Layyah out of shit because she didn't know how to handle her anger. That shit was played out. We were getting too old to be out here fighting over our supposed spouses. **It's too many people in this world to be trying to hold on to one that doesn't want to be held.**

"Hell yea. She acting like she good and she probably is; but I'd feel better if I had her with me."

"So what you wanna do nigga? You know I'm down."

"I don't know man. I know I need to help Lay but I feel like I need to be here for Ziah too. Layyah a fool. I don't want to have the two of them around each other. Layyah feel like she still got access to a nigga. Ion need her trying to fight Alayziah."

"I feel you. Well we ain't made it too far yet so we can turn around"

I sat in silence and weighed my options. It was already bad enough for me to have to leave Alayziah to go and see about Layyah. Now she need a nigga even if she don't realize she need a nigga and I still ain't doing right. I gotta go see about my woman.

"Aight B, turn around."

Alayziah

Jabari insisted that I stay at his house tonight instead of Marcel's. The only reason I agreed was because Jessica was here and I wanted to spend some time with her. By the time I got out the shower Jabari was done with my pasta and we all ate in silence. I can't lie, I wish Rell did come and see about me. Even though I told him not to.

Now I'm sitting up here with Jessica's head in my lap while she sleeps. She wanted me to get in her bed so we could watch TV and her ass was out by the first commercial.

The light tapping on the door grabbed my attention. I smiled at the sight of Jabari. He was a good man. And a good looking one too. I hope the chick he's messing with knows what she has in him.

"Alayziah…you have a visitor," he whispered to keep from waking Jessica.

"A visitor?" I mouthed. He nodded. Gently I lifted her head so I could slide from under her. Once I put a pillow under her head I walked towards the door.

"Who is it?" I wasn't leaving that room until he told me.

"Terrell."

"What? How did he find me?"

"I don't know. Ask that nigga."

Sensing his attitude, I walked away to avoid that turning into an issue. When I walked inside of Jabari's living room Terrell and Bishop were standing there looking good as fuck. They both were wearing sweats and tight fitting tees. Bishop's were black and baggy while Terrell's were gray and form fitting at the bottom because of their fleece material. Just the sight of him had my mouth watering.

"What y'all doing here?" I asked by the time I'd made it over to them.

Terrell just stared at me and smiled as Bishop shook his head. I looked down at what I had on and realized why.

"Why you got on these little ass boy shorts in this nigga house?"

Rell pulled me into him by the ball of hair on top of my head.

"Nigga, let my hair go."

"Fuck that. Why you got these little ass shorts on in this nigga house Alayziah? And I thought you said your best friend's name was Marcel. His name is Jabari. So who the fuck is this nigga?"

169

His smile had disappeared. He'd gone from happy to see me in lust to pissed off. I looked at Bishop for help but he lifted his hands up in submission.

"Aye…that's yo crazy ass nigga." Bishop leaned against the wall and pulled his phone out.

"Alayziah…"

"I was in the bed Terrell. With his sister. I didn't plan on getting up for the rest of the night but when he told me I had a visitor I just jumped out the bed. I wasn't thinking about putting no pants on."

He looked at me as if he was trying to gauge the truthfulness of my statement. When he was satisfied with my answer he let my hair go only to wrap his arm around my waist.

"How'd you find me?" I asked.

"I tracked your phone."

"Stalker ass nigga." I joked pushing him away from me. "I'm glad you came, though," I continued honestly. He smiled before pulling me back into him.

"Swear I can't keep my hands off of you Ziah. Did you bring some clothes or some shit with you?"

"Yea. Why?"

"You coming to Miami with me."

"What? I can't…"

"You quitting your job anyway. I'll have you back before your class tomorrow night. I'd just feel better if you were with me. Don't fight me on this."

"Please don't. We gone be stuck in this house until you agree," Bishop added without even looking up from his phone.

"Fine. Let me get my stuff and say goodbye to Jessica and Jabari."

"Hurry up. And don't think I didn't notice you avoided telling me who that nigga is to you either."

I flipped Terrell the bird as I walked back into Jessica's room.

Rell

"Wake up baby, we here."

Alayziah was stretched out in the backseat faking like she ain't hear a nigga. I got out, opened the door to the backseat, and leaned inside.

"Alayziah. I know your ass hear me."

She smiled but kept her eyes closed.

I kissed her silly ass on the cheek about a million times as she wrapped her arm around my neck and pulled me deeper into her.

"Get up baby, Layyah gone need somewhere to sit and I'm ready to get this shit over with."

"Alright, alright." Finally, she opened her eyes and looked at me. Widening her smile.

"Get up Alayziah." Running her fingers through my locs she bit her lip. "Alayziah…"

"Is this how you always plan on waking me up?" She asked sitting up.

"Nah. Next time Ima wake you up with this dick," I joked. She blushed and brushed a few strands of her hair from her face.

I heard Bishop yelling at Layyah and I shook my head. Trying to keep my nerves calm before she stood in front of me. Alayziah looked at Layyah through the window briefly before looking back at me.

"What?" I asked.

"Nothing. She just looks familiar."

"Well she's from Memphis so you probably saw her out and about."

Alayziah nodded as she stepped out of the car and stretched.

"And I ain't doing this shit again Layyah. You better leave that stupid ass nigga alone. A nigga ain't tryna be traveling like I ain't got a pregnant wife sitting at home," Bishop yelled as they made it to the car.

Layyah was half listening. She was too busy staring at me to pay him much attention. I didn't want to smile back at her but I couldn't help it. Didn't matter what Lay was going through, she always looked good. Alayziah turned around and looked at Layyah and Layyah stopped dead in her tracks. Looking from me to Alayziah she shook her head in disbelief.

"Really Terrell? You couldn't have me so you found the artificial copy of me?"

"The fuck are you talking about?" I asked as Alayziah laughed and stepped up. I wrapped my arm around her stomach. I didn't know if she could fight or not but I knew Layyah didn't fuck around.

"Alayziah you gone act like you don't know me?"

"I don't know you. How do you know me?"

Layyah looked up into the sky with a smile on her face. "That's right. We were a secret to you but we knew all about you."

"Mane look...I ain't got time to be playing with you. If you got some to say, say that shit. Otherwise shut the fuck up and get your yellow ass in the car so I can get back home."

Bishop laughed at Alayziah's outburst.

"You're my little sister Alayziah. We have the same father. Laymont is my father. Your father is my father."

Alayziah took a step back as the smile that was on Bishop's face disappeared. I turned around and looked at Alayziah. Her face was pale.

"Layyah...this ain't no shit to play about," I said with my eyes still on Alayziah.

"Why would I play about this Rell? How would I know her and her name if I wasn't telling the truth? You originally from Chicago right?"

Alayziah nodded.

"Well when your mother and father moved to Memphis our daddy met my mother. He was married to your mother. They were separated and he fucked off. They ended up getting back together and he broke it off with my mother. When she found out that he was married she decided not to tell him about me.

For years I thought my father was the same as my sister and brothers but we saw him out one day and he flipped. Talking about he couldn't believe she had a child without telling him. She told him that she loved him enough to let him go and work things out with his wife and she didn't want to complicate things so she stepped back and planned on raising me alone just like she did my sister and my brothers. I knew about you though because he kept coming around and shit."

Layyah took a step forward and Alayziah took another step back.

"I know this might be a lot for you to take in right now but it's the truth. Ask him."

Alayziah inhaled heavily as she opened the door to the backseat and got in.

"Bishop you mind driving? I need to sit in the back with her."

"Yea no doubt. You wanna take her to a hotel? She probably don't want to be around nobody right now."

"Yea that's probably best."

Bishop nodded and got in the driver's seat as I stood and stared at Layyah's inconsiderate ass.

"You just had to tell her that shit right now? You couldn't wait or find a better way of saying the shit?"

"Don't be mad at me because her daddy couldn't keep his dick in his pants. That's not my fault. I just felt some type of way when I saw you with her. I'm sorry."

"It's not me that you need to be apologizing to Layyah. It's Ziah."

"That's funny...that's what he calls her."

Alayziah

Before they dropped me off at my suite I made them stop me by the liquor store. I bought two bottles of strawberry wine and a pack of cigarettes. I didn't want to be drunk; but I did want to numb this pain.

I couldn't even bring myself to call my father to see if what Layyah was accusing him of was true. What reason would she have to lie? And if it wasn't true how did she know me? After finishing the first bottle I had enough liquor courage to call my father.

"Ziah...what's up princess?"

"Hey daddy. Listen, I'm going to ask you something and I want you to be honest with me...okay?"

"Of course baby girl. What's wrong?"

"Do you have any other children that I should know about?"

His silence was deafening. "You met her?"

Tears immediately filled my eyes. "Daaadyy..."

"I'm sorry baby. I never meant for you or your mother to find out. That was, that was during a very rough period in my life. Your mother and I were having some issues and we took a break from each other. I messed around and...being with Layyah's mother just made me realize how much I loved your mother. So I called it off. I didn't find out about Layyah until years later."

"Did ma find out?"

"I told her. She never met Layyah or her mother. Said she didn't want to have any parts of my infidelity. How did you meet her?"

"It's a long story and I really don't feel like getting into it. I just, wanted to call and see if it was true."

"I'm sorry baby."

"Me too. I love you. I gotta go." I hung up before he could respond. Leaning back in the bed I closed my eyes as tears fell from them. No matter how I try to live a peaceful life I swear it seems like shit comes to me from all fucking sides.

Rell

By the time we were done taking care of Layyah it was late as hell so Bishop decided to rent a suite next to Alayziah's and I was going to crash with her. I had her to leave a key to the room at the front desk because I didn't know how long we were going to be.

When I walked into the bedroom she was stretched out across the bed. Laying on her stomach. Her arm hanging off the bed. Clutching an empty bottle of wine in her hand. I ran my hands down my face and walked towards her. I didn't even know her ass smoked but she had eight cigarette butts in an ash tray on the side of the bed.

I sat on the edge of the bed as best as I could and ran my fingers up and down her spine until she stirred lightly. Her hair had come out of its band and it was all over the pillow. I massaged her scalp until she moaned.

"Have you eaten? You good?" She asked turning to face me. I chuckled.

"Don't worry about me. I'm good. How are you? Have you eaten?" I ran my hand across her stomach. When chills covered her skin I smiled.

"I could eat," she mumbled sitting up in the bed. Our faces were inches apart. Her eyes were puffy and I could tell she'd spent most of the time I'd been gone crying. That shit made my heart ache.

"What you want to eat baby?"

She shrugged and wiped her eyes.

"I don't care Rell. Anything close that will deliver. I need you next to me. Everything in my life is shaky right now. I need you to be my rock. I need you to keep me steady."

Her eyes were getting watery so she turned her head to the side.

I wrapped my hand around her neck and pulled her lips to mine. This time when I kissed her she didn't resist. In fact, she cupped my cheeks with her hands and welcomed me in. She pecked my lips back until I suck on her bottom lip causing her to moan. Sliding my tongue inside of her mouth I grabbed a handful of her hair and pulled back gently. Giving myself a better angle to introduce her tongue to mine. She moaned as she entangled her fingers inside my hair. Lifting her off the bed I placed her on my lap and started to suck on her neck.

"Rell…" She moaned as my hands found their way to her hips. "Take it off…" She continued trying to lift her shirt but I wouldn't allow her to.

My dick was hard as hell and I wanted to dig inside of her in the worst way; but I didn't have sex with a woman unless I could see myself marrying her. And I definitely could see myself with Alayziah for the long haul. I just wasn't sure if she was ready to say the same.

Standing I turned around and climbed on top of the bed. I laid her down and sat on my knees between her legs. Her eyes were half closed as she looked at me. After pushing her legs further apart I placed my forearms on both sides of her head as I kissed her deeply. Slowly. Passionately.

Her legs wrapped around me and she held my face. Making sure to keep me from ending our kiss again. I had to though. I had to make her feel better. After removing her panties, I crawled down until my eyes were staring at her pussy. Gripping her thighs, I pushed them back before licking and biting them both.

"Shit," she whispered as she arched her back and moaned. I continued to torture her with my teeth and tongue until I was confident she was going to have a few hickeys on her thighs.

"Rell…please…"

"Please what?" I asked before kissing her clit. I smiled as I looked up at her. "Tell me what you want me to do Alayziah. Let me hear you say it."

"Make me cum Rell. Make me cum."

Alayziah

I've shared my body with four men in my life. The first three I loved and thought I'd spend the rest of my life with. The fourth, Jabari, was so sincere and for me the whole vibe that we had was so intimate emotionally and mentally that I just had to feel him physically.

Now, with Rell, in between my thighs making my pussy cry, I just wanted him to make me feel...fuck it I just needed him to make me *feel*. He was looking at me with those chocolate eyes. Biting his lip. Teasing the hell out of me. He'd licked and sucked on my thighs so good he had my head spinning. The shit was such a turn on.

For him to be so close and yet so far away from my pussy was driving me insane. Now he was laying here, an inch away from it, just...looking at me.

"Why you doing this to me?" I asked and he smiled.

"This is your payback for slapping me when we met." He licked from my clit to my belly button cutting my reply off. "You didn't want my lips on you then remember?" Rell continued before licking my clit like it was an ice cream cone, slurping on it, and sticking his middle finger inside me.

I moaned and gripped his head tighter as he began to move his finger in and out of me. Licking my clit simultaneously.

His tongue went up and down the top of my clit so soft and slow and then he'd look up at me and go inside my pussy with it deep. Pull out my juices and suck on my clit so hard my legs shook each time.

The shit was feeling so good I couldn't even moan. Or scream. All I could was whimper with each breath I exhaled. The sight of my cum on his lips and chin was becoming too much for me. He looked at my pussy like it was a fucking masterpiece. And I swear he was treating it like it was.

"I need to feel you inside of me," I pleaded.

"Not until you're mine and mine alone."

"Rell..." I whined as he lifted himself from me.

"I know you my woman, but am I your man?" He pulled his dick from his pants and my pussy immediately throbbed at the sight of it. I didn't even answer him as my mouth opened slightly and I tilted my head.

"Alayziah…" I looked into his eyes briefly before returning my attention back to his long, thick, and curved dick. "Am I your man?" He asked again as he began to stroke it.

My hand found its way to my clit as I massaged it at the same speed that he pleasured himself. "Alayziah…"

"Yes. No. I can't Rell. I'm sorry," I rushed out removing myself from the bed and heading for the shower.

Lord knows I wanted to trust him. I wanted to love him and be loved by him. But I'm just so scared.

Rell

"I'll fuck it out of her if I must…but for now I'm trying to give her the chance to see my love for her before I go there. And if that don't work I'm just gone leave her ass alone."

I said to Bishop as he puffed on the blunt we were sharing. He nodded and blew smoke out as he handed the blunt to me.

"I feel you nigga. Al is a lot like Kai. I'd think they were sisters before her and Layyah. I still can't believe that shit. She just got a lot going on right now. She probably just don't want to get caught up with you."

"I understand all that shit, but I ain't tryna bring that girl no harm. I'm just tryna be here for her. I don't know why her crazy ass can't see that."

Bishop laughed but I was dead serious. I wanted Alayziah. *Bad.* But I wasn't gone chase her ass for too long. I'm too good of a man to be wasting my time on somebody that couldn't see that. Bishop was the nigga that chased. Shit was fun to him. Wasn't nothing for me to replace.

"So have y'all had that talk about y'all past relationships yet? Maybe if you talk to her about the shit and get her to open up she'll lighten up. You know Kai was giving me a hard time until I made her tell me about Courtney. When she got that shit off her chest she was open for a nigga."

"I'll see what's up. I got this chick coming in a few minutes though. Say she want me to produce her album. I tried to send her to Peyton and her sisters but she said she wanted to work with me."

"How are they doing anyway? I know you gave them Star and the rest of your clients at your label when you left."

"They doing good. Crazy as shit. Mane they make us look sane they have so much drama in their lives. That's probably why ole girl didn't want to work with them."

"Ion blame her. I have a hard enough time dealing with one crazy female. I can't imagine being around all three of them at the same time."

"How Kai doing anyway? I know she ready for BJ to get here."

"Nigga… I don't think her ass ever gone let me get her pregnant again."

I couldn't help but laugh. I knew Kai was giving him hell. Especially since he got her pregnant intentionally after he promised he wouldn't try to do that shit no more.

"What? What's wrong with her?"

"She just mad at me because I got her pregnant without us being married first. Said she wasn't ready and all that other bullshit. Ion care though. It's gone be worth it when I'm able to hold my lil nigga in my arms."

"I feel you. You know ma been on me about settling down and shit. Say she ready for some grandkids. I need you to let her have BJ."

"You know I'm down for that. But BJ just gone make her be on you more."

Before I could reply we heard light knocking on my door. I stood and went to let the woman in. When I let her in Bishop stood and prepared to leave but I shot him a look that told him I wanted him to stay.

I didn't know this female so until I got a feel for her I didn't want to be alone with her. I had too much shit riding on my union with Alayziah to be caught slipping with the next chick. Although she was looking good.

She was thick as hell. She had milk chocolate skin. Her hair was in a weave I could tell but she had it curled cute so I gave her credit for that. Her face was cute, but she ain't have shit on Alayziah. There was something about her face that was familiar. Like I'd seen her on TV or something but I just couldn't put my finger on it. After speaking to both of us she stood in the center of the studio and looked around.

"So, what's up Carmen? What exactly do you need my help with?" I asked pointing to the empty chair next to Bishop. After she sat down she looked at me and spoke.

"Well…I'm really a church girl, but some shit went down and I think I want to switch over to the R&B lane. I heard you was the hottest producer in Memphis so I wanted you to help me create a sound for myself."

"Aight…let me hear you sing."

She looked from me to Bishop before standing and smiling. Once she opened her mouth and began to sing I was impressed. Her voice was definitely churchy. She had that Kierra Sheard vibe but her voice was just a tad bit deeper. I could definitely rock with her on some Fantasia or Keke Wyatt soul shit.

"Okay, okay I hear you. You definitely can sing Carmen. Can you write?"

"Nah."

"Dance?"

"A little."

"Okay...what you think about using your choir background in your music and performances? Like Fantasia. She takes her listeners to church no matter what she's singing. That's your vibe. That should be your lane. Soul. Not R&B."

"I'm in. What do I need to do?"

"First you need to decide how you want me to help you. If all you want is for me to create some instrumentals for you and record you then that's all you'll get. You'll have to pay my hourly fee and make sure you list me as your producer. If you want to sign to my label and have me as your manager you won't have to pay me to record or write for you; but I will need fifteen percent of your record sales and what you make at your shows for the first year and ten percent afterwards for six more years. Matter of fact, I'm not even gone write for you. I'm gone let Kailani or Alayziah write for you. More than likely Alayziah since Kai is pregnant."

Her eyes lit up when I said Kai and Al's names and I didn't know if it was because she knew them or if it was because I was going to let a woman work with her.

"Sounds good to me. I want to sign with you if you think I'm good enough. But I will need some time to talk it over with my dad. I'm a PK and I know he's going to give me a hard time."

"That's cool. Why don't you talk it over with him and come back to the studio this weekend? I'll make sure Al is here so y'all can meet and see if y'all gone vibe with each other."

"Great. I'm so excited."

I stood and she followed.

"It was nice meeting you. You too."

She said to Bishop. He just nodded. I shook my head at his unfriendly ass and walked her to the door.

"Why you so rude nigga?" I asked sitting back down.

"Ion like her."

"Why not? You don't even know her."

"Just some about her. Ion like her."

"Aight. Ima keep that in mind."

Carmen

When I saw Alayziah and Rell interacting at her poetry set I knew he was going to pursue her. And she was putty in his hands. Which is why I decided to take him from her. Show her what it feels like to watch your man pine over someone else.

She took mine, so I'm definitely going to fuck with hers. I'm wrecking every area of her life until I've had enough.

And I don't think I'm ever going to get enough.

Alayziah

Layyah forced me to give her my number before we left Miami. She'd been sending me Facetime requests all week and I had yet to answer. I knew it wasn't her fault, but I just didn't want to deal with her. And the fact that she was in a relationship with Terrell before me really makes me not want to deal with her.

Yes, I've always wanted siblings but I wanted them with my mother and my father. I don't know how I feel about her yet. But one thing I can't deny is the fact that she looks like my father. They have the same light skin, jet black hair, and high cheek bones. I heard she was crazy so I figured it would be best for me to talk to her on the phone before her ass popped up in Memphis.

I'd been staying at a hotel until I was mentally ready to clean my apartment out and buy new furniture. Terrell had been harassing me about coming to stay with him but I declined. Ever since we spent the night together in Miami I haven't been around him as much. I just...didn't want to start something I knew I wasn't going to be able to finish.

I'm tired of loving and losing. I wish he would just let me go like Jabari did but his stubborn ass will not let me go.

He ended up giving me the money still so I did quit my job. I was about to head to the studio to see him but I stopped by Bishop and Kailani's house to check on her and get a feel for Layyah before I did. When I saw Bishop coming out the house with a mile wide smile on his face I got out of my car.

"What's up Al?" He asked taking me into his arms.

"Shit, what's up?" I spoke hugging him back lightly.

"Rell ain't got on you about your mouth yet?"

I started walking past him and towards their front door.

"He told me I can't curse when I'm talking to him."

"Sound like that nigga. Kai in the bed. She's expecting you though so gone on upstairs. First room on the right."

"Aight cool. See ya."

"Peace."

After admiring their décor in the front room for a brief second I walked upstairs and chuckled when I heard Kailani laughing.

"Girl bye. I am not getting in the middle of y'all. You can't make her fuck with you. Shit, I wouldn't fuck with your crazy ass either. Only reason I been your friend this long is because you won't let me go."

I peeked my head inside her door and smiled. She motioned for me to come in.

"She here now. No. I am not. No Layyah. No. If you want to talk to her call her phone. Ion care be mad. Bye. And you better be here in two weeks too. If I have this baby and you not here...alright, alright. Bye."

I laughed at their exchange as she patted her bed for me to sit down.

"Hey Al. Sorry about that. That was your crazy ass sister."

"Hey mama. It's cool. How you feeling?"

"Girl...I'm good actually. My feet are swollen pretty badly so Bishop won't let me do anything or go anywhere but other than that I'm cool."

"So Bishop Jr. is set to make his arrival soon hunh? I can't wait! I'm gone be all over your baby I'm letting you know that now!"

"I don't even care girl. You and Layyah can spend the night whenever y'all want to until he gets big enough to leave the house. What's up with y'all though? You still don't want to talk to her?"

I sighed heavily and leaned back on her bed. She naturally pulled my head on her lap and started playing in my hair like we'd been knowing each other for years.

"It's not that I don't want to talk to her. I don't know. I guess she just puts a bad taste in my mouth because she's the product of my daddy cheating on my mother. I know we had nothing to do with that and I shouldn't hold that against her...but I can't help it. Then she's Rell's ex? That just makes it even worse, feel me?"

"Yea I feel you. But don't even let that bother you. Rell wants nothing to do with her as far as a relationship is concerned. She cheated on him with my ex so he's done with her."

"Damn. That was foul. And y'all still mess with her?"

Kailani shrugged.

"Yea. She just grows on you. She crazy and selfish as hell but she don't mean no harm. She wasn't doing it to be spiteful she just selfish. And her mother raised her and her siblings to go after what they want and say fuck whoever stands in their way. Her mother never married and was never in a relationship with one man. She just used them for money and sex. So Lay definitely has it honest. I can't hold that against her; but I told her ass if she ever even thought about coming at Bishop I was gone kill her ass. Friend or not."

I laughed. I couldn't see Kai fighting but I guess people said the same thing about me.

"What's up with you and Rell anyway?" She continued. I shrugged. "You still giving him a hard time?"

"Kind of. He wants to commit, but I'm scared."

"Why?"

I shrugged again. "Just don't want to be hurt again. Not this soon at least. My heart can't take another break."

"I feel you. But I'm telling you Rell is a good man Alayziah. He's not on that love them and leave them shit. He's not gone cheat on you. He's not going to lie to you. If y'all don't work it'll be because you fucked up or because he gets tired of you not giving him your all or because y'all are too much alike. But Rell would never do anything to intentionally hurt you. He's too selfless. He'll hurt himself before he hurts you."

"And how do you know that Kailani? Just from seeing him get cheated on by Layyah?"

She stopped running her fingers through my hair momentarily before continuing.

"Nah. Me and Rell...we...fucked off."

I sat up so I could look her in her eyes. "What you mean y'all fucked off?"

"We had a thing for each other. We fought it for as long as we could but Bishop was taking me through so much shit and I was so vulnerable. And Rell was there for me. I can't explain our connection... we're like brother and sister and creative soul mates, but you don't have to worry about me either. I'm satisfied and committed to my husband. Had he not been acting so foolish Rell and I wouldn't have even entertained each other. We just got caught up."

"So that's why you fighting so hard for him to find somebody hunh?"

"Yes. I know firsthand that he's a good man. He deserves the best. He has so much love to give Alayziah. And if I honestly felt like you two wouldn't work I wouldn't have even introduced you to him."

"I hear you."

"Do you really?"

"I do."

"Then go and find your man."

Rell

Alayziah had been in the studio for a few minutes before I gave her my full attention. She was so stubborn it was frustrating. I decided to take Bishop's advice and see where her head was at before I gave up and fucked her and let the idea of having a relationship with her go completely. She had her feet up on my soundboard. Her head resting on the back of her chair. Taking a blunt to the head. If I wasn't feeling some type of way, the sight would be turning me on but since I was feeling petty I just stared at her ass until she looked at me.

"What Rell?"

"What's up with you mane?"

She rolled her eyes as she put her feet on the ground and sat her blunt in the ashtray.

"Ain't no point in me even smoking with you if you just gone blow my high," she muttered folding her arms over her chest and leaning back in her chair.

"You don't think we need to talk about this? I'm losing my patience with you Alayziah. I wouldn't give a fuck if I felt like you genuinely didn't want a nigga but I know you do. And I want you too. So what's up? What happened that's got you so shut down?"

I pulled her chair closer to mine.

"Rell I will never deny that I like you, I promise you I do. I just…I can't take another loss. I love so hard. I don't want to be hurt again. I've had niggas feed me abortion pills. Gay niggas try and marry me just so no one would think they were gay. And the last nigga…he was in a fucking triangle with a crazy ass bitch. I loved him so much."

"That's the one that died hunh?"

Tears fell from her eyes as she nodded yes.

"It wasn't even a year ago. I still think about him. Cry over him. It's not because I want him back or some shit like that…like I've accepted his death. I just can't believe how stupid I was for him. I never want to be in a position where I love and want a nigga so much that I'm out here looking so foolish. Nigga was straight up married and I was still messing with his lying ass."

She wiped her face and looked at me. "I'm scared Rell. I already like you so much. I know I'm going to love you deeply. I just don't want to and then you leave me. I can't take another loss. I'd go crazy."

She was starting to cry harder so I pulled her into my lap and arms. Held her until she calmed down a bit.

"I understand that you've been hurt before baby, but can you tell me one thing that I've done to hurt you?"

Looking into my eyes she played with my chin. "No."

"Can you tell me one thing that I've done to make you feel like you can't trust me?"

"No."

"Have I lied to you?"

"No."

"Do I have a wife or girlfriend stashed somewhere?"

"No Terrell," she whined laying her head back against my chest.

"Then why the fuck are you making me pay for what them grimy ass niggas did? I ain't them Ziah."

"I know."

"Obviously you don't, because you taking that shit out on me. And I've done nothing but try to help you and be here for you."

"I know Rell. I apologize." She lifted herself from my chest and looked into my eyes. "You not gone accept my apology?"

"Ion know yet."

Smiling she twirled one of my dreads around her pointing finger.

"Can I have you Alayziah? I'll treat you good. I promise."

"Okay Terrell. You can have me."

I smiled. "So you my woman?"

"Yes."

"And I'm your man?"

"Yes."

"Say it."

"I'm your woman and you my man baby."

"Because you wanna be or because I wore you down?"

She laughed. "Both. Crazy ass nigga."

"You like it though."

"I love it."

"Cool. Now get off my lap so I can play you this instrumental I recorded for you. I'm taking you out tonight."

"Recorded? You mean…"

"I played the piano and guitar and recorded it for you. I think you're going to love it."

Her eyes watered. "You did that for me Terrell?"

"Yea baby. I told you I got you. Whatever you need and want I got you. Didn't I tell you that?"

Biting the inside of her cheek she nodded.

"Thank you," she whispered sincerely before kissing my lips sweetly.

"No problem. Now move."

Alayziah

Clothes were thrown all over the bed in my hotel. I couldn't decide what to wear on my date with Terrell for the life of me. Maybe if I knew where we were going that would help a little but I was stumped. And it also didn't help that an unknown number had been blowing my phone up. I couldn't block it because I didn't know the number. And I couldn't cut my phone off because I was expecting a call from Terrell.

So I had to constantly push ignore or let the shit ring and it was aggravating as fuck. My phone began to ring again and I decided to answer.

"Hello?" I yelled. Silence. Then they hung up. I almost threw my phone across the room but I groaned and tossed it on my bed instead.

After staring at the clothes on my bed for thirty more minutes I took a shower and figured something would pop out at me when I was done. After my shower I let my body marinate in my apple body butter as I applied some eyeliner, mascara, and nude brown lipstick.

I put on a black bustier and boy short set before walking back over to my bed, closing my eyes and deciding to wear the first thing my hand grabbed. Turned out to be a cute white elbow sleeve knee length Bodycon dress.

The top was sheer and lace and the back was cut out. I decided to change my lipstick to a pinkish nude color to complement the pale pink pumps and clutch I was going to wear. I sprayed myself with my apple body mist and With Love by Hillary Duff perfume and unwrapped my hair. I'd flat ironed it earlier and I was rocking it bone straight with a part down the middle.

My phone rang again and I searched through my clothes on the bed to find it. This time it was Layyah.

"Yea?" I answered.

"Damn. I'm surprised your stubborn ass answered the phone."

I smiled unwillingly. "What you want Layyah? I'm getting ready to go out."

"With Rell?"

"Yea."

"Be good to him Al." I rolled my eyes. "Call me tomorrow…okay?" She continued.

"Fine Layyah."

"Have fun."

"Thanks."

As I ended the call Rell was knocking on my door. I stood there paralyzed for a moment. He knocked again. Running my hands down the sides of my dress I slowly walked towards the door. When I opened it and he grabbed his dick through his pants I bit my lip and took a step back. Took all of him in. Our attire was color coordinated.

He was dressed so simply but he looked so good. He had on a pair of wine colored loafers. White slacks that showed off his muscular legs beautifully. And a red wine and white checkerboard button down shirt that was form fitting and tucked inside his pants. His hair was in that high bun that made my nipples hard every time I saw it.

"Damn," he mumbled unbuttoning his shirt.

"What?"

"You literally just made me hot. You look so fucking good Ziah."

I blushed as he took his button down off. Underneath he had on a white v neck tee. Which was even worse for me because I was now able to see his tattoos and the outline of his abs.

"You look quite handsome yourself," I finally replied closing the door behind me. There was no way I was letting him inside with all of those clothes on my bed.

"So where we going?" Rell pulled me into his arms and kissed my forehead.

"You'll see."

Rell

She was looking so good I couldn't take my eyes off of her. Literally the whole ride to the restaurant I was staring at her every red light I caught. In fact, I was getting caught up on purpose. Just so I could have a moment to admire her beauty.

I'd rented the rooftop out at Twilight Sky Terrace so we could watch the sunset together and eat in peace. She must have been impressed because once we were escorted outside and no one else was out there she punched me in my arm.

"What girl?" I asked smiling.

"Rell I know you did not rent this rooftop out for us." She wrapped her arms around my waist.

Pushing her hair off of her shoulders and onto her back I kissed her neck softly. She moaned quietly and wrapped her hand around my neck as I made my way up to her cheek. Resting my lips on hers. After pecking them for a while I opened her mouth with my tongue and allowed mine to dance with hers.

My hands roamed her body until they found her ass. And squeezed. Pulled her deeper into me. She pulled away and looked into mine with lust in her eyes.

"You tryna make me weak." Alayziah away from me.

"How you figure that?" I asked with a smile as I took her hand and led her to a nearby bench.

"I've already asked you for the dick twice and you've turned me down Terrell. I'm not asking you again. So stop playing with me."

"Baby I'm not playing with you. That was because your ass didn't want to commit. Now that you mine you can have it whenever you want it. Shit you can get it right now if you want it."

She smiled and squeezed her legs closer together.

"And you won't think I'm easy?"

"Alayziah I dan already had my tongue all up inside that pussy. Mmm," I moaned at the thought of how good her pussy was.

She crossed her legs as my eyes made their way in between her legs.

"I know we moving fast and reckless but fuck it. I want you. And I ain't letting you go no time soon. Matter fact…bring that ass here. Come sit on your man lap."

Alayziah

I was smiling hard as hell as I climbed on top of him. The way he looked at me. Talked to me. Handled me. Had me crazy over him. His hands wrapped around my hips as he licked his lips and stared into my eyes. I wrapped my arms around his neck as he moved his hands up to my waist and grinded my pussy on top of his dick.

"Rell..." I moaned wrapping my hands around his wrists.

Trying to get him to stop. I was already so wet. I didn't know how much more I could take.

"Don't be saying my name like that Alayziah. That shit does something to me," he warned me as he slid his hands under my dress and ripped my panties off.

I moaned out loudly and threw my head back in ecstasy.

"Shit Terrell," I whimpered as his hands grabbed my breasts and squeezed.

"What I tell you about your mouth?" He asked lifting my dress up to my waist.

"Terrell..."

"I wanna see you wet my dick Alayziah. Can you do that?"

I opened my mouth to reply but nothing would come out, so I nodded my head yes.

"Why you getting quiet on me? You been talking a lot of shit since I met you. Don't get quiet now. I want you to talk to me while I'm inside you."

"Rell..." I moaned trying to get up. I was scared as hell. Getting head and making me cum was one thing. What I was feeling for him right now was on a whole other level. *I was scared of the dick.*

"Unh unh." He sat me back down on his lap.

"This what you been wanting, right?" My heart raced at the sound of his pants unzipping. "Take what you want," he continued.

Slowly I opened his boxers with one hand and pulled his dick out with the other. As soon as my hand touched it he moaned deep in his throat. Pushing my hand away he lifted me up and slid deep inside me.

"Aahhh..." I moaned as he whispered, "Shit."

I gripped the top of the bench behind his head as I made my way down his shaft.

"Don't move," he commanded.

"Rell..."

He grabbed my face and kissed me passionately.

"Fuck me," Rell whispered before sticking his tongue in my ear.

"Ssss shit Rell," I moaned feeling my orgasm build already. Sliding a little down the bench he rested his head against the back and stared up into my eyes as I began to ride him. Nice and slow. My hands on his chest. His on my hips. My pussy was burning up as it drenched his dick. I flung my head back as my lips and legs began to shake.

"Ride that dick baby," he said huskily. I moaned as he began to match my thrusts and play with my nipples.

"Ohhhh Rellllll..." I cried out as I came. He slapped my ass and massaged my clit. Making me cum even longer and harder.

"Mmmm fuck Ziah," he moaned grabbing my waist.

Standing up he sat me on the bench and pushed my legs back before entering me so deep he took my breath. My eyes rolled into the back of my head and my back arched as he moaned again. "Got damn Alayziah. You so wet baby. I love the way you nutting on my dick. Cum all on my dick baby."

Gripping my hair and pulling I surrendered to my second orgasm as my legs began to shake.

"Rell... you keep hitting my spot," I whimpered trying to close my legs. "Why you keep hitting my spot?" I asked as he opened my legs wider.

"Cause I'm the king," he confessed pulling out of me completely before ramming himself back in slow and deep.

"Ohhh fuck Rell, you the king baby! You the king! You the king!"

Rell

I handed her one of my t-shirts to put on. We'd made it back to my place and showered. Now it was time for part two of our date. Grabbing her hand, I led her into my den. I had about ten cans of spray paint lined against the wall.

"What's this?" She asked as I handed her a can.

"I want to do some graffiti on the wall. I want you to help me."

"That's dope as fuck Rell."

"Alayziah…"

"I'm sorry. I'm sorry."

I shook my head and slapped her on her ass as I picked up another can of spray paint. We were halfway into the mural, conversing and enjoying each other's company when her phone rang.

"You not gone answer that?" I asked her.

"Really I don't want to. Somebody has been playing on my phone all night."

"You want me to answer it?"

"Ion care."

I went to her phone and the nigga Jabari's name was flashing across her phone.

"It's Jabari."

"What he want? Answer it."

I smiled at her…glad she trusted a nigga to answer her phone. Let me know she ain't have shit to hide.

"Hello?"

"Um…may I speak with Alayziah?"

"She's kind of busy right now. Is it important?"

"Yea. Tell her it's about Jess."

I heard the nervousness in his voice so I took Al the phone.

After putting the call on speakerphone she handed me the can of spray paint. "Hello?"

"Hey…I'm sorry to bother you but it's Jess."

"What's wrong with her Bari?" Her brows wrinkled in concern.

"I don't know. She came home crying. Locked herself in her room. She won't talk to me. I figured it was some girl shit she might let you know. I don't want to call my mom and worry her yet."

"Um…okay. Let me get Rell to take me to my hotel to get my car and I'll be on my way."

"Cool. Thanks Alayziah." She hung up her phone and looked at me. "I gotta see about her baby."

"It's cool. Just take my car and come back when you're done. You know I don't want you staying at that hotel anyway."

"Terrell I am not moving in with you," she tossed behind her as she walked to my room.

"Why not? You let me inside so we practically married now. Might as well move in."

She stopped walking and turned to face me. I didn't mean to be smiling so hard because I knew she was tired of having this conversation but I loved irritating her. She looked so good mad.

"I'm sorry…did you slide an invisible ring on my finger while you were inside me?" Alayziah asked looking at her ring finger. I mushed her ass in the head and walked back into the den.

"Fuck you Alayziah."

"You already did. And you fucked me good too. I can't wait to get back so you can fuck me again."

I stopped walking and turned around to face her. This time she was the one smiling.

"Alayziah stop fucking playing with me. Ima start washing your mouth out with soap."

She walked towards me and fell to her knees. "You know what I want in my mouth Rell?"

My dick got hard immediately as I slid my fingers through her hair.

"What baby?"

"Your seeds."

I almost nutted when she said that shit.

"I knew yo ass was a freak," I said with a smile as I stepped back. "But you need to go and check on that nigga sister before I have you calling me the king again."

Her cheeks grew red in embarrassment and I swear I've never seen that happen before.

"Gone before I change my mind about letting you go." I lifted her to her feet. She was pouting but she turned around and went into my room to put her clothes back on.

"Damn," I mumbled heading for the shower in my guest room.

Alayziah

When I walked into Jabari's home I heard Jessica sobbing inside her room. Caught me so off guard I stopped walking and looked at Jabari. I could tell he'd shed a few tears as well. I held my hands out and motioned for him to come to me with my fingers. I held him and caressed his back for a few seconds before letting go.

"I'll let you know if she tells me anything." He nodded and walked outside. I walked to Jessica's room and knocked. "Pretty girl?" She stopped sobbing immediately.

"Allie cat?" She said walking to the door. When she opened it she almost ran into my arms. I smiled and wanted to cry at the same time. "Allie cat I miss you so much," she said into my ear. Her tears wetting my neck and hair.

"I miss you too pretty girl but you know I'm always gone be here for you. I'm only a phone call away baby girl. Talk to me. What's going on?"

With her arms around my waist she asked me, "Where's RiRi?"

"He stepped outside."

Releasing me she walked back to her bed.

"Close the door."

I did and walked over to her bed. After I sat next to her she looked at me.

"What is it Jessica?"

"I'm pregnant."

"What?!"

"Allie cat!"

"I'm sorry," I whispered and looked at her door as if I could see Jabari through it. "What do you mean you're pregnant? I thought you were a virgin? You told me you were a virgin."

"I was."

"Then how are you pregnant Jessica?"

"I didn't want to say anything because I knew Jabari would flip but, you know my sister that died, Jasmine?"

"Yea. What about her?"

"You know my mom has custody of her daughter?"

"Yea I remember Bari saying something about that. She stays with you and your mom right?"

"Right. Her baby daddy Chris is such a bum. He doesn't even take Christina out the house. He just comes over there to spend time with her. I've never liked him but after what happened with Jasmine I really couldn't stand him. So I started spending more time at Bari's house. That's why he set this room up for me."

Tears filled her eyes again.

"One day Chris wanted to come over and see Christina but my mom wasn't there. It was just me and Christina. I told her that I didn't want to be around him but she said that he had every right to see his child and that I should just let what happened go and do what was best for Christina."

She began to sob. I took her into my arms.

"He came over and...he raped me Alayziah. He made me promise not to say anything. He said if I did he would deny it and take Christina away from us and I couldn't let that happen. She's the only thing we have left to remember Jasmine by. So I just blocked it out of my head. But I missed my period this month. I've been throwing up all this week so I decided to get a pregnancy test. I'm pregnant Al. I don't want this baby. I can't keep this baby. I'm only sixteen."

Tears had begun to flow from my own eyes. My legs were shaking. My anger rising. I stood and began to pace.

"I'll tell Bari."

"No!" She jumped up and grabbed my arms. "Al he will kill Chris. Please. Don't tell him. I don't want him to go to jail because of me. Just take me to get an abortion."

"Jessica I can't ignore this. What if he's done something or will do something to your niece? We have to tell him baby."

"What if I get him to leave? What if I tell him that I'm pregnant and if I have the baby everyone will know that he raped me? What if I get him to promise to...to...just...leave? Please Allie cat. Don't tell Jabari."

"Jessica..."

"Please Alayziah. My brother will kill him. Please."

"Jessica..."

Jabari knocked on the door lightly and Jessica jumped.

"Y'all okay in there?" He asked. Jessica stared at me with pleading eyes.

"I'll make you a deal. You have to tell him that you were raped. But I will not tell him by who if you don't want me to. I'll get someone else to take care of Chris."

She nodded and hugged me tightly. "Okay Allie cat. Thank you. I love you."

"I love you too Pretty girl. I love you too."

Rell

"You want me to handle it?" I asked as I wiped her tears from her eyes.

She'd just finished telling me about Jessica. Not only was she raped, but the bastard took her virginity. Even though I didn't know her I knew that she meant a lot to Alayziah. So whatever she wanted me to do, I'd handle the situation. Wasn't nothing for a nigga to go back to his old street ways.

"No baby. I don't want you getting caught up in this. I don't want anything to happen to you."

"Don't worry about that. If you want me to handle it, I will. Even if I don't touch the nigga personally I'll get somebody who will."

She looked at me and smiled. "I just wish she'd tell her brother. He's over there sick right now."

"I bet he is. If a nigga violated my sister I'd be on a fucking killing spree right now. I know it's eating him up to not know who did it. I know you said you wouldn't tell him but you need to tell that mane before this shit drives him crazy."

She nodded and looked away from me. "I want to tell him but she's just scared that he's going to go to jail."

"Mane, I'll make sure that nigga don't go to jail. I'll have some niggas to handle it for him. But he needs to know."

Alayziah stood. "I'm sorry about ruining our night. You want to finish your mural?"

I pulled her into me and kissed her stomach. "You don't have to be so strong in front of me Ziah. I can see it in your eyes that this is bothering you. I'm here for you baby." Before I could get the words out she was falling into my arms.

"I failed her Rell. Why didn't she call me? I told her she could come to me for anything. And she's been walking around holding this weight on her shoulders alone."

"At least she told you tonight babe. We gone take care of it. I promise you that."

"I feel like I need to be with her."

"Absolutely. You want me to drop you off and pick you up in the morning? You know we got that session with the new chick I was telling you about."

"That'll work. Thank you so much Terrell."

"You don't have to thank me. This is what I'm here for."

Caressing my cheeks, she pushed my head back slightly and stared into my eyes.

"You're my Adam. You know that?"

I blushed as her fingers stroked my lips.

"Yea?"

"Yea."

"Recite it to me."

She inhaled deeply as I pulled her closer. "I wrote something just for you."

"Oh yea? Let me hear it." I said picking her up and wrapping her legs around my waist.

"You said the sun rises in my eyes but it sets as you stare into mine. And when you speak it's like music seeps from the crease between your top and bottom lip.

You don't have to demand respect because your character commands it.

You know the power you could release into this world with the seeds between your thighs if you ever implanted them between mine what a problem that would be if your seed brought forth life inside of me.

But the problem would be the solution. The cause would be the cure. And the combination of us would lead to a line of royalty that would reign forever more.

Your scent is just as sweet as the taste of your skin. You love me so good it makes me want you so bad it feels as if this should be a sin to be so satisfied.

I never thought I was capable of loving this way. You make it so easy to love you. Because of the way you love me. And your love is like the light of Christ shining on me. I hope I bring out the God in you because you bring out the woman in me. You make me want to respect, love and serve until my heart no longer beats.

Some might think we're moving too fast. But I've moved slower in the past. Obviously those relationships didn't last even though I thought the pain would. But you've loved on me more in a matter of weeks than any other man ever has.

And you have me for as long as you desire. And I pray you choose to have me until we both expire. But if for some reason you end up leaving and break my heart in two it wouldn't matter because I love you so much I still wouldn't mind sharing it with you."

Tears were welling up in my eyes. I didn't want to be a punk ass nigga and cry, but no woman had written anything so beautiful for me before. Sensing my emotions were on the rise she placed kisses all over my face as I held her close.

"That was beautiful Alayziah. That's how you really feel?" I finally managed to get out.

"Yes baby. That's how I really feel. I'm so grateful to have you." After wiping away the tear that fallen from my eye she kissed me deeply.

I pushed her off of me and stood. "Let's go."

"Go where?"

"To the studio. We gotta build on this vibe. Then I'll take you to her."

With no protest she wrapped her arm around mine and we walked down to my home studio in silence; but I was confident that what we were about to create was going to speak volumes.

Alayziah

Rell and I ended up being in the studio all night. I recorded six poems and two songs. By the time I made it back to Jabari's house it was five in the morning. He let me in and I went straight to Jessica's bed. I cuddled with her until it was time for her to go to school. She didn't want to go but I talked her into going so she wouldn't be sitting around the house all depressed all day.

When Jabari returned from taking her to school I was dressed and getting ready to head out for breakfast with Marcel. I hadn't been spending much time with him lately so I wanted to make it up to him before I went back to the studio.

"You leaving already?" He asked throwing his keys on his coffee table.

"Yea. I gotta meet up with Marcel before I head back to the studio."

He walked towards me and towered over me. I looked up at him and smiled.

"How you doing?" I asked.

He shrugged and put his hands in his pockets. "I'm okay. I'll feel better when I know who did this so I can take care of them."

My heart ached. "Jabari, she made me promise not to tell you; but I know who did it."

After taking a step back Jabari removed his hands and rubbed his face with them. "Who Alayziah?"

"What are you going to do to him?"

"The fuck you think I'm gone do?"

"Promise me that you'll call Rell before you do anything crazy Jabari. He and Bishop can help you. She doesn't want you getting into any trouble because of her. Besides your mother you're all she has. If you went to jail or were hurt, she'd carry that with her for the rest of her life. Promise me that you won't do anything without some help."

He walked towards me and wrapped his hands around my waist. I covered his arms with my hands and tried to remove them but he held me tighter.

"Bari..."

"Al I was there for you...be here for me. Love this pain out of me."

"Jabari I'm in a relationship now. I can't. I'm sorry."

"You're in a relationship?"

"Yes."

"With that nigga that came over here looking for you?" I nodded. "Alayziah, I need you."

"Call your girlfriend."

"It wouldn't be the same."

"Jabari..."

"Alayziah please." His lips found my neck and I moaned involuntarily.

"Jabari stop," I protested lightly. My spirit was willing to leave and be faithful to Rell but my flesh...my flesh was weak.

"Come on Al. I need to feel you. Please Al."

He fell to his knees and tried to pull my leggings down. I gripped his head and pulled him into me and then I quickly pushed him away.

"No Jabari! Get your shit together! When you're ready to handle this nigga call me and I'll link you up with Rell and Bishop. Until then, I'll get up with Jessica when she's at home," I yelled grabbing my keys and purse.

"I'm sorry Al. I'm so sorry. I don't know what came over me. I'm sorry for disrespecting your relationship. I'm just...in my feelings right now."

Sadness laced his voice. My anger began to subside.

"It's cool. I'm sorry for yelling at you. I appreciate you so much Jabari because you were there for me at one of the toughest points in my life. But I'm committed to my man."

"I understand. Thank you for being here for my sister."

I nodded before walking out. No more alone time with Jabari. This was too close of a call.

∞

On my way to breakfast with Marcel I called Rell to let him know about what had just happened with Jabari and me. I didn't want to keep this from him because I didn't want him to ever question whether or not he could trust me. I just prayed that he understood that Jabari was at a weak point and my sex drive almost got the best of me, but I quickly recovered.

If I lost him because of this, I can't even imagine how my life would be after experiencing him for this brief moment. He answered the phone and I couldn't help but smile at the sound of his voice.

"Baby," I spoke lightly.

"What's up, Ziah? Why you sound like that?"

"Sound like what?"

"Like you got some shit on your mind."

"I do."

"Let me ease it then. Out your mind just in time."

"You know that's one of my favorite songs."

"I know baby. That whole smash up Erykah Badu did fits you perfectly."

"How so?"

"Well, the first song on the *Out my Mind just in Time* smash up is *Undercover over Lover* right?"

"Yeap."

"That's you baby. You are an undercover over lover. You try to make it seem like you didn't want love and a relationship, but that was only because you desperately needed it. You are a relational being. You love hard as hell. You let that shit consume you.

Not everybody can understand and handle that, and that's why your relationships have failed in the past. You were choosing to give that love to men who couldn't understand and return it. They couldn't balance you out. You were feeding them with your love, but they left you hungry because they couldn't do the same."

I sighed heavily into the phone. "True."

"Then the second one she spits, *Here I am Alone* is what happens after you've given your all to those bum ass niggas who couldn't balance you. Had you feeling alone, insecure, crazy. Overthinking and overanalyzing that shit, had you thinking the problem was you, but it was never you baby. You are special.

You love hard, with your heart on your sleeve. You love unconditionally, and not too many people do that today. They don't want to be weak. They don't want to get played. They don't want to feel. They don't want to give. They just want to take, but you don't love that way. No matter what happens between us I will always respect you for that."

"Terrell, I didn't call you for this," I whined with tears filling my eyes. The fact that he knew me almost better than I knew me had me feeling even worse about what had just happened between me and Jabari.

"Then, she ends the three song suite with *Out my Mind just in Time*. She explains that the reason why she was feeling the way she was in the previous song was because she was thinking about what someone else had done to her, but she acknowledged the fact that in order for her to feel good and be at peace – she had to let that shit go.

She had to get that shit out of her mind just in time and free that space up for positive thoughts and energy. That's what I'm trying to do with you. Give you good vibes and memories. Get you out of your mind. Show you that you can't seek love and peace on the outside, it must come from within. You have to create that shit for yourself within yourself. That's the only way it's going to last."

"Rell, Jabari tried to fuck me, and I almost gave in. He was having a weak moment over this situation with Jessica and he asked me to love the pain out of him. He kissed me on my neck, but I pushed him away, then he fell to his knees and tried to pull my leggings down, I'm not going to lie for a second I did pull his head into me out of a reflex, but I pushed him away and got on to his ass. I'm not going to be alone with him ever again. He apologized for disrespecting my relationship, it's never going to happen again. I promise you that."

I waited for him to respond, but for a few seconds, all I heard was him breathing.

"Did you want to fuck him Alayziah?"

"No, it was just a reflex. You know I can be a horn dog sometimes. I don't want him or anyone else Rell, I only want you. I don't need anyone else. You take care of me on every level – physically, spiritually, mentally, emotionally, and financially. You're it for me Terrell."

"You sure about that Alayziah?"

"I'm positive. It was my pussy. It wasn't my heart reacting to him."

"Cool, where you headed?"

I looked at my phone skeptically. I wasn't expecting him to be this calm, not that I was complaining.

"That's it? You're not mad?"

"Why would I be mad? I'm secure in who I am and what I have to offer. I ain't sweating no other nigga trying to take my spot. You fuck around you a fool. I get that shit happens, your little nasty ass just had a natural reaction, but if it happens again..."

"It won't, with him or anyone else. I give you my word."

"Then that's all I need."

I smiled as I resisted the urge to tell him I loved him. Finally, it seemed as if I found the man who complements and can handle me.

Rell

When Alayziah told me that she was going to IHOP to pick up some breakfast before she came back to the studio I decided to meet her there. I was on my way back from Bishop and Kailani's crib. They thought she was going into labor last night so I went to check them out.

What Alayziah failed to mention, however, was the fact that she was meeting some nigga up here. Now I ain't the jealous type. But I am possessive. I don't share. And I don't play about what's mine. So when I first saw her hugging the nigga and cheesing harder than a rat my skin started sweating. But since she has yet to do anything to make a nigga not be able to trust her I decided to give her the benefit of the doubt.

I walked over to them and pulled her into my arms from behind. The nigga looked at me like I was crazy but I didn't give a fuck.

She was mine.

She moaned and wrapped her arm around my head and ran her hand down my neck.

"Hey baby." She turned to face me. I kissed her forehead but I kept my eyes on the nigga she was with.

"Who is this?" I asked as she wrapped her arms around my waist.

"This is my best friend Marcel. Marcel this is Terrell."

He nodded and I did the same. "Why you ain't tell me you were having breakfast with him? I came up here to surprise you and you already have a date."

"Well baby I didn't expect you to stop by. I was going to bring you something back. But since you're here you can still eat with us. Y'all need to get to know each other anyway."

"Nah baby you enjoy your breakfast with your friend. I'll see you in a little while."

"You sure?"

"I'm positive. Just bring me something back. You know what I like, right?"

She smiled as I gripped her ass. "Rell stop."

"Why? I ain't had none today."

"Rell it's…" She looked at her watch and chuckled. "It's only eleven o'clock."

"I know!" I yelled. "I need that on the regular. Swear your pussy is peace for a nigga. I need that peace Ziah."

Alayziah turned and smirked at her best friend. "Suga…"

"Get it Love."

"You want some now?" She asked after she turned back to face me. I was surprised she even offered it to a nigga. My dick swelled and she didn't make it no better when she pulled me into her and kissed me softly.

"Fuck yea. And I can get some when you get home?"

She laughed. "Rell you gone get tired of me."

"No the hell I'm not. I'll never get tired of you or that pussy. So you gone give me some when you get home?"

"Stop saying it like that. That is not my home."

"That is your home Alayziah. You don't need to be staying in that hotel when I got a four bedroom home. Even if you don't wanna lay up with a nigga you can crash in one of my extra rooms."

"Hotel? The fuck you staying in a hotel for?" Marcel asked. I was about to check his ass for cursing at my lady but since it was out of love and concern for her I let the shit slide.

"I meant to tell you but somebody trashed my apartment. Fucked my shit up. I've been staying at a hotel for a couple of weeks."

"Watch your mouth," I warned.

"Why Alayziah? You could've been with me. Why didn't you tell me? That's how we doing it now?"

"No Suga. I just got caught up. I meant to tell you that night but I called Jabari and he made me come over there. Then Rell came over and made me come with him to Miami. Where I found out I had a step sister. It's been a lot going on best friend."

"Shit, I see. You just dan forgot about me. That's cool though. I see how it is."

"Awww don't be like that Suga. You know I love you. It's just been so much going on boo."

"I hear you, but you need to catch me up so you can say goodbye to that quickie." He looked from her to me as he continued. "It was good meeting you Rell. I'll have her home to you in about an hour."

I chuckled at the nigga as I looked at Alayziah. "Baby look like you in trouble," I joked.

"I know. Tell him you want me to come home now," she whispered.

"Nigga I can hear you," Marcel said.

We all shared a light laugh before I kissed her.

"Thirty minutes. And don't forget my food." I said before walking away.

Carmen

She still hadn't figured out I was the one fucking with her. When I was last at her apartment I found her credit card information. Since she was still oblivious I decided to have a little fun by maxing her credit cards out. I couldn't find her bank information which was good for her; but what I did find I was about to blow up.

I was supposed to meet up with her and Rell today. I can't wait until she sees my face. With her man at that. Now I just have to figure out how to get him inside of me before she walks in.

Alayziah

Rell asked me to meet him at his studio downtown instead of the one at his house and that's when I remembered that he set it up for me to meet some chick he wanted me to write for. Said she could really sing. Said she had that soulful Fantasia vibe. Said she was a church girl that wanted to switch over. I wasn't too hype about meeting her simply because of the fraudulence I'd just encountered with Alex and Carmen but I was willing to put that aside to help him. With my writing and his producing, we were going to be the newest power couple in the industry and if I had to use this chick to get there…so be it.

When I pulled up to the studio Kai's face popped up on my phone. I answered immediately. BJ was going to be making his arrival soon so we all were on call.

"Kai…"

"Hey boo. You at the studio yet?"

"Yea. What's up? You good?" I asked starting my car back up.

"Yea I'm good. Bishop wanna talk to you."

Surprised I cut the car back off and looked at the phone. "Ummm, okay."

"Alayziah," he said in that voice that I knew Kailani loved.

"What's up nigga?"

"Aye, this chick Rell tryna get you to work with, Ion like her ass. You need to watch her."

I smiled. "Why don't you like her Bishop?"

"Ion know Al to be honest. I just got a bad vibe when I met her that day at the studio. Ion know if you get down like your sister or not but I just wanted to warn you just in case some shit pop off."

"Yea I heard she crazy. That runs in the family. I ain't worried about her. If she want it she can get it no problem. And even if she don't want it if she come for my nigga I'm serving her ass."

He chuckled but my face was dead serious. "Yea you definitely Lay sister. Damn I wish I could see you with her. You going in yet?"

"Nah I'm still in my car. Instigating ass nigga."

He laughed. "Mane fuck all that. Nigga need a little action every now and then. Kai boring ass don't even care about a nigga no mo. She used to be crazy about me. Now she don't care who look at me or try to get at me."

"That's cause your ass ain't crazy! Play with me if you want to Bishop," Kailani yelled in the background.

I smiled at their exchange.

"Mane I'm just playing. Watch your mouth nigga you ain't slick. Listen though Al, call me if you need me."

"Will do. Appreciate you looking out too."

"You good."

He disconnected the call and I sat there for a moment.

Trying to compose myself before I went inside.

After getting out of my car I dragged myself into the studio. I had a bad feeling about this. I don't know what it was but I just felt like some shit was about to go down. Stopping in the hallway I leaned against the wall and inhaled deeply. My phone began to ring and I pulled it out of my pocket to answer.

"Hey pretty girl."

I'd told Jessica to call me when she made it out of school. And of course, she called as soon as she walked out.

"Allie cat."

"What's wrong?"

"RiRi said you ain't gone be at his house when I get there. Why not?" I rolled my eyes. I knew Jabari did that shit on purpose.

"I'm at the studio boo."

"Well, will you come when you get out? We're off from the restaurant tonight so I was hoping we could watch a movie or something."

"Listen…you know I love you like a little sister and I'm always going to be here for you, but I'm not so sure if it's a good idea for me to be coming over as much anymore. I'm in a relationship now and I have to respect my man. But if you want to come to my place once I fix it up you can. And we can always go out."

"Allliiiee caaaat. How could you?"

"I'm sorry Jess. Your brother is a great guy…it just…wasn't meant for us."

"You didn't even try."

"We did. I know you might not understand it now but every one that you come into contact with isn't going to be your mate. Jabari and I...we have a strange relationship. We're there for each other tough, but I don't think it's meant for us to be in a relationship honey."

"It's not because of me is it? I won't call you as much if it is."

"No, no. No. That's not it at all. It has nothing to do with you don't even think that."

"Okay. Well, I need to meet this nigga."

I smiled. "You will meet him soon enough pretty girl."

"Okay. Have fun at the studio!"

"I will. I'll call you later."

"K bye Allie cat. I love you baby."

"I love you too."

I smiled as I disconnected the call. And I wore my smile all the way to the studio. But my smile immediately faded at the sight of Carmen. I saw Rell smiling and saying something to me but I didn't hear him. Everything in the room went silent as my eyes focused in on Carmen. She was sitting there smiling. As if we had no past history.

Before I could stop myself I rushed her and started beating her face in. Rell pulled me off but I punched him unintentionally and ran up on Carmen. Kicking her face until Rell lifted me into the air. He dragged me out and I could see his lips moving, but I still heard nothing. Nothing but the beating of my heart and Alex's last words ringing in my ears.

"It was always you Noelle. You were my one and only. I love you."

Rell

"Mane what the fuck is wrong with you! Have you lost your damn mind?" I screamed as I carried Alayziah out of the studio.

I didn't know what the hell had just happened. All I know is when Al came in the studio her ass pounced on Carmen so fast I couldn't even stop the shit. Then her skinny strong ass punched the shit out of me when I pulled her off. She better hope my jaw don't have a bruise on it or I'm gone beat her ass. Carmen might not have been able to get up with her but I wasn't gone play with her bipolar ass. When we made it outside I let her go. She still hadn't answered me. She was shaking so bad she sat down on the ground and started rocking.

"Alayziah, what the hell is going on?" I asked for the third time. Finally, she looked up at me with tears streaming down her face. Her hands trembled as she palmed her face. I squatted in front of her and tried to remove them, but she wouldn't let me.

"Baby...talk to me. Let me fix it," I pleaded. At first I was mad because she was fighting, now I was getting mad because she was so upset and there was nothing I could do about it. "Alayziah..."

"That's the bitch. That's the bitch he was with. He married that bitch. Like what we had wasn't shit. What is she doing here Terrell? You fucking her too?" She sobbed as she finally faced me.

"Hell nah I ain't fucking her. I told you she came at me on some music shit. Said she wanted me to produce her album so I agreed."

"Rell she's a fraud nigga. That hoe don't mean you no good. She means me harm."

I nodded as I lifted her to her feet. "Say no more. Get in your car and don't get out when I bring her out here."

"Rell..."

"Gone Alayziah. And don't get your ass out the car."

Cursing me out under her breath she stomped over to her car and slammed the door once she got in. I walked back into the studio and Carmen was gone. She must have parked in the back of the studio because there was no way she could have left without us seeing her.

After cutting the lights off and locking my shit up I made my way back outside. Figured I was going to have to fuck this aggression out of Alayziah. But before I did I was going to have to call Bishop. He wasn't gone believe this shit. The nigga was right about Carmen all along.

Alayziah

Rell wanted me to follow him back to his place but I didn't. I was pissed. *Carmen tried it!* I bet her ass was the one that trashed my place and had been blowing my phone up. Her ass was definitely going to have to be handled. I drove to her and Alex's old home hoping she still stayed there but she didn't so I called Alex's brother Terrance to see if he knew how I could find her.

"Al…what's up ma?"

"Terrance you will not believe what just happened."

"What? You good?"

"Yea nigga I'm good. Carmen ain't though. I just beat her ass. And when I see her I'm beating her ass again. You know where she staying now?"

"Damn, nah but I can find out for you. What happened? Where you at? Meet me somewhere."

"Aight. Where you wanna meet?"

"I'm going to Fox and Hound in about an hour with a few of my niggas. You can meet me there if you want."

"Cool. I'll see you in a few."

Rell

I'd been blowing Alayziah's phone up and she hadn't answered since she ditched me on the expressway. That was cool though. I was gone make her ass pay for it when she came home. For now, I was over Bishop and Kai's house. In his man cave. On my third blunt. Shit wasn't even calming my nerves like it normally did. I was too worried about my baby.

"Damn nigga, that shit bruised already," Bishop said looking at the side of my face. I rubbed my jaw absently and shook my head.

Alayziah had a mean right on her.

"Nigga she caught me so off guard with that punch I couldn't even protect myself." I laughed lightly.

"I told you some was up with Carmen. You know anything about her and the nigga?"

"I mean...she told me little bits and pieces. All I know is she was talking to the nigga and she loved him but he married somebody else. Died shortly after. The way she talks about it seem like her and the nigga might've had a chance to work the shit out but he died before they could."

"Damn."

"I think Carmen was the one that was in her apartment too. Bitch is crazy. She's mentally crazy. Al is crazy like Lay. Popping off any minute. But Carmen, she stalker crazy. Al better watch that shit. You can't fight everybody. Ain't no telling what Carmen up to. And I ain't tryna have to body that bitch. But I will."

"Shit I feel you. Might need to do that shit anyway. Her ass needs to be dealt with. Preferably before my son get here."

I sighed heavily. I couldn't make any moves until I talked to Alayziah. I decided to call her again to see if she'd answer. When she didn't I asked Bishop to get Kai to call her. He shot Kai and text and she called him. He put her on speakerphone.

"Bae..."

"Yes Bishop?"

"Call Al and see if she'll pick up."

"Rell still ain't getting no answer?"

"Duh. Why would I tell you to call her if she was answering his calls?"

"Shut up Bishop. You're such an as…"

"Such a what?"

I shook my head at them and chuckled.

"Nothing."

"That's what I thought. Call her."

"Aight. Hold on."

I sat next to Bishop. Unsure of how to feel. If she answered I was gone be pissed. If she didn't I was gone be pissed. Now was not the time for her to be pulling no disappearing acts.

"Baby?" Kai said as she clicked back over.

"I'm here."

"Kai…you good?" Alayziah asked. Before Kai could answer I grabbed Bishop's phone and jumped up.

"Aw so you can answer her phone calls but you can't answer mine?" I yelled.

"Rell…"

"Don't Rell me. Where the fuck you at Alayziah?"

"Fox and Hound."

"Fox and Hound? With who?"

Took her a while to respond, but when she finally did she whispered, "Terrance."

"And who the fuck is that? Alayziah you gone make me pop a fucking vessel and strangle your ass mane."

"He's Alex's brother. I was trying to see if he could get me Carmen."

"Fuck that. Take your ass home."

"But Rellll…"

"Now Alayziah. I ain't playing with your ass. Don't be at the house when I get there and watch what happen."

I hung up before she could even respond. I gave Bishop his phone back and sat back down. After running my fingers through my dreads and groaning I relit my blunt and tried to calm down before I headed home.

"Swear I thought I was done with this shit when I cut Lay's ass off," I said more to myself than Bishop.

"Damn nigga. I thought Alayziah's ass was gone be stress free for ya. Thought she was gone be a quiet lil normal junt. Fooled yo ass."

"Mane what! It's cool though. She's worth it."

"Is she?"

"Hell yea. She's to me what Kai was to you."

"Damn. Go see about your woman then. Break her. Make her fall in love with you. Then that ass will be on some act right."

"You already know how I do. She getting it tonight."

Carmen

"How long are you going to be gone baby? You know I don't mind watching my grandbabies but we will be in revival next week. I can't have them running all over the church."

I rolled my eyes as my mother spoke. She was holding my youngest daughter in her hands as I packed my bags. Alayziah was going to be looking for me so I had to get away for a few days to come up with my next plan. I wanted her dead. Period. And I was going to do whatever it took to make that happen.

"Ma...I don't know how long I'll be gone but it won't be long. A week tops."

"A week? You can't wait until after revival? You're in some kind of trouble aren't you? Does this have something to do with your face? You need to go to the police baby."

"No ma. And trust me, if there was someone else I could leave my kids with I would. But seeing as my husband is no longer here you're all I have."

"I know baby. You know I don't mind. I'll just...I'll make it work."

I stopped packing long enough to hug her before I returned my attention to my bags.

"How is Alex's parents doing anyway?"

"Fine Ma. Just fine."

"Baby..."

"Ma please. It's bad enough that you let your husband practically run Alex away from me and into Alayziah's arms. I really don't want to talk to you about this.

"That is enough Carmen. I get that you're hurting. But I will not allow you to disrespect me. Especially when I'm trying to help you. Alex didn't leave you because of your father. He left you because he wasn't the man for you. None of the men that you've chosen to give yourself to have been. Your father saw that. Now the way he went about expressing that to you may not have been the best but baby he did it out of love."

I didn't respond. I couldn't respond. I was tired of having this conversation with her. With myself. Alex was mine. He was supposed to be my forever. Alayziah ruined that. She had to pay.

I was scared as hell when I made it back to Rell's place. I didn't know what he was going to do to my ass when I got there. He was pissed and he had every right to be. I know I probably had him worried sick but I just needed some space. I needed to talk to someone that understood what was going on.

I didn't even want Rell to know about that part of my life because I was ashamed. Embarrassed. But when I saw her, something inside of me flipped. I called Kai to see how much trouble I was in and she laughed as I cut my car off.

"Well Al...I will say this; our men are crazy. So just...don't do anything to fuel his anger. Just listen and keep the peace. What would possess you to ditch him though crazy?"

I chuckled lightly and shook my head. "Girl I don't know. I just... I don't know. I wasn't thinking straight. I was caught up in my feelings and I started thinking about Alex. She just irks me to my soul Kailani. Every time I see her I think about Alex. How much I loved him. Wanted him. Adored him. And she fucked that up. She should have just let him go."

"Al..."

"I know I know if he wanted to leave he would have. I guess I just hate that she had him for as long as she did and I couldn't. That eats at me Kai. And every time I see her, it pisses me off."

"Let me ask you this, is your hatred of her and love for Alex greater than what you feel for Rell? Because you're going to lose him if you don't get a grip."

I exhaled deeply. "You're right. I'm going to go in and see how much trouble I'm in."

"Alright boo. Call me if you need me to talk some sense into him."

"Thanks."

"No Bishop. Stop instigating," Kailani said as she disconnected the call. I chuckled as I unbuckled my seatbelt.

When I made my way to Rell's front door I knocked and took a step back. He opened the door slightly and stared at me.

"Thought I told you to be here before I got here?"

"I'm sorry." He stalked my body with his eyes in silence. "You not gone let me in?" I asked. Stepping off to the side Rell allowed me entrance. When I made it inside he closed the door behind us.

"You mad at me?" I asked walking into his living room. He didn't say anything, and that was unlike him. He always had some smooth or smart shit to say. I turned around to face him and he just…looked at me.

"Rell…" His hand wrapped around my throat and he pulled me into him.

"You don't respect me."

My eyes watered. I'd never wanted him to be angry with me or disappointed but shit, I couldn't help it.

"I do respect you baby."

"No you don't Alayziah. You don't take me or what we have seriously."

"Yes I do Terrell. I promise I do."

"Then why don't you fucking listen to me? Do you know how scared I was? All fucking day I've been calling you and texting you and you didn't respond. I didn't know what the fuck happened to your ass.

Did you not take into consideration that you'd just gotten into a fight with a crazy ass bitch that I don't know anything about? I didn't know where she went or how she got there. Anything could have fucking happened to you and I wouldn't have been able to do anything to protect you. Do you know how helpless that made me feel? How bad that shit hurt Alayziah?"

I blinked my eyes a couple of times fighting back my tears as his grip around my neck tightened. "Do you?"

"I'm sorry." Was all I could think of to say. I didn't think he'd care this much. Or that it would bother him this much.

"You sorry?" He asked shaking me a little bit. I nodded my head and closed my eyes.

"Alayziah I can't function like this. I'm not tryna be with your sister all over again. If you can't handle your emotions and let that shit with that nigga go tell me. We can be done tonight."

"But I don't want you to be done with me Terrell."

"Then fucking act like it woman."

"Yes, King." His grip around my neck loosened.

"You ain't getting off that easy. I'm about to punish that pussy. Fuck that nigga outta your system. Go into our bedroom and strip. Take a shower. Get on that bed on all fours. I been waiting to get you on your knees."

Rell

As I waited for Alayziah to get out of the shower I went through her cell phone. I had to get this shit with Carmen taken care of ASAP. I went through her recent calls and found the Terrance niggas number. I stepped into my home studio and called him.

"You good Al?" He asked.

"This ain't Al. This her nigga."

"Rell?"

I smiled. She'd told him about me. "Yea."

"What's up nigga? She was telling me about you earlier."

"That's what's up. What's this shit going on with her and this Carmen chick? I need some insight."

"Man...my brother Alex met Carmen a while ago. They started off as friends and shit. My brother, the nigga craved love and a family. Carmen had three children and my brother instantly stepped up and played the daddy role.

So they started kicking it tough and eventually he proposed. But her daddy didn't like my brother once he found out who my brother used to be in the streets. So he tried to get Carmen to leave him. They started beefing tough. Then he met Al. Nigga instantly changed. She was there for that nigga. He fell for her on sight. She was good to and for him. But he just couldn't let Carmen's ass go. He broke up with her and tried to see what was up with Al but he was still messing off with Carmen.

She ended up getting pregnant and he thought the baby was his so they got married. He tried to cut Al off but he ran into her and started talking to her again.

Then, Al went to a church service he and Carmen was at. Carmen confronted Al. Al snapped on her pregnant ass. Punched her and everything. She found out that they were married and she tried to cut him off but he wouldn't let her go. He chased her for months. He ended up divorcing Carmen and he found out the baby wasn't his so he planned on making it up to Al but... my bro ain't have the chance to make it right with her. He uh...he was in a horrible car accident and...the whole time that nigga was in the hospital Al was there. Right by his side.

227

Nigga wanted nobody but her. And she was there. But he ain't make it. So Carmen mad at Al because she felt like Al took Alex from her. And Al mad at Carmen because she feel like Carmen stood in the way of her being with my brother."

"Damn."

"Al is a good girl man. She's like my brother. They crave love. They desperate for the shit. And anybody that gives them an ounce of it they cling to. Whether they good for them or not. That's why my brother couldn't let Carmen go. And that's why Al couldn't let Alex go.

His ass didn't deserve her but they loved each other in a twisted kind of way that only they understood. Shit was so unhealthy. I honestly believe that's why my brother was taken. Ain't no way in the world he was gone let her go. Ain't no way in the world Carmen was gone let him go."

"I appreciate you telling me all this. That shit makes sense now."

"No problem. I'd do anything for Al for how she was there for my brother. I'm working on finding Carmen now. I'm killing her ass when I find her. I never did like her ass."

"I'm about to call you from my line. Lock my number in and let me know when you find her."

"Bet."

After I disconnected the call and stepped out of the studio I heard the water in the bathroom cut off. I called Terrance's number from my phone and let it ring enough times for it to show up before I hung up. He sent me a text saying he got it so I put my phone in my pocket and made my way to my woman.

Alayziah

After my shower I did as I was told and crawled into bed. I was using some of his cocoa butter lotion until he made his way upstairs. When he did I put the lotion on the floor and got on all fours. I watched him slowly walk over to me as he rubbed his hands together.

"Don't look at me I'm still mad at you." He commanded lightly.

"Relll..." I whined lifting myself up. "I apologized!"

"Shut that shit up."

Biting my lip, I fought the urge to moan. Damn this nigga was turning me on heavy. I got back in position and rested my forearms on the bed. My forehead on the bed. Hair flowing past my shoulders. After undressing he crawled behind me and gripped my waist with one hand as he pulled my hair and lifted my head off of the bed with the other. This time I couldn't hold my moan in as he bit my neck.

"Shit Rell," I whispered as he slapped my ass.

"You like that?" He asked slapping my ass again.

"Yes baby. I love the way you handle me."

"Yea?" He started licking down my spine and placing light bites over my ass.

"Mmmmm yes Rell. Yesss..."

After pushing me further into the bed he spread my ass cheeks and ran his pointing finger from my asshole to my clit. I jumped involuntarily and tried to scoot up in the bed but he gripped my waist.

"Where you think you going?" He asked spreading my legs wider. He slid under me. Positioning his face between my thighs. His tongue found its way to my clit. His pointing finger inside my pussy.

He alternated between licking and sucking my clit. Biting and blowing. Pushing his finger in and out. Fast and slow. Then he began to make the come here motion with his finger inside of me. Sending me into my first orgasm of the night. But this was no ordinary orgasm. I felt my entire body heat up. And I had the strongest desire to pee. I quickly jumped off of his face but when I did clear liquid squirted out of me as I moaned out in pleasure.

"What the fuck was that?" I asked breathlessly falling into the bed. He smiled as he grabbed my ankle and pulled me back to him.

"You squirted," he said laying me flat on my back.

Rell wrapped my legs around his waist. Put the tip of his dick at my opening. Grabbed two handfuls of my hair. Entered me slow and deep. So deep I couldn't speak. But he talked to me.

"Look at me baby."

I opened my eyes slowly and saw love and care inside of his. The passion. The hurt. The yearning. I cupped his face and kissed him deeply. His tongue was so deep in my mouth I thought we'd choke each other. I'd never been kissed so passionately before. Slowly he pulled himself out of me. Left the tip in as he kissed me. Plunged deep inside of me. I threw my head back in delight.

"Ohhhhh my uhhh..." My legs began to shake. He slapped my breasts lightly before sucking them and sending me into my second orgasm.

"Mmmm Rell!" I screamed out as he continued to punish my pussy with his long and deep strokes.

"Fuck Rell...stoppp..." I pleaded. I couldn't take it. It was feeling too good. Too good. Too slow. Too deep. *Like he was digging up any memories of any man that had been in me. Completely erasing them and claiming me.* He moaned sweetly into my ear and breathed deeply and I swear I've never heard anything sound so good in my life.

"Alayziah..." He moaned in my ear. "Alayziah..." He moaned as I grabbed his dreads and pulled his head back. "Shit, don't do that." Rell pushed my legs back until my feet were touching my ears.

"Aaaahhhh..." I moaned as he entered my deeply. "God I love you," I said as he sucked on my neck.

"You love me or you love the dick?"

With soft strokes to his chest I smiled. "Both. But I was talking about you Terrell. I love you."

Looking into my eyes he smiled.

"I love you too Alayziah. Swear I do."

Massaging my clit with one hand he played with my nipples with the other.

"Shit King," I moaned as my legs began to shake.

"I feel good inside my pussy?" He asked making me cum yet again.

"Yes King. You feel soooo good. You the King of this pussy baby. Fuck."

"Watch your mouth girl." He pulled out of me and put me back on my knees. Entering me deeply he said, "Fuck me back Ziah. Show me how much you love this dick."

He started slow and deep. Then he sped up his movements. I matched his strokes until I could no longer moan and he couldn't stop moaning.

I came and was about to tap out until he said, "Don't you stop. I'm coming."

I couldn't take anymore. My legs were too weak so I pushed him out of me and sat on the bed before taking him into my mouth.

"Shit Ziah…" He moaned grabbing my hair and flinging his head back. "Suck it baby. Just like that. Just like that. Play with that pussy while you get your man off."

I started moaning and the vibration of my throat sent him over the edge as he tried to push me off of him but I didn't stop until he'd deposited all of his seeds in me.

"You tryna make sure a nigga never let you go hunh?" He asked as we collapsed on the bed.

I nodded yes as I stroked his chest.

"You staying tonight?" Rell continued as he wrapped his arms around my waist.

"Yes baby. I'm moving in if you still want me to."

He pulled me onto his chest and slid inside me again. "There is nothing that I want more."

Rell

I'll admit, Kai was my dream girl. But sometimes a dream don't have shit on your reality. And this morning, I woke up to my reality.

Alayziah.

And having her in my arms was better than any dream I'd ever had. She was laying slightly on my chest. Her hair all over her head and my neck. And her hand was holding a handful of my dreads. I don't know how her ass managed to hold them in her sleep but somehow she did. I caressed her back lightly after I pulled her on top of me completely.

"Good morning," she mumbled letting my hair go and running her hand down my face.

"Good morning baby. Sorry to wake you. I just wanted you closer."

"It's cool. You hungry?"

"I could eat."

"You got something for me to cook?"

"Yea breakfast is the only time of the day I eat here."

She pulled the top part of her body off of me and sat on my lap. For a moment we just stared into each other's eyes. Smiling. A nigga could definitely get used to this. I ran my hands up her thighs before cupping her ass and grinding her pussy against me slightly.

"Stop bae or I'm not gone be able to fix breakfast."

"Ion care. Ima still eat." I flipped her over and crawled between her legs. She smiled and grabbed my hair as I spread her thighs.

"You be the 6. I'll be the 9," Alayziah said closing her legs. Her ass ain't have to tell me twice. I laid on the bed and held my hands out for her, but she stopped when my doorbell rang.

"Who the fuck is that?" I asked in frustration.

"Ion know. This your house."

"Our house. Don't get amnesia now since the dick dan wore off."

Smiling she rolled out of my bed.

"I haven't changed my mind Terrell. I'm here and I'm yours. I'll start breakfast when I'm done in the bathroom."

I nodded as I watched her naked ass walk into my bathroom. Once she closed the door I got up and grabbed the bottle of water that was sitting on my dresser before heading for the door. It was one thing for my girl to smell my morning breath.

I didn't want nobody else to have to. Even though it would have been their fault for popping up at a nigga house this early in the morning anyway. When I opened the door and saw Layyah standing on the other side I took a step back.

"Damn nigga. The hell happened to your face?" She made her way inside without waiting for my invitation.

"Your sister is what happened to my face."

"What you do to her?" Layyah turned to face me.

"I ain't do shit to her."

I smiled at the thought of what happened last night. She rolled her eyes and walked down my hallway.

"Where she at? I need to talk to her."

"How you know she was here?"

"I didn't. I don't know where she stay so I was just gone make you take her to me."

"She stay with me. What you doing here anyway?"

"What? I was with you for a year and you hardly let me spend more than two nights here in a row. I'm here for Kai and BJ. You know she's due to have him any day now."

"Yea. Well. I'll get her for you." I turned to walk away but her calling my name stopped me. "Yea?" I said turning back around to face her.

Avoiding my eyes, she asked, "You love her yet?"

"I do. You know it don't take me long to decide whether to give a woman my love or not."

"So I really have no chance now hunh?"

I looked at her ass like she was crazy.

"Layyah get fucked up if you want to. Don't come for my man," Alayziah warned calmly. I didn't even hear her walk up. I guess she wanted to see where our conversation was going to go.

"I was just asking because I need closure Al."

"Aight." Alayziah walked in between the two of us and looked at me. "Terrell do you want to be with my sister?"

"Fuck I need with her or anybody else when I got you?"

Shrugging she turned to face Layyah.

"There's your closure. Stay in your lane Lay. I'm about to cook breakfast. You want some?"

Alayziah

I decided to go to my apartment and take out all of the trash and start cleaning up. Yes, I agreed to move in with Rell but that was temporary. I wasn't moving in with him until we were married. I'd already had sex with the nigga. If I moved in with him there was no telling when he would propose and make us official.

Since Rell had a few clients to record before he could get to me I decided to call Marcel so he could help me out. Between his new relationship and my new relationship our friendship had definitely been slacking. So much so that when we were together, it was kind of awkward. I don't know why.

We were sitting across from each other at my kitchen table. Drinking bottles of water. On our phones and looking everywhere but at each other. When I finally couldn't take it anymore I asked him, "Suga what's up with us?"

He sighed heavily as he sat his phone down. "What you mean Love?"

"Marcel you know what I mean. This…is weird. We're never weird. What's up?"

"You want the truth?"

"Always."

"Alayziah you know you my baby. And I want to always see you happy, but…I'm worried about you. And I just can't sit around and watch you live the way you are and seeing the damage it's doing to you. It's bothering me."

My face scrunched up as I pushed my seat away from the table. "The hell you mean the way I'm living?"

"See, this is why I didn't want to talk to you about this. I knew you were going to be overly dramatic."

"I'm not being overly dramatic. I just don't understand why you would even say that. Help me to understand."

"Okay. First it was the nigga that you dated before my cousin. The nigga you were pregnant by. Then it was my cousin. He still a no good ass lying and cheating nigga. Then it was Andrew, the gay nigga. Then it was Alex, the married nigga. Now it's Terrell, your sister's ex."

"Hold up right there. I didn't even know I had a sister before I met Terrell. And what we had was already building before I met her. So don't even include him in the number. But what does that have to do with the way I'm living? Marcel I'm living and loving. That's what we're supposed to do right? I can't help it that the niggas I chose to date weren't any good."

"That's just it Love. You can choose. You just be choosing recklessly. Take Alex. You knew he was engaged when you entertained him. Even if he might have lied in the beginning when you found out that he was still messing with the bitch you should have let him go then. But you stayed. And the nigga ended up playing your ass. Same thing with Drew.

You thought he was gay because you brought it up to me but you stayed with him too. And Jabari...I don't know what the hell that was. Now with this new nigga you haven't even been knowing him for two months and you already staying with the nigga and having sex with him. You fall in love so fast Love. I just don't want to see you get hurt anymore. You need to slow down. Be single for a while. Or at least take things slow with Rell so you won't make the same mistakes."

I scratched the side of my face before folding my arms across my chest. "So you saying I'm a hoe?"

"Not at all Love. I'm just saying, you reckless with your heart."

"Well, thanks but...this is just the way I was built. I love hard. And I'm not changing. You know my situation with Terrell and my living arrangements. And as far as the time frame of me having sex with him is concerned, how long does it take to choose to love someone Marcel? I love Terrell. And he loves me. I know you might not be able to understand it from the outside looking in. But yes, I love him. And I love Alex. And that will never change.

I chose to love these niggas. And it's not about what they say or do or give or how they make me feel. My love has nothing to do with them. Alex didn't understand that. But Terrell does because he loves just the same. So I'm not slowing down or giving him up for anything or anyone in this world. Not even you. If my relationship with him bothers you that much, we might need to chill with this friendship because he isn't going anywhere."

"So you gone choose that nigga over me?"

"It ain't even a choice baby. It shouldn't be. That's my nigga. You my best friend. Y'all ain't even in the same lane."

He nodded as he stood. He walked over to me. Kissed my temple and stared at me for a second before grabbing his phone and leaving. I groaned heavily as I grabbed my phone.

Terrell's ass better do right since he may have just costed me my best friend. After I dialed his number I put the call on speakerphone and sat in on my table.

"Ziah...where you at baby I need some Peace."

I blushed. For whatever reason he decided to name my kitty cat Peace.

"Why Terrell? What's going on?"

"These niggas I'm recording. Niggas suck man. Then they expect me to work a fucking miracle. Got my head throbbing."

"Awww baby you got it. You the King that's why they came to you."

"Look at you. Where you at though? You gone be able to slide through so I can slide in you for a few seconds? We ain't gotta have sex. Just let me put it in for a few seconds."

"Terrell that is not going to work."

"Yes it will. I'll behave. I promise."

"Nigga why you just lie like that?"

He laughed. I laughed. "Alright. Alright. What's going on though? Aren't you with Marvell?"

"Marcel nigga. You know his name quit playing."

"Whatever, you know who I mean."

"He left. He mad at me."

"Why? What happened?" I heard his chair creek as he sat up and I smiled at his concern.

"He don't wanna be my best friend anymore. He said I love too recklessly and he don't want to see me get hurt again."

"Type of shit is that?" I shrugged as if he could see me. "So what that nigga say? He just left?"

"He was like I need to slow down with you or be by myself for a while, but I was like nah. Losing you ain't even an option."

"Baaabyy... I don't want to be the reason you lose your best friend. But...I'll be your best friend. I promise you won't even notice he's not in your life anymore. If you want me to talk to him or some shit though I will. I'm with you no matter what."

"I'm good. It will work itself out in its own time. If not, it was fun while it lasted, feel me?"

"Nah ion feel you but I'm trying to."

"Terrell!"

Rell

Alayziah and Layyah were pacing in front of me like crazy. Bishop texted me to let me know that BJ was ready to come so we met Layyah up here. Now they were wearing a hole in the floor in front of me and it was taking all the patience I had to not snatch them both by the hair and sit their nervous asses down. Bishop came waltzing out and I stood and walked towards him. Stopping midway to turn and look at them. They both were on my heels and one of them stepped on the back of my shoe.

"Will y'all chill? Stepping all on me and shit."

Alayziah smiled and Layyah mugged me.

"We sorry baby." "Nigga, shut up." They replied simultaneously. I shook my head and turned around to face Bishop.

"What's up nigga?" I asked.

"She can have one more person in the room. It's time."

"Okay…who y'all want?"

Bishop looked at all three of us and sighed. "You nigga."

My eyes bucked.

"Me? Ion know nothing about birthing no babies."

"You ain't got to birth no baby country ass nigga. We just gotta stand there and hold her hand and tell her she's doing good the nurse said."

"Fine, but if she starts screaming too loud and shit I'm ghost."

Carmen

My plan would soon be in full effect. I was worried that I wouldn't have a way to get to her now that she knew I was coming for her. But thanks to one of the men in her life practically handing her to me I was going to soon get my full revenge. Since she wanted my husband so bad, she was about to meet him in hell.

Alayziah

Layyah and I were sitting in the waiting room and we were a nervous wreck. Layyah was sitting next to me with her forearms resting on her thighs and her head hanging. I was sitting so far down in my chair the back of my head was where my back should have been and my ass was almost out of the chair.

My legs were shaking and I couldn't help but wonder how long this was going to take. I'd never been in the hospital while someone was giving birth before. Usually I just got the call or text that the baby had been born; but this shit was nerve wracking. I closed my eyes and shortly after Layyah began to speak.

"Al, what was it like growing up with pops?"

Surprised by her question I opened my eyes, sat up and looked at her. "It was cool. He's...a great dad." She nodded as she looked away. "I'm sorry you didn't get to grow up with him."

"It's cool. I mean, it ain't...but it is what it is."

"Well, you can have a better relationship with him now if you want."

"What about you?"

"I mean; I don't really have anything against you personally. Just don't come for my man."

"I'm not. Me and Rell are past over. He made it very clear that he was done with me. Besides, I'm with Mike."

"The nigga we had to come to Miami for?"

"Yeap." She blushed and I shook my head at her crazy ass.

"Lay..."

"I know it might seem crazy but that's my baby. He cheated on me because I cheated on him. I was scared to commit honestly, but after almost losing him for the second time I want to do whatever it takes to make it work."

"I hear you."

"So what's up with you? I want us to really get to know each other, but for now give me the basics about my little sis. You know you were born because of me. Pops felt so bad about what he did with my mother that he took yours on a weeklong vacation and that's when you were conceived."

"Layyah only you would take credit for somebody's birth. But um, I just started back going to school. I've got two more years before I have my Bachelors in Creative Writing. I want to use it to teach, but the ultimate goal is to make it as a poet and writer.

I'm working as a copywriter, well I was until Rell made me quit. Um, I, I don't know Lay. I'm just living. I'm working on a poetry CD and DVD with Rell. That's actually how we met. Kai invited him to my poetry set and he wore me down."

"You really like him hunh?"

"I do. My best friend and I had this little spat because he doesn't understand me and my love. But Terrell does. We vibe in such a way that throughout the day I can't tell if I'm thinking for me or for him. He gets me. He handles me. He appreciates me. He adores me Lay. Why wouldn't I want to spend my life with him?"

Sadness filled her eyes temporarily but she quickly put her poker face back on.

"Well, he deserves to be happy Al. And if you bring him that I'm glad you two found each other."

"What about you? What you got going?"

"Shit. I ain't into the arts and dreaming big and all that shit like y'all. I'm just a normal girl living a normal life. My family moved to Cali. When the shit went down with Kai and Rell I moved there but I came back when Mike started snooping around trying to find out who killed Courtney."

"Courtney? Who is Courtney?"

"Girl...that's a long ass story."

"We got time."

Rell

"Well when is he gone let me come and see the baby? He's been home two whole weeks and I ain't had time to see BJ yet."

I sighed as my mother asked me the same question that she'd been asking me since BJ was born.

"Ma, Bishop and Kailani don't mind you coming over. You just want to come when ain't nobody else there so you can hog BJ but I'm telling you that ain't gone happen no time soon."

"I bet it's not. That little boy is the most handsome little thing. He's got Bishop's eyes and Kailani's color and cheeks. Oh he's going to be a heartbreaker. Speaking of which, when you gone give me some grandbabies?"

"I don't know Ma." I stood and took my plate took the sink. It was time to bounce when she starting bringing this shit up.

"Well are you dating anybody? I'm so glad you didn't get Layyah pregnant. I couldn't take her for the rest of my life."

"Ma…"

"I'm just saying baby. I told you she wasn't good for you."

"That you did." I sat back down and pulled my chair closer to hers before I continued. "Honestly Ma, I know I've found the one. She's amazing. She's creative. She's beautiful. She's corny funny. She's submissive and respectful, but she don't take no sh- no stuff from me or anyone else. She's passionate. She's everything Ma."

"Well if she's everything to you why haven't I met her yet?"

"It's been a lot going on but you'll meet her soon."

"Y'all having sex?"

"Ma…"

"What? That's how I know you serious about a woman. You having sex with her?"

"Ma I am not talking about my sex life with you man."

"I'll take that as a yes. You really like her hunh?"

I nodded as the wheels in my head began to spin. Me and Al have been getting it in on the regular. No condom. And I never pulled out. I needed to see if she was on birth control. If not ma might have a grandbaby on the way sooner than we thought.

Carmen

I wasn't sure how Rell was going to react to seeing me, but we had a contract. I signed to his label. So for the next seven years we were going to be tied to each other. When I pulled up at his studio I made sure to ride around the entire building to see who all was there. Since I didn't see Alayziah's car I went on in. As soon as I opened the door this nigga pulled a gun on me. And Bishop wasn't far behind with his. I immediately raised my hands and yelled.

"Don't shoot! I'm not here to cause any trouble. I just want to work Rell. We signed a contract, remember?"

"Fuck you and that contract. Did you think you was gone get away with the shit you been doing to my girl?" He asked stepping towards me.

"Rell, I told my mother where I'd be this afternoon. If I don't call her every hour she's going to call the police."

Slowly he lowered his gun. Bishop stubbornly kept his in the air.

"Bishop…" Rell said.

"Fuck that. Her mama don't know shit about me. She came for Al she came for you. She came for you she came for me."

"I told her about you too Bishop. I'm not stupid."

"Ion believe you." he said taking a step towards me. I took a step back.

"I can call her. I told her that you were here my first time coming. If anything happens to me she's going to the police and tell them I had beef with Alayziah, her boyfriend Terrell, and his best friend Bishop. I don't want no problems with y'all. My problem is with her. And that don't have shit to do with what's going on here."

"That has everything to do with what's going on here. The fuck? That's my woman!" Rell yelled lowering Bishop's gun.

"Rell, I just want to sing."

"Alright. I got some for your ass. You ain't stupid but I ain't either. Section L paragraph 6 of your contract says that at any point I can ship your ass to The Cannon Sisters and still make my profit off of you. So don't think about stepping foot in my studio again. And if I catch you anywhere near my woman again I'm not gone touch you. I'm touching everyone around you. Play with me if you want to Carmen."

He pulled his phone out and made a call. I stood there to see what he was up to even though I was clearly unwanted.

"Layyah, where you at? Meet me at the studio. I got some shit I need you to handle." Ending the call, he returned his attention to me. "Aye if you don't want to get your ass beat I suggest you leave. Now."

"Nah, let her ass stay. I wanna see Lay tag into her."

I didn't know who this Lay character was but seeing as I was dressed in a skirt and pumps I decided to leave. Not because I was scared, but because I was a lady. I didn't do this fighting shit on the regular. But I definitely knew how to get even.

"He treating you good?" Jabari asked. I had Jessica to come with me to pick out some new furniture for my apartment. What I wanted for my living room area had to be custom made so I decided to have the entire order shipped to me in a few weeks.

I was sitting on the steps in front of my apartment waiting for him to pick her up. I offered to take her home but since he was at the restaurant he decided to come and pick her up. After we hugged goodbye and she walked to the car he sat next to me and asked me the same question he'd been asking me every time he saw me.

"Jabari why do you always ask me that? I don't ask you about your woman every time I see you."

"I ask you because I know what you've been through Al."

My heart softened.

"He's treating me really good Jabari."

He nodded. We sat there for a few minutes before he spoke again.

"I want you to know that I appreciate you so much Al. For being here for my sister, and me. I didn't tell her that you told me about that nigga, but I took care of him."

"What?!" I yelled. "I told you to tell me Bari. Why would you handle that alone? Knew I shouldn't have told your ass."

"Look, I took care of the shit. That's that. I didn't want anyone else involved. I'm good."

"Fine Jabari."

"Let me get her to the house. Has she made her appointment for the...uh..."

"Yes."

"When is it?"

"She's going to get the abortion Friday Jabari."

"Good. Then she will be able to put this behind her."

"I guess."

He stood and walked away. I took that as an opportunity to call and check on Marcel before I headed back to Rell's. I was just about done getting everything that Carmen damaged out of my crib, but I still had a little ways to go.

"Hey Love. What's up?" Marcel answered.

"You really through with me hunh?"

"You know I could never let you go. I just figured you needed some time to get over what I said."

"Did you really mean that? Is that really how you feel?"

"Yes Alayziah. I don't want to lose you, you know that. Maybe after some time has passed and I see that things are going good between you and Rell I'll come back. But when you hurt I hurt and I ain't tryna deal with that shit again."

"I can respect that."

"I love you."

"I love you too."

I disconnected the call and stood. After grabbing my purse and keys I headed for Rell's.

"Why the fuck y'all just now telling me about this bitch? I would've handled her ass the first morning I was in town!" Layyah yelled after Bishop and I finished telling her about Carmen.

"Shit we really ain't had time. Besides I thought it was over after Alayziah beat her ass. Today was the first time I saw her since then," I replied as Bishop shook his head and laughed at Layyah's flaring temper.

"Aight. That's cool. So where she at now?"

"Ion know. Her ass just ups and disappears."

"Ion like that shit. She needs to be handled. What y'all gone do? I can beat her ass all day but if Al already dan whooped her ass it's obviously gone take more than that to make her back off."

"True. What you wanna do nigga? I'm down," Bishop added.

I sighed heavily and shook my head. Last thing a nigga wanted or needed was to catch another body. Especially a mother with four kids.

"Ion know yet. We just gone have to catch her slipping. In the meantime, I'm gone keep her close to me. She ain't scared of course, but I'll be better at peace knowing she was nearby."

"I feel you. When you find that bitch let me know and I'm on her."

"I already know."

Alayziah

I was surprised as hell when Terrell asked me to meet his mother. Even though we were in a committed relationship I still wasn't expecting him to be on this meet the parents shit so soon. But Terrell, he wasn't just a real nigga. He was a real man. And he was doing everything he could to make things between us go right.

I figured tonight would be the night that I told him that when my furniture arrived I was moving back to my apartment. He wanted to take me out on a date after we met up with his mother so I was having the hardest time trying to find something to wear yet again. I wanted to be sexy for my boo but I wanted to be presentable for his mother.

We went paint balling the day before so I had some bruises on my arms and legs. I really didn't want to be showing my body but last night as he made love to me he made it perfectly clear that no matter what happened to my body over time he would love me unconditionally.

Especially while I was barefoot and pregnant. Crazy ass. I could tell he was a little disappointed when I told him that I was on birth control but I had no doubt in my mind that when the time was right he and I would be married with tons of babies crawling around here.

"Baby!" I yelled. I was tired of trying to figure out what to wear by myself.

"What?"

"Come find me some to wear while I take a shower."

"You ain't even took a shower yet? Thought I told you to be ready at six?"

"Terrell...if you come find me some to wear I can get ready faster."

"It's six thirty and your ass nowhere near ready?"

"Terrell!"

Rell

Almost two hours later my baby was making her way to me. I smelled her perfume before I saw her. We went paint balling and to the mall yesterday and I got her some new perfume. Dolce and Gabbana Light Blue. Shit smells good as hell. Made me want to eat her ass up there in the store. I looked up when her scent filled my nostrils and stood. I definitely made the right choice picking out her outfit.

I chose a grey jersey romper. It was loose fitting at the top but tight at the bottom. It was a one shoulder piece with the back cut out. I made her put some flats on because I loved looking down on her. I loved when she looked up at me.

Her honey colored eyes already glowed but when she looked up at me and let the sun hit them...swear I didn't need anything else in this world.

As usual she didn't have on much makeup, which was quite fine with me. I preferred her face natural. She did have on some mascara and eyeliner and some purple lipstick. Her slick ass knew that was my favorite color. And her hair was pulled into a slick bun. She smiled and walked towards me as I continued to take all of her in.

"Baby you're beautiful," I mumbled pulling her into me. She blushed as she looked up and into my eyes.

"You're quite handsome yourself King." I blushed before trying to take her lips into mine. "Nu unh Terrell. You gone smear my lipstick," she protested pushing me away.

"Mane you can put some back on. Put some purple lip stain on then. You know I'm gone be nibbling at them Megan Good lips all night."

"Terrell my lips are not that big."

"Whatever. Just hurry up. Don't be back there long."

"Nigga don't rush me. It's your fault I got to start over anyway."

"Start over?! Alayziah if you don't wipe that lipstick off and put some lip stain on..."

Alayziah

This is why I hated going out with Terrell. He looked so good he made me lust after him so bad. All I wanted to do was go back home and rip his clothes off. And being that we were spending the first part of our night with his mother that just made the shit worse.

Usually I could steal a few feels and kisses and be satisfied but now I couldn't even do that. He'd been standing at the passenger door of his car waiting for me to get out for the longest. My shaky ass was scared. I did not want to meet his mother. He said she was going to be cool...but that didn't make me feel better.

"Ziah come on before you have me smelling like outside," he whined.

Pouting I unbuckled my seatbelt and twisted to the right to sit my legs out the car. I looked up at him.

"Do I have to?"

"Yes big baby. Come on. My mama cool. She gone love you." Rell grabbed my hand and pulled me out of the car.

"We staying long? You look good as hell Terrell."

"Ima let that slide since you complimenting a nigga."

"It ain't like I said fuck." He slapped my ass so hard the little bit of meat I had jiggled. "Ow!" I yelled turning around. I was about to slap him out of reflex but he grabbed my hand and pulled me into his chest.

"You showing out tonight. You need some dick?"

"Yessss."

Chuckling he grabbed my ass and squeezed lightly. Taking the pain away instantly.

"You want a quickie in my old room?"

"Hell no! Your mama will think I'm a hoe. Besides, that's disrespectful."

"Come on baby. It'll be fun to sneak around. See how deep and hard I can go inside that pussy and how slow and soft I can rub on that clit without you screaming out."

My pussy literally throbbed. "Terrell stop playing with my emotions." I tried to pull away but he wouldn't let me.

"I'm dead serious Ziah. Try me."

"No just come on so we can get this over with so we can go home."

"We ain't going straight home. I got us a spot reserved at Pinots Palette."

"The place where you paint and drink?"

He shook his head and smiled. "Yes Alayziah. It's bring your own beverage."

"Yay! I've always wanted to go there."

"I know. I listen."

My heart melted and I was putty in his hands at that moment as I wrapped my arms around his waist.

"I love you Terrell."

"I love you too. Now come on so my Ma can fall in love with you too."

Unwillingly I allowed him to lead me into his mother's home. After he let us in he started screaming like a mad man.

"Ma! Ma!"

"Boy, why are you yelling like you crazy? I'm in the kitchen."

I smiled as he took me into the kitchen. I was walking slow and he was walking fast so our arms were spread out as he held on to my hand. When we made it to the kitchen I smiled hard as hell. His father was sitting at the table looking just like his ass. Only difference was his hair was cut short and he was a little darker than Terrell who inherited his mother's skin tone and love for dreads. Hers were a mix of gray and black that rested just at the top of her butt.

"What's up pops?" Rell spoke releasing my hand to dap his father up before hugging his mother. "Y'all this is my Queen Alayziah. Alayziah this is my mother Diana and my father Terrell."

"It's nice to meet you both," I spoke shyly.

"Girl come on over here and give me a hug. You family if my son brings you to meet us." His mother said with open arms. I walked over to her and she took me into her arms and gave me the biggest, longest, warmest hug I'd had since my mother died. She didn't release me. She kept her arms around my waist but she pulled the top part of her away to look into my face as she talked.

"Now Prince told me that your mother died. I know I will never be able to take her place but I want you to know that I'm here for you. You're my daughter now. Anything you need you come to me, okay?"

Tears immediately filled my eyes as I nodded. I didn't mean to get emotional but Lord knows I missed my mother. So for her to offer herself to me as that influence…

"Look what you dan did Diana. The girl ain't been here for more than a minute and you already got her crying," his father said causing us all to laugh.

"I didn't mean to," she said wiping my tears away. "Prince go get her some jolly ranchers out the candy bowl. I ain't got no peppermints."

"Ma we are not at church and she is not a child. You ain't got to give her no candy just because she crying. You so old and down south," Rell teased pulling me away from her and taking me into his arms.

"Boy shut up. Dinner will be ready in about ten minutes. I got some rolls on the table and it's a bottle of Port chilling in the fridge," his mother said returning her attention to the stove. "Can you cook baby?" She asked me.

"Yes maim."

"I'll have to have you over here with me next time then. We cook for our men in this house. What you doing tomorrow?"

"Umm…nothing really. Just hitting the studio with Rell."

"Why don't you come by then? We can cook and go shopping or something."

"Yes maim."

"Ma how you just gone steal my girl like that?"

"Oh hush. I'm not gone have her all the time."

"Mane whatever." Rell pulled me out of the kitchen.

"Young lady you smoke?" His father asked stopping us.

"Yes sir."

"Cool. We'll have to burn one before you leave."

I looked at Rell and he shook his head as we walked out.

"Yes sir," I said when I composed myself. He completely caught me off guard with that shit I couldn't even reply right off the bat.

"Yo, your parents are cool as…" I stopped myself as he led up a set of stairs. "Your parents are cool!"

"I told you you ain't have nothing to worry about."

"Where we going? I'm hungry and she said it's rolls on the table."

"I'm hungry too greedy ass."

"Rell…" I whined. "Ion want to."

"Yes you do. Stop fronting."

"Reellll…"

"You really don't want me baby?" He asked when we made it upstairs and into his old room.

"You know I want you."

"Then give me some Peace. Ziah I'm so turned on right now. I want you so fucking bad. She already know we fucking."

"Terrell!"

"I ain't tell her, she figured it out." I crossed my arms over my chest as he sat on his bed. "Please baby," he whined pulling me into him.

"Fine. Lock the door. Five minutes."

Jumping up he said, "Hold up," before he ran downstairs and returned.

"What you do?" I asked as he locked the door behind him. Before he could answer I heard Ann Peebles blasting from downstairs. I smiled as he walked towards me.

"Now you won't have to worry about them hearing us."

"Now she really gone know we having sex since you dan turned some music on."

"You want me to cut it off?" Rell turned me around and unzipped my romper.

"No." I pouted pulling my romper down and climbing into the bed. "Five minutes." I added.

"It's gone take me five minutes to eat you."

"No eating then."

"Ugh," he groaned as he took his pants off. I took my bra off and waited for him to remove my panties. I loved when he took them off of me. He crawled between my legs and took my panties off before laying on top of me and kissing me sweetly. His fingers found their way to my pussy as he gauged my wetness. Pleased he slowly slid himself inside of me. I bit down on his lip to keep from moaning.

"Why are you so wet Alayziah?" Rell questioned as he stroked me slowly. Softly. Sounds of my pussy gushing immediately filled the room. I opened my mouth to say some smart shit back but I was scared that I was going to moan so I kissed him instead.

"Mmmm…" I moaned into his lips as he went deeper inside of me. "Don't do that," I whispered wrapping my legs around him.

"Do what baby?" His lips covered my nipple. Licking it with the tip of his tongue just the way he knew I liked. Shit got me so hot and wet.

"Stop playing Rell before I get loud."

"Get loud then baby."

He lifted himself from off of me.

Instead of going deep as he was before he punished my g-spot. Caressing my clit at the same time. I tried to close my legs but he wouldn't let me.

"Stop fighting it," he ordered wrapping his hands around my neck.

"Rell..." I whispered opening my legs wider.

"I know you like this rough shit."

"Yes King...Fuck Rell...you hitting my spot," I panted as I tried to fight my orgasm.

"Cum Alayziah. I'm waiting on you," he pleaded stroking me faster.

"Shit Rell. Slow down before I... I..." It was too late. My legs began to shake as I came. "Shhh Shit!" I yelled as he came inside of me.

"Fuck Ziah," he grunted falling on top of me.

I rubbed his back softly.

"I cannot go back down there. You gone have to bring my food up here."

Rell

Alayziah was sipping on her cup of wine as the teacher gave us the rules for the class. Which weren't really rules. Just the normal, raise your hands if you have questions and don't laugh at anyone's work, type of shit. My palms were sweating hard as hell as she pulled the class painting up to show us what we were going to have to paint. Alayziah looked at me and smiled in excitement.

"Thank you for bringing me here baby," she said before kissing my cheek. I was so nervous I couldn't even reply. I just nodded.

"Okay class. We have a couple's portrait that we're going to paint today. It's a little more advanced than what we normally do but I want you all to have fun with it and do the best you can."

The teacher said unveiling the canvas painting she'd done of me and Alayziah. Her emotional ass dropped her cup of wine and covered her mouth in surprise. Luckily we were sitting in the front so no one was next to us or they would've been mad as hell. I laughed as the teacher picked the plastic cup up and I apologized to her.

"Good call on giving her plastic," the teacher said.

"Oh my God." Ziah looked at me with tears in her eyes. "Terrell!" She yelled standing to her feet and hugging me. "This is beautiful baby! Thank you so much!" She continued kissing my lips a few times before walking towards the painting to get a better look as the room filled with awwws and ooohhhs from the onlookers.

I stood and walked behind her.

"Baby this looks so much like us. Wait…" She stepped as close to the painting as she could. Tilting her head her eyes focused in on her hand. "Rell I don't have a ring on my ring finger. Why is that there?"

Alayziah turned to face me. I kneeled.

"Because…I want to change that." I said reaching into my pocket. "Alayziah you're…me. You complement me in a way that no other human being has complemented me before. You make me feel like a man baby. You appreciate me. You respect me. You love me. You value me. And I know this might sound selfish but I want you to do this to me for the rest of my life. And I promise if you do I'll shower you with so much love and affection you will drown in it. So what do you say? You gone ride with a nigga for life?"

"Until we hit the grave."

I smiled and slid the ring on her finger. Trying to shake the tears from my eyes.

"Ummm…just so we're clear…that was you asking her to marry you and her saying yes…right?" the teacher asked as I stood.

"Yes. Yes." I said.

"She said yes!" She yelled and everyone stood and applauded as I took her into my arms and kissed her passionately.

Alayziah

After three days locked inside with Rell I called my girls up for a ladies' night. First I had a girl's day with Jessica and then I met Layyah at Bishop and Kailani's place to get ready for our night. It would be her first time out since she had the baby and we were amped! I'd just finished putting the final touches on my outfit when she lightly tapped on my door.

"You almost ready future Mrs. Prince Terrell Brown?"

I smiled as I walked to the door and let her in. "Girl, I still can't believe Terrell proposed!"

"I can! You were made for him." Kai stepped completely inside of the room.

"Y'all ready to go?" Layyah asked walking in.

"Damn. Y'all do favor." Kailani looked from me to Layyah. I didn't see it. She did look like my dad but not like me. I was brown and she was yellow. I was slim and she was slim thick. We did have the same grade of hair and the same lips. Same dimples. Maybe we did favor...a little.

"I guess." I grabbed my phone to see if Rell had texted me back yet.

"You don't want to look like your big sister?" Layyah asked sitting on the bed.

Layyah was bad as hell I can't lie. I guess I was still just getting used to having a sister.

"It's not that Lay."

"Leave that girl alone she wanna look like herself," Kailani said looking herself over in the mirror. She was wearing a flowing red backless maxi dress. Her hair was in its natural state pulled into a bun. She had on some bad chunky gold earrings with a naturally made up face. Her gold eyeshadow and ombré brown and dark gold lipstick complemented her skin very well. The simplicity of her outfit and makeup had her looking flawless without even trying.

Layyah had on a high waist short set with a crop top that accentuated her curvy hips. The black against her skin looked good as hell. Her hair was in loose curls with a part down the middle. On her face she had on nothing but a black matte lipstick. Her ass wasn't even trying hard and I knew she was gone kill.

I was dressed in a white crop top with a pair of high waist light ripped jeans. I had on a pair of black and red pumps with a black and red clutch. My hair was bone straight with a part down the middle. Maybe that's why Kailani said Layyah and I favored. And on my face I did my usual eyeliner and mascara with a bold red lip.

I looked at them and smiled. Just a few months ago I had no female friends. Just Marcel. Now I had a sister by blood and a sister friend. My eyes glossed up as I stood.

"Let's go y'all I'm about to be in my feelings." I walked towards the door.

"What's wrong?" Layyah asked walking towards me.

I shrugged. "Just…thinking about my life. A few months ago I was heartbroken in this crazy ass triangle. Now I got a man who adores me. You two beautiful ladies. I'm just blessed."

"Awww," they said simultaneously as we group hugged. The ringing of my phone stopped us.

"Hey baby," I said answering Rell's FaceTime request.

"Let me see you." I rolled my eyes and tilted my phone to give him a full view of me.

"Damn you look good. When you coming home?" He continued.

"Thanks babe. We leaving now so probably in a couple of hours."

"Aight. Y'all behave. Don't get too drunk. And don't be out there fighting."

"I'm not Terrell. We too cute to be fighting tonight."

"Whatever, that ain't stopped y'all crazy asses before. I love you. Call me on your way home."

"I love you too babe."

Rell

Bishop's lonely ass called me to come over his house soon as the girls left. I didn't mind though because after being locked up with Al celebrating our engagement a nigga needed some fresh air. This was the first time he was alone with the baby so I knew he wanted me there because he was nervous too. Even if he didn't want to admit it.

"I'm surprised you ain't got Al pregnant yet." Bishop flipped through through channels on the TV.

"Mane…it ain't for a lack of shooting my seeds in her. She on birth control though."

"I should've known it was something like that. How does it feel to be engaged my nigga? This gone be your life soon." He claimed grabbing one of BJ's blankets from off the couch and throwing it at me.

"Ion think it's really hit me yet. Ion think the shit gone hit me until I see her pretty ass walking down that aisle. That's what a nigga waiting for. I'm ready to sign them papers. Shit, we can go down to the courthouse Monday for all I care. I'm just ready for her to have my last fucking name."

"I feel you. That's how I was with Kai. After I proposed to her the first time and she turned a nigga down I was heartbroken. I wasn't gone stop until she was legally mine. It's cool to fuck around and shit but it ain't nothing like having somebody at home that you know gone always hold you down."

"I feel you. And she fits with Kai so well. Then she's Lay's sister. I still can't believe that. She fits our little family perfectly."

"I can't believe that shit either. One Layyah is bad enough. Her crazy ass. I still remember when Al punched your ass though. I wanna be there when y'all have y'all first fight."

"Nigga I'm the King of my house. All I gotta do is fuck that shit out of her and she good. That's the only time she act up is when she want some dick."

"Whatever nigga. Wait until she really gets your ass. And when she gets pregnant? Oh my God."

"Kai only gave you a hard time because you trapped her ass."

"Mane whatever. I ain't trap Lani. She wanted to have my seed. She was just taking too long."

I shook my head at his crazy ass as he pulled his phone out. Talking about our women always made us miss them.

"Lani...where y'all at?" He asked after dialing her number. "Some niggas been tryna get at y'all? Don't nobody care about Layyah's ass she single. I'm talking about you and Al. Aight. Make me come up there if you want to. So? You better let them niggas know before they even get to y'all table. Hold your hand up and let them niggas see that ring. Keep playing Ima take BJ to Diana and be up there on your ass. You think I'm playing? Aight."

He hung up the phone and looked at me. "Why we let them go out together?"

"Nigga I know you not finna go up there? Leave them folks alone mane. They can't help it that they look good."

"Aight. Since that's how you feel I guess you don't care that it's one nigga that's been buying your fiancée drinks and tryna get her number all night then hunh?"

I chuckled lightly as I stood. "Let's go."

Alayziah

I didn't believe that Bishop and Terrell were going to come to the lounge we were at so when Kai and Lay tried to get me to leave I declined. I had already had my limit of three drinks and I was feeling mighty good. Cheesing hard as hell.

The same guy had been staring at me all night and would not take the hint that I was not interested. I was flattered though. I tried to throw him off on Layyah since she was on a break from Mike but her ass wasn't going. One day she was in love the next she was ready to kill Mike. I just stopped trying to keep up with their relationship status.

When my drink buyer came to our table again I sighed heavily and looked from Kai to Lay who both had attitude all over their face.

"Mane if this nigga come over here one more time..." Layyah said sitting up in her seat.

"I know right. His ass just don't let up," Kai added.

"I know you ain't talking. You had that light skinned nigga practically begging you to let him buy you a drink."

"So he eventually took the hint. This nigga here ain't catching shit."

I chuckled as he stood in front of our table. Before he could even speak I said, "I'm engaged man."

"But you ain't married yet. I still have a chance."

"No you really don't."

"I don't know what type of man would let a woman as fine as you out anyway."

"One that knows he has absolutely no competition. I'm well satisfied."

"Damn. She told you," Layyah said instigating.

"Just...give me five minutes of your time and I promise I won't bother you anymore," he pleaded.

"Uh oh. Look who just walked in." Kai pointed towards the door.

"Shit..." Layyah added sitting deeper in her seat.

"You might wanna go my nigga," Kailani continued.

"Why?" He asked turning slightly to face her.

"Unh unh don't turn towards me. I don't want my husband thinking you here for me."

"Kailani!" Bishop's country ass yelled. "Who the fuck is this nigga?" He asked walking towards our table.

"Nigga shut yo loud ass up. He ain't even for me. He for Al." Her ass snitched quickly as she stood.

"His ass ain't for me either," I said following her.

"Oh so you entertaining this nigga knowing you got a man at home?" Rell grabbed my ass and pulled me into him.

"No baby. He just wouldn't go away. I told him I was engaged."

"And well satisfied," Lay added standing. I smiled at her and shook my head.

"She told you she ain't wanna holla and you still pushing up on my lady?" Rell asked pushing me to the side.

"I ain't mean no harm. Her giving me a hard time just turned me on I ain't gone lie. But I don't mean any disrespect." Ole boy took a step back.

"Rell let's just go. You don't have to fight over what you already have."

He looked at me intensely before nodding. "Aight. But y'all three...y'all don't get to go out alone no more. Not unless one of us is with y'all."

"Terrell! That's not fair!"

"Whatever. A nigga ain't tryna catch a case playing with y'all. Show me the nigga that was tryna push up on you," Bishop said grabbing Kailani's arm.

"He gone," she lied.

Layyah and I sniggled a little too hard because he looked back at us.

"Stop lying Lani."

"I ain't lying Bishop."

"Then why they laughing?"

"Ion know. Ask them. They just crazy."

"Why y'all laughing?" Bishop asked Layyah and I.

I nudged her in her stomach so she could answer.

"Uh...we were just thinking about... how the nigga begged for her number before he left."

He looked like he ain't believe her but he let the shit go as he wrapped his arm around Kailani's neck and walked her outside.

"Did you drive baby?" I asked Rell as he, Layyah, and I walked out behind them.

"Yea. You coming home?"

"Yea. Lay you gone be straight for the night?"

"Yea I'm good," she replied sadly.

"You miss Mike don't you?" I asked. She nodded. "Just go back home. I'm sure y'all can work it out. Or leave his ass and move on."

Once we made it outside she grabbed me and pulled me in for a hug.

"Call me if you need me...k?" I said.

She nodded as I kissed her cheek. I don't know if it was really her relationship with Mike that was wearing her down...or the one she had to watch me have with Rell.

"You wanna come over for a movie?" I asked. I couldn't resist.

Rell

Waking up with Alayziah and Layyah in the same house was weird as hell. They fell asleep on the couch last night so I took Layyah to the guest room before putting my baby in bed with me. I woke up before the sun rose. Just had a weird ass feeling in the pit of my stomach. I looked to my right and Alayziah was laying on my heart as usual.

After sliding from under her I went down the hall to the guest room to check on Layyah. When I did she was on the edge of the bed. Crying. I started to go and wake Al up but it seemed like she needed comfort now. I went over to the bed and sat next to her. She looked at me and smiled lightly wiping her face.

"What's wrong Lay?"

"Nobody else knows this."

"Knows what?"

"I'm moving back to Memphis permanently. You know I've been going back and forth because of my relationship with Mike but, I'm moving back home."

"Why? What about him? What about your shop? What happened?"

"I'm just tired Rell. I'm tired of being with men who can't give me what I need. I can't even have a healthy loving relationship because I'm so fucked up. You were the only man to ever really care about me and I cheated on you. Mike says he cares, but he don't care about me. He cared about the old me but not me. He swore he didn't want to change me, but that's all he's been trying to do since I got back with him."

"You just ain't found the man for you Lay. When the right man comes along, he gone make you want to be faithful. He's going to be so different that you're going to just... know... you're going to know that he's the one for you. He's going to give you the love you need. He gone pull that selfishness out of you. Ain't nothing wrong with wanting to have some fun, your ass just need to be single while you're doing it."

She chuckled as I brushed her tears away.

"I just feel like I'm never going to get it right. At this point, I don't even have the desire to. I'm never going to find a man who can handle me and make me want to do right. Then I have to watch you and my sister. Y'all are so good together and it eats at me. Not because I want you back, but because I know I could have had that with a good man and I ruined it."

"Every good man ain't the man for you Layyah."

"I know, and I will never come at you like that, not that it would do my any good, it's just hard being here. I feel so alone."

"You are not alone. You got Al, Kai, me, and Bishop."

"Yeah, but y'all got each other. Who got me?"

Her tears started to flow again and I sighed heavily as I caressed her thigh.

"Just wait on him Lay. In the meantime, leave Mike's ass alone for good. You don't need somebody that's gone make you want to be worse; you need somebody that's going to make you want to be better."

She nodded as she covered her hand with mine.

"Rell, I'm so sorry."

"We past that. You don't have to apologize anymore. We good. You're my sister now and I love you. I got you."

"Okay, go before you make me cry even more," she said pushing me off the bed.

"Aye, check this out... you remember when I first bought my studio downtown?"

"Yeah, what about it?"

"When I first got it, it was a shoe store. The nigga that I got it from sold it because his business was expanding. He's cool as hell... Maybe I could..."

"No. I am not letting you hook me up with anybody."

"Why not? Don't you think I would know if someone would be a good match for you or not? I know you Layyah, and I know what you want and need. You need a nigga that's gone be able to handle you and make you submit, not a nigga you can walk all over."

"Kai said I don't need a man that's gas to my flames like you. She said I need water to balance me out."

"Kai ass only said that because that's what she thinks she does for Bishop, but her ass just as crazy as him. Sometimes you do need water, but sometimes you have to fight fire with fire. A fire needs oxygen and nourishment, which can be other leaves, grass, and shit to build, right?

So, if you kill that source of oxygen and the leaves that nourish it you create a controlled burn. That controlled burn keeps the fire from spreading. Once the fire is contained then it can be put out, but if you let the shit burn all willy nilly or just try and throw some water on it the flames will spread and cause more harm than good. Yes, you need water to contain you, but first, you need a nigga to handle you with some flames and sustain you."

She nodded and licked her lips as if she was in deep thought.

"Let me think about it," she mumbled.

"Cool. You good?"

"Yeah, I'm good. Thanks, Rell."

"Anytime."

Alayziah

I woke up to my phone vibrating like crazy. The first time someone called I let that shit go to voicemail but they called right back. Groaning, I grabbed my phone angrily but softened when I saw Jabari's name.

"Yes, Jabari?" I said groggily.

"Al…are you busy?"

"I mean…I was sleep. What's up?"

"It's Jessica. She's been acting strange since she had the abortion. I was out of town last night but she was supposed to be at my place. When I got in, she wasn't here. I called my mom and tried to see if she was there without alarming her, but she isn't there. She isn't answering her phone. I tracked her location. I was wondering…if you could go and pick her up with me. I don't know what I'm about to walk into."

I sat all the way up in bed after he said Jessica's name. I sighed heavily and ran my fingers through my hair.

"Aight, Bari. Let me take a shower really quick and let my fiancé know what I'm doing and then I'll head out your way."

"Fiancé?"

"Yes, Jabari. Terrell and I are getting married."

"Damn. That's good, Al. I'm genuinely happy for you."

I smiled and placed my feet on the floor. "Thanks. Let me hop in the shower and I'll be on my way."

"Cool."

"Where are you going?" Rell asked as I ended the call.

"To find Jessica with Jabari."

"Mane, they stay in some shit."

"I know right. That's my little sis though."

"Speaking of sisters… take some time today to see about yours."

I looked at him skeptically. "Why?"

"She going through some shit right now."

"And she talked to you about it instead of Kai or me?"

"Not intentionally. I woke up this morning and found her crying."

"Crying? What the hell is wrong with her? Is it Mike?"

"Kind of. Just…take care of this shit with them and then see about her."

The softness in his expression and voice warmed my heart. Even though she did him wrong he still cared about her.

"I will baby."

"I love you. Call me when you get to that nigga and call me when you on your way to her. Matter fact...do I need to go with you?"

"I'm sure it's nothing baby, but if you want to come you can."

"Just text me the address to where y'all gone be and I might slide through there."

"Cool."

After my shower I threw on some basketball shorts and a baby tee and made my way to Jabari's place. When I got there he was sitting on the porch waiting for me. I parked my car on the street and made my way to his car. He met me there.

"Hey... sorry," he said lightly standing in front of me.

"It's cool. She still ain't answering?"

"Nah. I'm just gone go to the address her phone is at and see what's up."

"Cool."

We got inside his car. After he put the address into the GPS I texted it to Rell.

"So... besides being engaged what's new?" Jabari asked.

"Um, I don't know, Jabari, still working on my poetry CD. I recorded some of my songs to send out to some labels to try to get on as a songwriter. You?"

"We're opening a second restaurant so that's cool."

"That's great, Jabari. What's up with you and your girl?"

"Man... she's cool. I don't see it going anywhere though."

"Why not?"

"Jessica don't like her."

I chuckled. "Why not?"

"She ain't you. You got her spoiled."

My smile faded.

"You ain't gotta close up. She knows nothing will ever be between us. She just...really likes you."

"Well, I love her like a little sister. That will never change, but that shouldn't keep you from being in love and happy."

"It won't. I'm just going to give her some time to get you out her system. Me too. I told you Al, I just wanted to see you loved and happy, whether it was by me or not. I meant that shit."

I nodded. "How far away are we?"

"About fifteen minutes away."

"Cool."

Rell

I scooped Bishop up before heading to the address Al sent me. I just didn't feel right sending Al off to handle some shit with that nigga alone. It wasn't that I didn't trust him...fuck it. *I didn't trust him.* I didn't know him, and as much drama as he and his little sister stayed in, I just wanted to keep my baby safe. Bishop and I made light conversation as I drove to the address she gave me. We were a couple of streets away when I texted her to see what was going on. She didn't reply. I sighed heavily unintentionally before throwing my phone in the cup holder.

"What's wrong nigga?" Bishop asked.

"Shit. She ain't texted me back yet."

"Your ole impatient ass."

"Mane...I know I am so I'm tryna be cool about it."

"You think she's in danger or some shit?"

"Nah. She trusts the nigga and she loves his sister. Ion know. I know he still wants her. Maybe that's what it is. Ion know."

"I feel you. We almost there. Y'all need to set some boundaries if you feel that strongly about her dealing with the nigga."

"We gone have to do some. He can't be calling her all times of the day. They gone have to get their shit together. Especially once I knock her ass up."

"Lord have mercy. That's gone be a sight to see. Your over protective possessive ass already crazy now. I can only imagine how you gone be then."

I just smiled. His ass was right. That was gone be some shit.

Alayziah

When we made it to the house that Jessica's GPS on her phone led us to, Jabari said he was going to try to call her once more before we went in. When she didn't answer, we got out and headed for the door. He knocked but no one answered.

"Stay here." He said walking to the side of the home.

I waited there for a second before pulling my phone out to call Rell. That's when I noticed he called me. As I let the phone ring Jabari held one finger up to his mouth and motioned for me to come with him. I hung the phone up, put it back in my purse, and walked towards him. When I got to the back of the house he'd already gone inside. I followed suit. After I walked inside the home I closed the door lightly. I turned around and saw Carmen standing in front of me.

"Do you know how long I've been waiting for this?" She asked. I was so caught off guard that I couldn't even respond. I just looked at her crazy ass. "Do you?" She screamed.

I scanned the rest of the room for a sign of Jessica but she wasn't there.

"Jabari," I called out calmly. He slowly walked into the room. His face was laced with sadness.

"I'm sorry. She saw me kill Chris. She has been following me. You. Us. She said if I didn't help her trap you she was going to go to the police," he rushed out.

I nodded in understanding. I wasn't messed up about him snitching. A nigga will do anything to keep his freedom. What I was pissed about was the fact that he didn't appreciate all that I'd done for him and his sister enough to warn me.

"It's cool Jabari," I said nonchalantly throwing my purse to the floor.

"So what's up, Carmen? What's your beef? You wanna kill me cause I fucked your man and beat your ass?" I stepped towards her but stopped when she cocked her gun.

"No, bitch! I want to kill you because you took him from me. He was my last chance, Alayziah. My last chance to be happy. Do you know how hard it was for me to find a man who accepted me and my children as his own? And dealt with my crazy ass daddy? And you took Alex from me."

I laughed lightly and shook my head.

"Carmen, I didn't take your man. He married you," I reasoned.

"No. That piece of paper and ring didn't mean shit to him. He still wanted and chased you. That's why I killed his ass."

My heart dropped. My ears had to be deceiving me. I know she couldn't have said what I thought she said. She must be stone cold crazy. She had to have lost her mind. Alex died in a car accident. *The hell she mean she killed him?*

"The hell you mean you killed him?" I asked taking another step towards her.

"Stop fucking moving Alayziah. You make me nervous when you move. Be still! I can't think with you moving."

"Fine. Fine. Just talk to me. Tell me what you mean. You said you killed him. Alex died in a car accident Carmen."

"I know, but I put sleeping pills in one of his bottles of tea. That's why he fell asleep at the wheel. We took vows Alayziah, that nothing but death would separate us. Not you. Not his family. Not my father or my baby's daddies. Nothing but death. So, since he divorced me and planned to be with you I made sure death separated us, but now, you get to join him."

I inhaled deeply before rubbing my face. Shaking my head as tears fell from my eyes. Running my fingers through my hair, I felt like my heart was pounding, trying to get out of my chest. Chills pierced my skin but I was hot on the inside, so hot my palms began to sweat as I stared into her eyes.

"You killed him? You took him from me?" I asked calmly.

"Seemed fair to me. You don't agree?" Carmen smiled.

I opened my mouth to reply, but as I did, the door was kicked down behind us. Without even looking to see who it was, I took that as an opportunity to tackle Carmen and take the gun from her. After tossing it across the room, I started bashing her fucking face in. I have never been so angry in my life.

Yes, I was happy, in love, and satisfied with Terrell and what I had with Alex could in no way compare to what I have with Terrell...but still...I loved him with all of me. I gave him access to my soul and that wasn't something that could be easily forgotten. It was one thing for me to think that his death was just an act of God that neither of us had any control over, but to know that she took it upon herself to play a part in his death, took away what little rationality I had. I'd hit her so many times I was tired when a pair of arms wrapped around me and I knew by the grip that it was my baby.

"That's enough Ziah," he said calmly pulling me away from Carmen.

I didn't even protest. Her face was already swelling beyond recognition. Bishop pulled his gun out and aimed it at Jabari.

"You want this nigga or can I have him?" Bishop asked Rell as Jabari lifted his hands in the air.

"I want him," Rell said putting me on my feet.

"Wait...wait...I know it looks like I set her up, and in a sense I did, but I wasn't going to let anything happen to her. I only did it because she threatened to go to the police about me killing the nigga that raped my sister. I've been recording the whole thing. My camera is on top of the fireplace," he said in one breath.

Rell walked over to the fireplace and pulled the camera down. After stopping the recording, he played it from the beginning. I walked over to Jabari and slapped him.

"You couldn't fucking warn me?"

"I'm sorry Al. Please, don't be mad at me. I wasn't going to let her harm you."

"Where's Jessica?"

"She's at my mom's. She's safe."

"I get that you did what you felt like you had to do... but this shit is just too much. For you to use my love and care for Jessica against me was low Jabari. Do you know how scared I was that something had happened to her? You couldn't think of another fucking lie to use?"

"I'm sorry Al. I knew you wouldn't come for me. I'm sorry."

I shook my head in disgust as Bishop made Jabari go outside.

"What we gone do about her?" I asked Rell grabbing my purse.

"What you wanna do? We can do this the legal way and take her and this tape downtown and let her serve her time or we can do this the illegal way and dead her ass right here and now."

Tired of the fighting, drama and death, I looked down at Carmen, as she lay unconscious.

"Call the police."

Rell

The past two weeks had been mad crazy. After the whole situation with Carmen was over and done with, Alayziah had a look of peace about her that I hadn't seen before. I don't think it was so much about Carmen but about the closure the situation gave her with Alex. She visited his grave and his parents after Carmen was arrested and even introduced me to his brother. I didn't sweat the shit because I knew she needed it. I didn't want her taking that baggage into our union.

Her new furniture had arrived and instead of her moving back into her apartment until we were married, I convinced her to put her new furniture in my home. *Our home.* I let her completely redecorate the whole thing so she could truly feel like it was hers.

Bishop's sister Imani decided to move to Memphis for a little while since her divorce from Brian was finalized. Turns out, when she went back home after spending some time at Bishop's house before he and Kai married, she found his ass cheating. Now, they have split custody of the twins and she's trying to get as far away from him as she can.

I thought it would be a good idea for her to move into Al's old apartment and they both agreed. She was going to spend the week here in Memphis and fly out to Dallas on the weekends to be with her kids or have Brian bring them down.

Layyah finally told Al and Kai that she was done with Mike and moving back to Memphis for good. They couldn't be happier because their little trio was going to be together on a regular basis. All in all, shit was good right now. All I had to do was give Al her dream wedding so she can get off her birth control and give me my son – soon.

Alayziah

"Baby... can we get married here? I've always wanted a garden wedding," I asked Rell as we walked around the Botanic Garden.

"Anything you want baby," he replied squeezing my hand.

He led me down this concrete trail that led us to a secluded part of the garden. When I saw Marcel standing near the river I stopped walking abruptly. I looked up at him and he smiled.

"What is he doing here?" I asked.

He shrugged.

"To walk his best friend down the aisle, I guess. What type of husband would I be if I married you without your other best friend being here?"

Tears filled my eyes as I buried my head in his chest. "Rellllll..." I whined as he wrapped his arms around me. "Baby, you're the fucking best!" I yelled as I sobbed.

"Watch your mouth..."

Epilogue

When Rell surprised me with our garden wedding, my joy was complete. To have a man as good and as fine as him was more than a blessing to me. Rell loved me just as hard passionately and unconditionally as I loved him. I was so happy I let my guards down one last time to get to know him. Lord knows I didn't want to though.

I was so scared of being hurt again that I almost missed out on the man of my dreams, the man of my reality, the man that was all mine!

I looked around the garden as my family of friends congregated. Rell and I had about an hour or so left before we had to head for the airport and I wanted to take that as an opportunity to pass the love torch.

Jabari and Jessica came for the wedding but left shortly after. Kai convinced Khalil to come down and see Imani so they were in the cut chilling, cheesing all in each other's face. Rell told me about some nigga he knew that he thought would be perfect for Layyah. When I saw a light-skinned nigga saunter in that I'd never seen before I figured that was him. I grabbed Rell's arm to gain his attention.

"What's up baby?"

"Please, tell me that's the nigga you got for my sister," I whispered.

Homeboy looked good. He had the same light skin as Layyah. His muscles were exposed because he was wearing a v neck black t-shirt. He had coal black wavy hair and a thick ass beard full of curls. Swear I've never seen that shit before. His lips were pinkish red in color and when he smiled at Rell he flashed a set of pearly whites. *Good Lord.*

"Ion go for light skinned niggas but he fine as hell," I continued.

"What you say?" Rell asked pulling me behind him.

"I mean, he fine for Lay, you know you're the only man who catches my eye."

"Mane whatever. You ain't never said no shit like that about me before."

"Rell you a damn lie. I tell your ass you handsome, fine, and looking good all the time."

"Who you cursing at?"

"Your crazy ass. You know I love you."

"What's love got to do with it?"

"Baby I promise you fine as hell. I wouldn't trade you for him or anybody else in this world. Just the sight of you gets my panties wet, especially when you have your hair up in a bun like this."

I pulled him down to my lips by his bun, his dick swelled against me immediately.

"Well, I know that ain't Layyah," the light skinned nigga said.

Rell pulled away from me and licked his lips as he stared at me.

"Baby…" I said nudging him towards the light skinned nigga. "Introduce me to your friend Rell."

"You know you paying for that when we get in the car right? I'm spreading them legs as soon as we get out there."

"Come on then. Hurry up and introduce them."

Finally, he acknowledged his friend and they dapped it up.

"What's up, nigga?" Rell spoke.

"Shit what's up? So this the wife?" He asked looking at me.

"Hell yeah," Rell said proudly. "Baby, this is Israel. Israel, this is my good thing Alayziah."

"It's nice to meet you," he spoke taking my hand into his.

"You as well. You here for my sister?"

"Yeah I guess so. Where she at?"

I pointed towards Layyah and Israel grabbed his dick through his pants. I chuckled and took a step back. His ass was gone be just like Terrell and Bishop.

"Damn, she looks good as fuck," he mumbled walking towards Layyah.

I followed behind him. Terrell followed behind me.

"Who is that?" Kai asked.

"Girl," was all I could say as I blushed. Kai handed BJ to Bishop and walked towards us.

"Nosey ass," Bishop said.

Layyah watched us all walk towards her skeptically. I couldn't imagine how crazy we all looked. When Israel made his way to her he looked back at us. Chuckling, he shook his head and looked at Layyah. Her mouth opened slightly as she looked him up and down.

"What we about to get into?" Israel asked simply.

Layyah looked from him to Rell then me.

"Who is this nigga?" She asked me.

I shrugged.

"You ain't gotta ask them, ask me," Israel said gently pulling her attention back to him by grabbing her chin and turning her face towards his.

"I shouldn't have to ask you. When you approach a lady you're supposed to introduce yourself," Layyah replied pushing his hand away from her face.

"Had I came at you like the average nigga would you have paid me any attention?"

"Hell nah," Kai and I said simultaneously.

"Aight, let's go," Rell said grabbing both of our hands.

"Hold up, I wanna hear," I whined as he dragged us away.

"Mane, leave them folks be. She gone call you and tell you what happened anyway," he said giving Kai's hand to Bishop and leading me out.

"But Ima have to wait a whole week." I pouted.

"Trust me when I get your ass to Turks and Caicos Layyah and Israel won't even be the last thing on your mind."

"You so nasty," I replied looking back at Layyah once more.

"You like that shit though."

"I do King. I love you."

"I love you too."

The End for Terrell and Alayziah

The Beginning for Layyah and Israel, and Khalil and Imani

To follow up with the crew check them out in *Teach Me How to Love*

Again.

CPSIA information can be obtained
at www.ICGtesting.com
Printed in the USA
LVOW01s0252190417
531316LV00008B/190/P